TERROR OF THE
MOUNTAIN MAN

TERROR OF THE MOUNTAIN MAN

William W. Johnstone
with J. A. Johnstone

PINNACLE BOOKS
Kensington Publishing Corp.
www.kensingtonbooks.com

PINNACLE BOOKS are published by

Kensington Publishing Corp.
119 West 40th Street
New York, NY 10018

PUBLISHER'S NOTE
Following the death of William W. Johnstone, the Johnstone family is working with a carefully selected writer to organize and complete Mr. Johnstone's outlines and many unfinished manuscripts to create additional novels in all of his series like The Last Gunfighter, Mountain Man, and Eagles, among others. This novel was inspired by Mr. Johnstone's superb storytelling.

All Kensington titles, imprints, and distributed lines are available at special quantity discounts for bulk purchases for sales promotions, premiums, fund-raising, educational, or institutional use. Special book excerpts or customized printings can also be created to fit specific needs. For details, write or phone the office of the Kensington special sales manager: Kensington Publishing Corp., 119 West 40th Street, New York, NY 10018, attn: Special Sales Department; phone 1-800-221-2647.

PINNACLE BOOKS, the Pinnacle logo, and the WWJ steer head logo are Reg. U.S. Pat. & TM Off.

ISBN-13: 978-0-7860-2125-3
ISBN-10: 0-7860-2125-X

First printing: December 2014

10 9 8 7 6 5 4 3 2 1

Printed in the United States of America

First electronic edition: December 2014

ISBN-13: 978-0-7860-3692-9
ISBN-10: 0-7860-3692-3

Prologue

Vallecillo, Nuevo Leon, Mexico

The villagers were going about their daily business when Colonel Taurino Bustamante Keno and his *Ejército Mexicano de la Liberación* came riding in. There were more than fifty men riding in a precise military formation. Carrying rifles, and with bullet-filled bandoliers angled across their chest, they made quite an imposing and frightening sight.

As they approached the town, playing children ran to their mothers, men working in the field hurried back to their wives, and the merchants locked their doors. The street emptied quickly so that the only living residents of the town to welcome them were the barking dogs that nipped at the heels of the horses.

Keno fired his pistol into the air, several times.

"Why do you run?" he shouted. "*Los hombres de este pueblo!* Come to the *plaza del centro* now! If the men do not come, I will send my soldiers to your houses, and we will kill the women and the children!"

Gradually the men of the village began to come out, one at a time, until soon the town square was crowded with them. All were unarmed, and all were looking on, with fear, at Keno and his men.

"There," Keno said, a wide smile spreading across his face. "Now that you are here, I ask you for your help. We need money, so I am declaring a tax on this village. A tax of ten thousand pesos."

"Ten thousand pesos?" one of the men shouted. "This is a poor village. What makes you think we have ten thousand pesos?"

"I know that you do," Keno said. "And perhaps that is a great deal of money for you to raise. But we need it, you see. And I am sure that you would like to support the *revolución popular.*"

"It is not a people's revolution!" the same villager shouted. "We don't want a revolution. The government does not send *Federales* here to steal from us. Only you, and your Mexican Army of Liberation does such a thing."

"I told you, *amigo*, this is a tax."

"If you have guns and you take money from us, it is not a tax. It is stealing!"

Keno nodded at one of his men, and they shot the protesting villager down. The other villagers shouted out in shock and alarm.

"Do you see what happens to traitors of the revolution?" Keno asked. "Now, please, raise the tax among you, as I have asked. Then, when that unpleasant business has been taken care of, we will barbeque goat, and have a fiesta."

For a moment longer the men just stood there, still transfixed by having seen one of their neighbors shot down so casually.

"Hurry, my friends, do not make us wait!" Keno shouted with a wave of his arm. "Hurry!"

As the villagers hurried to raise the money Keno had demanded, Keno and his men proceeded to the cantina. The cantina, like the other business establishments in town, had closed and locked the doors when the fifty or more *bandidos* rode into town. Finding the door locked, Keno signaled to a couple of men, and they broke through the door. With the door out of the way, the men rushed inside and began grabbing bottles of tequila and whiskey, and filling mugs with beer.

"Where are the *putas*?" Keno shouted. "If the *putas* do not come, we will burn this place!"

A few minutes later five very frightened prostitutes arrived.

"You," Keno said, pointing to the youngest and most attractive. "I will take you."

He went into the back with the young girl while his men made arrangements to share the remaining four.

During the war with America, when Keno had been a very young man, his commanders learned quickly that he had courage, and would not hesitate to kill. He was given the mission of carrying on a deadly guerrilla warfare against the Americans in Texas, and he was most effective. Keno was a hero then, and all Mexicans honored and respected him.

After that war he was given a commission by the Mexican government, and during the French intervention in Mexico, Keno, as he had in the Mexican-American War, fought well. He was present when Maximilian was executed, on June 19, 1867.

After that war ended the other soldiers returned to ranching and farming, but Keno did not. He promoted himself to colonel, kept many of his soldiers with him, raised even more, and under the auspices of fighting a revolution for the people, instead began stealing from them. His military skills had not diminished, but now, instead of using them in service of his country, he was using them for his own enrichment and self-aggrandizement.

Some of the men of the village held a meeting to try and determine what they should do.

"We must do something," the leader of the group said. "We are not animals, to be treated like sheep."

"What can we do, Orozco?" another asked.

"Why do you ask, Rivas? Are you not a man? You know what we must do. We must fight them."

"We should go to the *Federales*," another suggested.

"We have gone to the *Federales*, Cruz, and what did it gain us?" Orozco asked. "We get nothing from them. There are only two of them. They can do nothing. We must fight him ourselves."

"And how shall we fight them, Orozco? They have guns and knives. We have we have scythes, and hoes," Rivas insisted.

"I don't know," Orozco admitted in frustration. "I don't know."

Chapter One

Southwest, Missouri—1882

"We're getting pretty close now," Smoke said.

Smoke and Sally had been two days on the train since leaving Sugarloaf Ranch at Big Rock, Colorado, and he was sitting in the window seat, looking out.

"Do you see anything you recognize?" Sally asked.

"Yeah," Smoke replied. "I have been right here, on this creek, before."

"You sure it was this creek?" Sally teased. "We've seen at least a dozen or more creeks, streams, and rivers since we came into Missouri. Are you sure it's this creek?"

"I'm sure," Smoke said, as he recalled the last time he had been at this same spot.

Smoke could feel his stomach shaking from the shock waves of the explosion. The underpinnings of the trestle were carried away by the planted charges, but the superstructure remained intact for several more seconds, stretching across the creek with no visible means of support, as if defying the laws of gravity. Then, slowly, the tracks began to sag and the ties started snapping, popping with a series of loud reports, like pistol shots, until finally, with a resounding crash and a splash of water, the whole bridge collapsed into the creek.

"Now, that's the way to do it, boys," Asa Briggs said with a broad, happy smile. "The Yankees won't be movin' troops over this railroad for a while."

It was just over twenty years ago when that trestle had been destroyed, one of the casualties of war. However, as the train passed over the creek on a rebuilt trestle, Smoke could remember the event as if it had been yesterday.

Smoke was in Missouri for the first time since he and his father had left back in 1865. He and his father had left together, and now they were returning together. Smoke had exhumed his father's grave, and Emmett Jensen's remains were in a beautiful ebony and silver coffin in the baggage car ahead. Smoke was bringing him home, to Missouri, to be buried next to his mother.

"It's just something I want to do," he had told Sally when he came up with the idea.

"Then we shall do it."

"We?"

"Yes, we. I want to see where you were born, Smoke, and where you grew up."

"I didn't grow up there that much. I left home when I was still no more than a boy."

Sally chuckled, and ran her hand through his hair. "What makes you think you're grown up now?" she asked.

"Why would I want to grow up?" Smoke teased. "The only thing that happens when you grow up is you get old."

The conductor came through the car then and stopping at the seat occupied by Smoke and Sally, leaned over to speak quietly.

"There is a table available in the dining car now, Mr. Jensen. I've asked them to hold it for you."

"Thank you," Smoke said, and he and Sally got up to walk back to the diner. They were met by a smiling porter, who escorted them to a table which was covered with white linen cloth and decorated by a vase of flowers. The menu displayed fare as varied as that found in the finest restaurants in the country. Darkness fell outside, a single candle lighting the distance between the couple.

Sally reached across the table to lay her hand on Smoke's hand.

"I'm glad you've decided to do this," she said. "I know that you have spoken about how you had to bury your mother."

"In a feeding trough," Smoke said in shame and embarrassment. "I had to bury her in a feeding trough. But she'll have a fine coffin now. I should have done this long ago, Sally. I should have moved Pa back to Missouri and put them down next to each other, years ago."

"It's never too late," Sally said.

"I guess not," Smoke said. "It isn't as if they are aware that they had to wait so long."

After dinner they returned to the car, now brightly lit by the gimbal-mounted lamps between the windows.

Sally began reading, while Smoke sat in musing silence, the darkness outside limiting his view to that of the golden squares of light which, projected through the windows, were sliding by at almost thirty miles an hour along the gravel ballast beside the tracks.

Suddenly the train braked sharply, eventually grounding to a shuddering, screeching, banging halt.

Curious as to why the train stopped so suddenly, Smoke looked out the window to see what he could determine. Because of the dark, he saw nothing.

"What is going on? Why have we stopped?" someone asked.

"I nearly broke my neck! The railroad is certainly going to hear from me!" another complained.

"Smoke, what is it?"

"I don't know," Smoke said. "Could be a break in the track. Could even be a train robbery."

"Surely not?"

"Why not? We're in Missouri, after all. And this is where Jesse James sort of perfected the operation."

"But Jesse James is dead."

"So I've heard," Smoke said. He pulled his pistol from his holster, then let it rest on his knee, covered by his hat.

No sooner had Smoke done that than a man burst into the car from the front. He wore a bandana tied across the bottom half of his face, and he held a pistol which he pointed toward the passengers on the car. "Everyone stay in their seats!" the armed man shouted.

"Smoke!" Sally said.

"Ever'body get their money out. We're goin' to have us a collection, you know, like what happens in a church?" The gunman laughed. "You just do what I tell you to do, and there won't nobody get hurt," the gunman shouted.

"Except you," Smoke replied.

"What did you say?"

"You will be hurt, if you don't step off this train now, and go on your way," Smoke said calmly.

"Mister, are you crazy? You do see that I'm holdin' a gun here, don't you?"

"In fact, I do see it," Smoke said. "But it isn't going to do you any good. Now put the gun away and leave the train."

"Yeah? An' if I don't?"

"I'll kill you," Smoke said.

"Abner, I think maybe you'd better get in here," the gunman called.

Another gunman stepped in, to join the first. "What do you need?" he asked. "What's going on?"

"You see that feller down there, about halfway on the right?" The gunman chuckled. "He just told me that if I don't get off the train now, he's goin' to kill me."

Smoke continued to sit quietly in his seat, fixing an unblinking stare on the two men who were standing at the front of the car.

"Is that right, mister? Is that what you said?"

"That's what I said."

"Lady, maybe you'd better find somewhere else in this car to sit," Abner said to Sally.

"Why?" Sally asked.

"Why? 'Cause we're about to shoot that fella you're sittin' beside, 'n' it would be a downright shame if you was to get hit when we start shootin'."

"He's my husband, and I have no intention of moving. Besides, you won't be shooting."

"We're not foolin', lady. Do you think we won't shoot?"

"Oh, I think you'll make the attempt, but your effort will be unsuccessful."

Sally's cool, and unflappable comments, spoken without the slightest indication of fear, or even anxiousness, shocked the other passengers in the car, and had a very unnerving effect on the two men.

"What the hell, let's just shoot both of them," Abner said. He and the other gunman, who had been addressed as James, both raised their guns to fire, pulling the hammers back as they did so.

Two shots rang out, but the shots didn't come from the train robbers' guns. Instead they came from Smoke, who had lifted his pistol from his lap and fired twice before either of the outlaws could get even one shot off.

During the gunfire, women screamed and men shouted. As the car filled with the gun smoke of the two discharges, Smoke jumped up and ran out through the back door of the car. Leaping from the steps down to the ground, he fell and rolled away from the train, out into the darkness.

"Abner! James! What's goin' on in there?" someone called. "What's all the shootin'?"

In the dim light that spilled through the car windows, Smoke saw the gunman who was yelling at the others. As he ran through the little golden patches of light cast by the windows of the cars, it had the effect of a lantern blinking on and off so that first he was in shadow, then brightly illuminated . . . then shadow . . . then illuminated. Smoke waited.

"Hold it right there!" Smoke shouted. "I've got you covered. Put down your gun and throw up your hands."

"The hell you do," the gunman shouted. Realizing that he was illuminated by light shining from the train car, he moved out into the shadow to fire at Smoke, or at least, where he thought Smoke might be.

Smoke used the flame pattern to return fire. He heard the gunman let out a little yell, and he knew he had hit him. He got up, then ran quickly through the dark toward him, his gun at the ready.

His caution wasn't necessary. The man was lying on the ground, dead.

The immediate danger seemed to be over, and as far as he knew, the three men he shot had been the only ones involved.

After another moment the conductor left the train and was soon joined by a few of the braver passengers. By now even the engineer, fireman, and the messenger had come down and the train crew and passengers stood around the body that lay belly-down alongside the train.

"There are two more dead inside, besides this one out here. Any others that you know of?" the conductor asked the engineer.

"No," the engineer replied. "They was only three of 'em what stopped me, 'n' if you say they's two more of 'em inside, well, that would be all of 'em."

"Did they get anything?" one of the passengers asked the messenger, who had come down from the express car.

"No, they didn't get that far. The shooting started

before I opened the door, and the next thing you know, they were gone."

"Who was it that done all the shootin'?" the engineer asked.

"It was him," one of the passengers said accusingly, pointing at Smoke. "And, if you ask me, it was damn foolish of him to do it too. They was women and children in that car, 'n' with all the bullets flyin' around, why it's a wonder there wasn't some of 'em hit."

"There were only two bullets," Smoke said. "And they weren't flying around. They hit exactly what they were supposed to hit."

"Why did you start shooting?" the conductor asked.

"Because they were about to shoot me," Smoke answered.

"So you say. I'm not so sure about that," the conductor said.

"Well, I'm sure, because I saw it," one of the other passengers said. "The two brigands in the car pointed their pistols at this gentleman, and announced quite clearly for all concerned, that it was their intention to shoot not only him, but his wife as well."

"Judge Clayborne. Were you in the car where the shooting took place?" one of the other passengers asked.

"I was."

"What the hell, Eugene," the messenger said to the conductor. "As far as I'm concerned, this man may have saved a few lives, besides which, the robbers didn't get one penny of money. Mister," he said looking directly at Smoke, "I, for one, thank you."

Smoke nodded, but didn't say anything.

"Why'd you stop, Lyman?" the conductor asked.

"None of this would've happened if you hadn't stopped."

"Didn't have no choice," the engineer replied. "They put a barricade across the tracks." Lyman glanced toward a couple of the stronger-looking passengers. "Fact is, we can't move from this very spot till the track has been cleared. You two men want to bear a hand in gettin' the barricade moved?"

"Sure thing," one of the two answered, and both passengers went to the front of the train with the engineer and fireman, to begin clearing the cut timber from the track.

When Smoke returned to the train car the response toward him was measured.

"What a strange reaction these people are having," Sally said. "Don't they know you just saved their lives?"

"I wouldn't take it that far," Smoke said. "Besides, I fear that most of them think I endangered their lives by doing what I did."

"Nonsense," Sally said. "I'll soon set them straight on that."

Smoke reached out to put his hand on Sally's arm. "I'd rather you not do that," he said. "I would like for my return to Missouri to be as quiet as possible."

Despite the situation, Sally laughed out loud. When she did so, several others in the car stared at her accusingly.

"As quiet as possible," she said. "You just stopped a robbery in progress by shooting three of the robbers. Don't you think it's a little late to 'enter Missouri quietly'?"

Smoke chuckled as well.

"If you put it like that, I suppose you are right."

"If I put it like that? How else am I going to put it?"

It took less than fifteen minutes to get the track cleared, then, with a series of jolts that eventually smoothed out, the train started up again.

About half an hour later the train began to slow, and Smoke pulled the curtain open to look outside. He saw a small house slide by, a dim, golden glow shining through the windows.

When the train came to a complete stop, Smoke and Sally stepped out onto the brick platform at the Galena Depot and looked around.

Behind them the train was temporarily at rest from its long run, but it wasn't quiet. Because the engineer kept the steam up, the valve continued to open and close in great, heaving sighs. Overheated wheel bearings and gearboxes popped and snapped as its tortured metal cooled. On the platform all around him, there was a discordant chorus of squeals, laughter, shouts, and animated conversation as people were getting on and off the train.

When Smoke looked toward the rear of the train he saw that the three bodies had been taken down from the last car and were being laid out side by side at the far end of the platform. Already the curious were beginning to gather around them.

Smoke had brought his and Sally's horses all the way from Big Rock, and he and Sally walked toward the attached stock car, away from those who were congregated around the men he had shot. They waited there as the horses were led down the board incline that had been lifted to the door of the car for that express purpose. The horses recognized them, and nodded and whickered in appreciation and relief that they had been reunited.

"Good-looking animals," one of the employees said.

"Thanks. Is Grant's stable still open?"

"Grant? Where you been, mister? Emil Grant died ten years ago. It ain't Grant's no more. It was bought out by Dave Kern."

"Davey Kern?" Smoke smiled. He remembered Kern from when they were in school together. "Well, that'll be just fine. I'll be glad to leave my horses with him. Will there be someone there now?"

"I expect there will be. He keeps someone on duty there all night long."

"Is the stable still in the same place, up on the corner of Maple and Fourth?"

"Still there." The depot man looked at Smoke more closely. "You from here, mister? 'Cause if you are, I don't recollect you."

"You wouldn't likely," Smoke said. "I was just a boy when I left and that was a long time ago."

As they were speaking, Smoke saw his father's coffin being removed from the baggage car and placed, carefully, on one of the iron-wheeled carts. He handed the reins of his horse to Sally and walked over to it.

"This belong to you?" the baggage master asked as Smoke approached.

"Yes."

"It isn't empty, is it?"

"No, it contains the remains of my father. I've brought him here to be buried."

"What do you want done with it for now?"

"Can you keep it here, until I can make arrangements for it?"

"I reckon I can, but it'll cost you a quarter a night for me to put it up here."

Smoke gave him a dollar. "I should have all the arrangements made by the time this is worked off."

The baggage master took the money, nodded, then motioned for one of the other men to move it into the depot baggage-storage area.

Chapter Two

After making arrangements for his father's coffin to be safely stored until he was ready for it, Smoke walked down to the far end of the station platform where the bodies of the men he had shot had been laid out as if on display. Each one had his arms folded across his chest. The eyes were open on two of them, the third had only one eye open, the other having been destroyed by the entry of the bullet.

There were two men standing there, looking down at the bodies. One was the well-dressed passenger from the train, the one the conductor had referred to as "judge." The other man, who hadn't been a passenger, was also wearing a suit, and was smoking a cigar. A star, attached to the lapel of his suit jacket, identified him as the sheriff.

"This is the man who did it, Sheriff," the judge said.

The sheriff took his cigar out of his mouth and spit out a few pieces of loose tobacco before he spoke.

"You shot these men, did you?" he asked.

"I had enough people who saw me do it that it

would be rather foolish of me to deny it, don't you think?" Smoke replied.

The sheriff chuckled. "You have a point there," he said.

"There is no sense in you seeking an indictment on this man, because I will not grant it," the judge said.

"I've already been told by half a dozen others what happened, Judge. You don't have to worry about it, I won't be bringing any charges against him." The sheriff stuck the cigar back in his mouth and looked at Smoke again. "I do have one question, though."

"What would that be?" Smoke asked.

"Why? Why did you take a chance like that?"

"They were robbing the train."

"So I heard. But what business is that of yours?"

"It would have been my business if they started taking money from the passengers. I was one of the passengers."

"That's correct, Sheriff," the judge said. "Jimmy Dill announced the moment he stepped onto the train, that it was their intention to rob the passengers, regardless of what might have been in the express car."

The sheriff stuck the cigar back into his mouth and stared at Smoke for a long moment. That was when Smoke recognized him. This was Paul Sadler. But Smoke had changed a lot more than Sadler had over the intervening years, so he knew that while Sadler might find him familiar, he probably wouldn't be able to place him.

"Are you going to need me anymore, Sheriff? I need to get my horses down to Kern's livery, then get checked into the hotel."

"No," the sheriff said. "Truth is, the railroad, and the town, owe you a debt of gratitude. Will you be stayin' long?"

"Just for a few days," Smoke said. "I'm here to take care of some personal business."

"If I run into you in the saloon, I'll buy you a drink."

Smoke nodded. "I'll appreciate it."

"Damn, I didn't even ask him his name," Sheriff Sadler said as he walked away. "And I should have. He's damn familiar-lookin' to me."

"A man like that doesn't stay unknown for long," the judge replied. "I expect we'll learn his name soon enough."

Once arrangements for the horses were made at the Kern Livery Stable, Smoke and Sally checked into the Bracken Hotel.

"Mr. and Mrs. Kirby Jensen," the hotel clerk said as he read the entry. "Welcome to Galena."

"Thank you," Smoke replied.

"Why did you use the name Kirby?" Sally asked after they went upstairs.

"A couple of reasons," Smoke said. "One reason is because Kirby is how I was known when I still lived here. But primarily it's because back here, I doubt that anyone has connected the name Kirby with Smoke, and I'd just as soon nobody is able to do that. I'd like to keep this visit as quiet as I can."

"Ha! After that private war you had before we

arrived here, just how long do you think it will be before someone puts two and two together?"

Smoke smiled. "Who's going to put two and two together? I grew up here, remember? Math never was a strong suit around here."

"You're awful," Sally said, laughing as she threw a pillow at him.

The next morning a slight breeze filled the muslin curtains and lifted them out over the wide-beamed planking in the floor. With Sally still asleep beside him, Smoke moved to the window and looked out over the town, which was just beginning to awaken. Water was being heated behind the laundry and boxes were being stacked behind the grocery store. A team of matched mules pulled a fully-loaded freight wagon down the main street.

From somewhere Smoke could smell bacon frying, and his stomach growled, reminding him that he was hungry.

"Sally, come on, get up!" he called. "Are you planning on sleeping in for the entire day?"

"I could be talked into it," Sally replied sleepily.

"I'm hungry. Let's go have some breakfast."

After breakfast Smoke and Sally went down to Welch's Funeral Home. They stopped just before they went in, because standing outside the building, and strapped to boards to hold them up, were the three bodies of the men Smoke had killed on the train the night before.

"I wish they wouldn't do that," Sally said.

"Yeah, I'd just as soon not see them. But it could have been us."

"Oh, don't be silly. They wouldn't have put us up here," Sally insisted.

The mortician, Gene Welch, stepped outside. "These three men tried to rob the train last night," he said. "If you would like, you can have your picture taken beside them. It'll only cost you a quarter."

"You're charging people to have their picture taken beside these bodies?" Sally asked, incredulously.

"Yes. The money isn't for me, you understand. It will be used to purchase coffins to bury these poor unfortunates."

"I thought the county paid for their burials," Smoke said.

"Yes, but county money is taxpayers' money, so you might say that I'm just looking out for the people."

"Do people actually have their pictures taken in such a way?" Sally asked.

"Oh, yes, you would be surprised at the number of people who do. And often, they will pose with a gun, as if they were the ones who actually shot them. Of course, everyone knows, now, that they were shot by one of the passengers on the train. But twenty, or thirty years from now, who will know the difference?"

"Yes, who will know the difference?"

"Evidently you didn't come to have your picture taken, so, how may I help you?"

"I used to live near here, some time ago," Smoke said, "and I have brought my father back to be buried here. My mother is also here, but she is buried on our old home place. I would like to have her exhumed and brought into town. Then I want to have her and my father buried side by side, right here in the local cemetery. Can you handle that for me?"

"Indeed I can. How long has your mother been interred?"

"It's been over twenty years now."

There was a shocked expression on Welch's face. "Oh, my. You do understand, don't you, sir, that if the coffin has been in the ground that long, unless it was a very good one, that it may well have deteriorated to the point that by now it will be difficult to move and rebury it."

"She's not in a coffin. I'll be wanting to buy one from you."

"Very good, sir. Oh, I'm afraid this is most indelicate, but there is no other way but to come right out and say it. If she wasn't in a coffin, I must assume that she also wasn't embalmed."

"I buried her myself," Smoke said. "I put her in a feed trough and closed it up with a door. I'm pretty sure there will be nothing left but bones, but whatever 'there' is there, I want it moved to town."

"Yes, sir, I'll take care of both of them for you. Would you like to view our coffins, to pick one out for your mother?"

"I'll let you do that. I want the best."

"Yes, sir," Welch said with a big smile. "That would be our Eternal Cloud. It is guaranteed for five hundred years."

"Five hundred years?"

"Absolutely."

"Suppose I want to do this again in five hundred

years, and I find that the coffin has deteriorated, will you give me my money back?"

"Of course, that's what a guarantee . . . uh . . ." As if just realizing what Smoke said, Welch got a strange expression on his face. "Uh, of course, five hundred years would be . . ." He stopped, unable to complete the sentence.

"Never mind," Smoke said. "Once I get them here, I don't plan to move them in the next five hundred years, so I'll just have to take your word for it."

"Yes, sir," Welch replied, not catching the sarcasm. "Uh, may I have your name, sir?"

"It's Jensen. Kirby Jensen."

"Very good, Mr. Jensen, I'll take care of everything."

"Good, thank you. By the way, do you know the name of the man who actually killed these outlaws?"

"No, I'm afraid I don't. All I know is that it was one of the train passengers. For all I know, he may have gone on."

"Yes," Smoke said.

When they left Welch's Funeral Home, they started down to the stable to get their horses.

Sally laughed, quietly. "You want your money back in five hundred years? Smoke, sometimes you can be downright cruel, you know that?"

"Well, if it's a guarantee for five hundred years, why not get my money back?"

Sally laughed again, louder this time, and, playfully, she hit Smoke on the arm.

"Oh, hush."

* * *

A stable employee had taken their horses last night, but Dave Kern himself was there today. Smoke smiled, because he was certain he would have recognized him, even if he didn't know the name.

"We've come to get our horses."

"All right. And your name, sir?"

"Don't you recognize me, Davey?" Smoke said. "I'll admit that it's been a long time."

Kern stared at him for a long moment, but without recognition.

"The name is Jensen. Kirby Jensen."

Now a huge smile spread across Kern's face. "Kirby Jensen! Well, I'll be." He stuck out his hand. "It's real good to see you again, Kirby. Old Mr. Byrd said you 'n' your pa sold him your land 'n' your mules, then rode out of here. But you never come back, and there ain't nobody in town never heard from you, your brother, your sister, or your pa and ma again."

"Ma and Pa are both dead," Smoke said. "I've come here to bury them. Is Mr. Byrd still alive?"

"Oh, yeah, he's still alive. But he don't live here no more. He lives down in Texas now, bought hisself a ranch down on the Rio Grande. His son Sam owns the farm now. Not only his farm, but the old Gimlin place as well."

"What about Marv Gimlin?"

"Him 'n' his wife is both dead. His daughter, Mollie, married Sam Byrd, which is how Sam Byrd come by the land. You plannin' on goin' out to see 'em?"

"I thought I might."

"Well, I'm sure he'll appreciate that. He's good folks, even if he is about the richest man around here." Kern called one of his employees in, and gave him a couple of numbers. "Tony, go get these two horses saddled and bring 'em up front, will you?"

"Yes, sir, Mr. Kern."

"You're goin' to bury your folks here, are you? Well, that'll be nice. I know there's lots of people around that remember your folks just real kindly. By the way, where's your sister at? I always thought she was a real pretty thing."

"She died last year. She was living in Kansas," Smoke said without giving away any more information.

"That's too bad. Like I said, she was a real pretty thing."

"Mr. Kern, they's a fella out here wantin' to rent a buckboard," someone said, sticking his head in the office then.

"All right, I'll be right there. Excuse me, Kirby. Have you come back to stay? Or just to take care of your ma and pa?"

"Just to take care of them," Smoke said. "I'll be getting on back home as soon as that's done."

"Well, I do hope I get a chance to see you again before you leave. Tony will have your horses up here in a moment. If you'll excuse me, I'd prob'ly better see to the man who's wantin' to rent a buckboard. Ma'am, real nice to see you," he said with a nod, just before he went outside to see to his customer.

"Do you miss this town, Smoke?" Sally asked, when they were alone. "I mean, do you ever wish you were still here?"

Smoke chuckled. "Sally, if I had wanted to be here, I never would have left in the first place. Why would you even ask such a question?"

"Well, it does seem like a very peaceful little town. And we have enough money, you could sell the ranch and we could buy a nice home here. Or, we wouldn't even have to sell Sugarloaf. We could let Pearlie and Cal run it."

"Sally, not that I want to, but are you telling me that if I wanted to move here, you would be willing to move here with me?"

Sally put her hand on Smoke's arm. "You're my husband, Smoke. Wherever you go, I will go."

"That's good to know. But you can put your mind at ease about coming here. I left this part of my life behind me, many years ago."

"Mr. Jensen?" Tony said. "Here's your horses, sir."

"Thanks," Smoke said, tipping the boy half a dollar.

"Gee! Thanks!" Tony replied with a huge, grateful smile.

Chapter Three

Unable to fund his revolutionary army by robbing the small villages in northern Mexico, Colonel Taurino Bustamante Keno decided to move his operation across the border into Texas. And whereas in Mexico, his targets were often entire villages, his first foray into Texas would be against a small ranch.

He led his men across the Rio Grande, finding a ford that was easily passed. The long stream of horses behind him frothed the water and kicked up splashes that gleamed in the moonlight.

Earlier, one of his men had found a ranch about five miles north of the river. It was isolated, and there was one field where the cattle were under the watch of only three men. It would be a simple thing, Keno decided, to take the cows and herd them but five miles back across the river.

Under the canopy of brightly shining stars which were scattered across a black velvet sky, two hundred and fifty head of cattle, belonging to a rancher named William Pike, were resting. Some slept standing, some lying down on their sides, but most were leaning forward on their chests and forelimbs. The two hundred and fifty head had been separated from the rest of the herd because tomorrow they would be driven to Brownsville, then loaded onto a ship.

From somewhere within the herd a calf bawled anxiously and its mother answered. In the distance a coyote sent up its long, lonesome wail. The herd was approached by Keno and the men who were riding with him. When they crested a low-lying ridge, Keno held up his hand to call his formation to a halt.

On the range below, around the shapes and shadows that made up the small herd, rode three cowboys. One was much younger than the other two. Known as "nighthawks," their job was to keep watch over the herd during the night and, to pass the time, they were engaged in conversation.

"Billy, when are you goin' to let Big Lucy make a man out of you?" one of the older cowboys asked the youngest one.

"What do you mean?"

"Tell 'im, Roy. Tell 'im what I mean."

"Come on, Billy, you know exactly what Mitch means," Roy said. "When are you goin' to let Big Lucy take you up to her room and break you in?"

"Why would I have to get broke in with Big Lucy? Why couldn't it be with one of the others, one that's nearer to my age?"

"I'll tell you why. 'Cause Big Lucy ain't a-goin' to let

you anywhere near her girls till she's sure that you know what you're doin'," Mitch said.

"And if you don't know, why, she'll show you," Roy added.

"I don't want to be taught by someone like her. She's ugly."

"Hell, boy," Mitch said. "That's the whole point of it, don't you see? If you can do it with an ugly woman, you can do it with anyone."

"Besides which, if you blow out the lantern, you won't even be able to see her anyhow," Roy added with a chuckle.

The two older cowboys laughed at Billy's obvious discomfort.

At that moment, from the other side of the herd, several of the cows began bawling.

"What the hell is goin' on? Somethin' has them cows spooked," Mitch said.

"A wolf, maybe?" Billy said. "I'll ride over and have a look."

"We'll all go," Roy said.

As the three started around the herd they saw what was happening. Riders were cutting away the herd.

"Rustlers!" Billy shouted.

At that moment, gunshots erupted in the night, their muzzle-flashes lighting up the herd.

"Jesus! What's happening? Who is it? They're all around us!" one of the cowboys shouted in terror, firing his gun wildly in the dark.

The three nighthawks tried to fight back but they were badly outnumbered. In less than a minute, all three had been shot from their saddles and then the night grew still, save for the restless shuffle of the herd of cattle as they were being taken away.

Keno smiled in the darkness, then followed the herd back toward Mexico. This would be the best payday yet.

Stone County, Missouri

The only thing about the Byrd farm that Smoke recognized was the gate. The house was new, considerably larger than the original house had been. This was a two-story house with Corinthian columns that spread all across the front. The barn was new as well, and out in the corral, he saw at least two dozen mules. He thought about Ange and Rhoda, the two mules his pa had owned, and that he had worked with. Ange and Rhoda were less than ten years old when he and his pa sold them to Mr. Byrd. Since mules could live to be forty years old he knew that it was possible that they could both still be alive.

"Do you remember Sam?" Sally asked.

"I remember him, but I'm not sure he'll remember me," Smoke said. "He was about seven years old when I left."

Riding through the gate, they dismounted at a wrought-iron hitching rail in front of the house, and tied off their horses. A very pretty young girl stepped out onto the front porch.

"Is this the Byrd place?" Smoke asked.

"Yes, sir, they are my mama and papa. I'm Ellie Mae Byrd. Are you here to see them?"

"I sure am, if they are available," Smoke said.

"I'll go get them," Ellie Mae said.

"Thank you, dear. That's very nice of you," Sally said with a wide smile.

Ellie Mae returned the smile, then disappeared into the house. A moment later she returned with her parents.

"Can I help you with something, sir?" the man asked, clearly curious as to who might be calling on him.

"Sam, I would have never recognized you or Mollie. But I believe I could be excused for that, since the last time I saw you two, neither one of you were as old as this young lady."

The expression on Sam's face grew even more perplexed. "Do I know you, sir?"

"You know me. You just don't remember me. But maybe this will spur your memory. How did Ange and Rhoda work out for you?"

"Ange and Rhoda?" Sam smiled. "Well, I'll be. I know who you are. You have to be Kirby Jensen. Am I right?"

Smoke chuckled. "I thought you might remember."

"Ange and Rhoda are doing fine."

"Don't tell me you're still working them."

"Nah, they don't work anymore. Now they're living a life of leisure."

"Sam, Mollie, this is my wife, Sally."

"It's a pleasure to meet you, Mrs. Jensen," Sam said.

"It's Sally," Sally corrected. "And we've already met your lovely daughter," she added, smiling at Ellie Mae.

"Say, would you like to see your mules?"

"What do you mean, my mules?" Smoke said. "You've had them a lot longer than I ever did."

"I know, but Pa has always referred to them as the

Jensen twins," Sam said with a chuckle. "So I still think of them that way."

"Yes, if you don't mind, I'd love to see them."

"I'd like to come along as well," Sally said. "I've heard about these marvelous creatures for our entire marriage."

"Sure, come along," Sam said. "They've got their own corral."

The two mules were standing on the far side of the corral when they approached.

"Ange! Rhoda!" Sam shouted. "Come here and say hello to an old friend of yours!"

The two mules ambled over, and when they got close enough, Smoke leaned across the fence and stroked Rhoda's face.

"Hello, girl," he said. "Do you remember me?"

Both Rhoda and Ange stared at him with their big, liquid, brown eyes.

"You know what? I think they actually do remember you," Sally said.

"Why shouldn't they remember me? I remember them. Besides, mules are smart."

As Smoke stroked the faces of the two mules, he recalled a time with them.

Kirby had been plowing for two weeks, averaging an acre and a half per day. It was the middle of May and he had the ground broken on twenty-one acres, which was just over half of the farm. With both his pa and Luke gone to war, what he would plant this year was entirely up to him, and he planned to do twenty acres of corn, ten of wheat, and ten of oats.

Kirby was thinking about this when he got the whiff of an awful smell.

"Hell's bells, Ange!" he swore at the mule. "Ain't you got

no better sense than to fart in a man's face? Damn, you are the fartin'est one mule I've ever seen. Why ain't you more like Rhoda? She don't hardly ever fart. I guess she's more of a lady than you are a gentleman."

Kirby picked up a clod of dirt and threw it at the offending animal.

He was just reaching the end of the row when he saw Janey approaching.

"Whoa," he called.

Janey was carrying a canvas bag.

"Hi, sis," he said. "You're bringing water, I hope."

Janey smiled. "No. I brought you something better." She reached into the bag and pulled out a jar of tea.

"It's sweetened," she said as she handed it to him.

Kirby had worked up quite a thirst during the plowing and he took the sweetened tea with grateful hands, then took several deep, Adam's apple–bobbing swallows, until more than half of it was gone. Finally he pulled the jar away and wiped his mouth with the back of his hand. He smiled at Janey.

"Damn, that was good. If you weren't my sister, I'd marry you," he teased.

"I told you, I'm never goin' to get married. And I wouldn't marry you, even if you weren't my brother. You're too ornery."

Kirby drank the rest of the tea, but saved the last mouthful, and spit it out toward his sister.

For most of his life, Smoke and Janey had lived apart. In fact, he didn't even know where she was until, by accident, he learned that she had finally settled down with a good man. But, by the time he learned that, it was too late. She had already died.*

---

*See *A Lone Star Christmas*.

"What do you say we get back to the house?" Sam suggested. "I expect Molly will have lunch ready by now."

"I hear your pa owns a ranch down in Texas," Smoke said over lunch. "Isn't he a little old to be ranching?"

"Ha! Don't tell him that! He's seventy-two years old, but he gets around like he's no more 'n fifty or so. If you remember Pa, he always could outwork any two men."

"Oh, I remember him well. And you're right, he always was a hardworking man. Cattle?"

"Yes, sir. He's runnin' about thirty thousand head of Herefords."

"That's a pretty large spread."

"The biggest in the county," Sam said, proudly. "If you are ever down that way, you should stop in to see him."

"Maybe I will," Smoke said. "A man with a spread that is large enough to run thirty thousand head is almost always in need of remounts."

Sam's eyes opened wider. "How'd you know that?"

"Well, it's just common sense."

"No, I mean how did you know that Pa is needin' horses right now? I just got a letter from him yesterday, complainin' about that. He says he needs about two hundred head, and there aren't any available anywhere close by."

"I can sell him two hundred head," Smoke said.

"You have horses?"

"Do we have horses?" Sally replied. "Sugarloaf is the biggest horse ranch in Colorado."

"Well, now, that's good to know," Sam said. "If you don't mind, Kirby, I'm goin' to send Pa a telegram and see if he is still lookin'."

Kirby smiled. "I don't mind at all," he said. "Raising and selling horses is what I do. In fact, I would greatly appreciate it if you did get in touch with your father. And when you do, please give him my regards. He was always very good to me, and my family."

"I'll be glad to. By the way, I'm curious, what brings you back to Stone County after all these years?"

"I left something on our farm," Smoke said. "And since you own the land now, I figured that I should come to you before I go get it."

Sam looked puzzled. "Kirby, there's nothing there. Even all the buildings have been torn down."

"This will still be there, if I can find it."

"Well, you are certainly welcome to go look for it."

"You said you tore down all the buildings. Have you plowed over the ground where they were?"

"I'm afraid so," Sam said.

"My mother's grave was on a little Lodge overlooking the creek."

Sam smiled, and nodded his head. "You don't have to worry about that. Your mother's grave is still there. I put a fence around the area just so my hands would know not to disturb it."

Smoke smiled, and nodded. "That is very decent of you, Sam. I appreciate that."

"I remember your ma and pa well, Kirby. They were always very nice to me, and to my little sister."

"Ah, yes, Katrina, I remember her. Where is she now?"

"Katrina went to Texas with Pa. She's teaching school in San Vicente."

"Is she now? Sally was a schoolteacher."

"Did you like being a schoolteacher?" Ellie Mae asked. The question was her first contribution to the conversation.

"Oh, yes, I enjoyed it very much."

"I'm going to be a schoolteacher someday, just like Aunt Katrina."

"Wanting to be a teacher is half of what it takes to be a good teacher," Sally said.

"And being smart?" Ellie Mae asked.

Sally chuckled. "That does help."

"Aunt Katrina is a good teacher."

"Now, how would you know that, Ellie Mae?" Sam asked. "You've never been in her school."

"You said she was smart, didn't you?"

"Yes, I did say that."

"And Aunt Katrina wanted to be a teacher. You heard what Mrs. Jensen just said. You have to be smart, and you have to want to be a teacher to be good. So, Aunt Katrina is a good teacher."

Sally chuckled. "Mr. Byrd, you cannot argue with that logic."

Sam laughed as well. "No, I don't guess I can."

"And with a mind that works like that, it's my guess that Ellie Mae is going to be a good teacher as well," Smoke said.

Chapter Four

After lunch, Smoke and Sally rode out to the forty rolling acres of land that had, at one time, been his pa's farm.

"This is it," he said, taking in the land with a sweep of his hand. "This is where I grew up."

"Oh, what a pretty little stream," Sally said.

"That's Finley Creek," Smoke said. He smiled. "That is the most valuable part of the whole farm, and it was the only thing that enabled us to raise something other than rocks."

"I see a fence over there on that Lodge. That must be where your mother is."

"That's it, all right," Smoke said. Riding all the way up to the fence, Smoke and Sally dismounted, then walked inside the little square formed by the waist-high, white picket fence. There was no longer a mound of dirt to indicate that anyone was buried there, but there was a grave marker. It wasn't the one that Smoke had erected, but it too was no more than a wooden marker with the barest information.

Smoke took off his hat and stood there for a

moment, looking down at the grave. Sally reached over to put her hand in his.

"Ma," Smoke finally said. "It's me, Smoke." He chuckled. "No, I don't reckon you'll recognize that name, seeing as I never come by it till long after you were gone.

"And this is Sally, my wife. You'd love her, Ma, I know you would."

"Hello, Mrs. Jensen," Sally said quietly.

"Call her Ma."

"Hello, Ma."

"Now, Ma, I know you've been resting comfortable down there for more than twenty years, but I've got something in mind that you're going to appreciate. Tomorrow I'll be coming back out here, and the first thing I'm going to do is put you in a coffin that's decent, then I'm going to take you into town and bury you in the cemetery there, alongside Pa. I brought him back with me. That way, the two of you can be together, from now on.

"Of course, I know that the two of you are together already, and Janey too. I'm glad to say that Janey turned out to be a fine woman after all. But I expect you and Pa knew that a long time before I ever found out."

Smoke pointed out where the house and barn had been, then he stopped and was quiet for a moment. "This is where it happened," he said. "This is where Ma was killed by Angus Shardeen. I stood by and let it happen."

"You didn't *let* it happen, Smoke," Sally told him.

"You were just a boy, you were unarmed, and there were too many of them."

"Yeah," Smoke said. "I've tried to tell myself that."

"I know it's little recompense, and it didn't bring your mother back. But at least you had the satisfaction of seeing justice done with regard to Shardeen."

"Yeah," Smoke said again, and this time he nodded with a satisfied expression on his face. "Yeah, justice was done."

Sally leaned over to kiss him.

"Are you thirsty?" Smoke asked. "Because the water in that creek is the best-tasting water you're going to find anywhere."

"Well, I can't pass that up, can I?"

Smoke emptied his canteen, then went over to refill it with fresh water from the creek. He took the first drink just to make certain it was as sweet as he remembered, then he passed the canteen to Sally.

"Uhmm, you are right," she said after taking a swallow. "This water is as good as the water from Abrams Creek, back home."

Smoke pointed out the fields, already green with new growth, and told about how, as a boy, he walked behind Ange and Rhoda as they pulled a single-point plow.

"I started behind a plow when I was twelve years old," Smoke said. "That was hard work for a boy."

"I'm sure it was," Sally said. "But it made you the man you are today."

Rain started just after they returned to town, then continued into the night. In the distance, lightning flashed and thunder roared and the rain beat down heavily upon the roof of the hotel, then cascaded down off the eaves before drumming onto the porch overhang, below.

Smoke stood at the window of his hotel room, looking down on the street of the town. He saw very few people outside, and when someone did go outside they would dart quickly through the rain until they found a welcome door to slip through. The town was dark, the rain having extinguished all outside lamps, and the inside lamps provided only the dullest glimmers in the shroud of night.

The room behind Smoke glowed with a soft, golden light, for he had lit the lantern and it was burning very low. Though Smoke had spent many a night sleeping on the prairie in such conditions, this was one of those nights where he appreciated being under a roof.

"Are you coming to bed, Smoke? Or, are you just going to stand there staring out the window all night?"

Smoke turned to look at her. There was a pensive expression on his face.

"I've come a long way, Sally."

"I know you have, sweetheart."

"As soon as we get this done, I'll be ready to go back to Sugarloaf."

"But this is something that needed to be done," Sally said.

Smoke nodded. "Yes..I know it is probably a foolish gesture, but I think it will bring me some peace, after all these years."

"I think it will, as well."

* * *

While Smoke and Sally were at breakfast the next morning they were approached by an old man. Smoke recognized him at once and, smiling, stood to greet him. "Dr. Blanchard!" he said.

"Hello, Kirby," the old man replied. "You're a mite changed from the last time I saw you."

Smoke chuckled. "And a lot from the first time you saw me."

Dr. Blanchard laughed out loud. "Yes, I would say so."

Smoke introduced Sally. "This is the man that brought me into this world. Pa brought him out to the house when it was Ma's time."

"It's very nice to meet you, Dr. Blanchard," Sally said.

Dr. Blanchard nodded. "I'm pleased to meet you, ma'am."

"Won't you join us?" Smoke asked.

"I'm afraid I haven't time to join you right now. The reason I stopped by is because I was talking to Gene Welch, and he said that you were planning to bury your parents in the cemetery here in town."

"Yes, sir, I am. My ma and pa have been apart for a long time, and I thought it might be good to get them together again."

"I've spoken with the mayor and few others in town, especially those of us who have fond remembrances of your mother and father, and that would be everyone who knew them," he added. "We were wondering, Kirby, if you would mind if several of us came out to the interment to pay our respects."

"Of course I wouldn't mind," Smoke said. "Why, I

would be very honored to have people there. And I know my ma and pa would be."

"Mr. Welch has it scheduled for two o'clock tomorrow afternoon. Is that right?"

Smoke chuckled. "I suppose so. I hadn't really given him a specific time, but if that is the time he has chosen, I'm sure it will be fine."

"Good, because that is the word that has already gone out."

"Word has gone out? I don't understand."

Dr. Blanchard chuckled. "You haven't seen the newspaper, have you?"

"No, I haven't."

"You might find it interesting," Dr. Blanchard said. Then, after a long pause he added, "Smoke."

"Smoke?"

"That is how you're called now, isn't it?"

"How did you know?"

"As I said, you might find the article in the paper interesting. Good to have met you, Mrs. Jensen," Dr. Blanchard said with a nod as he turned to leave.

"I guess I had better get a copy of today's newspaper."

Train Robbery Attempt Foiled

The Kansas City Special was visited by three men on Monday last, motivated by the idea that they could get rich by robbing the passengers and the express car. However, the would-be robbers, who have since been identified as Abner Doby, Burton Kennedy, and Clem Givens, did not count on the presence of a passenger of particular note. Had they known that one of the passengers was none other than Smoke Jensen, they no doubt would have attempted to employ their nefarious scheme elsewhere.

Smoke Jensen, better known as Kirby Jensen to those friends and neighbors who remember him as a onetime citizen of Galena, proved that the stories that have been written about him are accurate. When he was challenged by the brigands who were attempting to rob the train, he responded by the skillful employment of his pistol, the balls thus energized being unerringly accurate, and taking terrible and fatal effect upon the three who would have robbed the train.

Mr. Jensen, and his wife, Sally, are currently visiting our fair city. He has returned to Galena, the domicile of his youth, in order to bury his parents in the city cemetery. His parents, Emmett and Pearl Jensen, were once farmers, just north of town. They were well known, well liked, and respected by neighbors and citizens of the town and county alike.

According the Gene Welch, the burial will take place at the Garden of Memories Cemetery at two o'clock on Wednesday afternoon. And all of our citizens who remember these good people are urged to be present for the interment so that proper respect may be paid.

"Well, so much about keeping quiet as to who I am," Smoke said as he passed the paper across the table to Sally.

Sally read the article quickly, then looked up with a smile. "I didn't really think you would be able to keep it quiet," she said. "Let's face it, Smoke. Like it or not, you are quite a well-known man."

Smoke returned to the funeral parlor to speak with Gene Welch.

"I see that you have the burial scheduled for two o'clock tomorrow afternoon."

"Yes, I hope that is all right with you."

"It will be fine, assuming you can get my mother's remains back in time."

"I'm sending a couple of men out today to recover your mother's body. Would you like to go with them? Or be here when she is brought in?"

"No," Smoke said, holding up his hand. "That won't be necessary."

"Would you like to see the coffin we have selected?"

"Yes."

Welch took Smoke and Sally to his display room and showed them the Eternal Cloud. It was highly polished mahogany, with a red felt lining.

"I think your mother will be very comfortable in this," Welch said.

"I'm sure she will be."

"It is quite a beautiful coffin, Mr. Welch. You did a wonderful job in selecting it," Sally said.

"I'm glad that you are pleased," Welch replied. He cleared his throat. "I, uh, am hesitant to bring up money but . . ."

"But you want to be paid," Smoke said. "Understandable. How much do I owe you?"

"The coffin in one hundred and fifty dollars, it is

twenty-five dollars to disinter your mother, and another fifty dollars to open the two graves. I suppose you will want grave markers."

"Yes, of course."

"Nice, marble markers will cost you fifty dollars apiece. That includes their names, date of birth and date of death."

"That's three hundred and twenty-five dollars then?"

"Yes, plus my fee. Normally, I charge fifty dollars, but that includes embalming. There will be no embalming of your parents, of course, so I will charge only twenty-five dollars. For each," he added.

"Sounds reasonable," Smoke said as he counted out the money. "I want to thank you for all you have done," he added.

"It has been a pleasure to work with you," Welch said.

Smoke had initially thought that the reburial of his mother and father would be a very quiet and nearly private event. Then, when it appeared in the paper he figured there might be a few who would show up. But to his surprise, there were several hundred people at the cemetery. Many, he was pleased to see, were older people who remembered his parents and had come to show their respect for them. But as turned out, there were just many who were here to see Smoke Jensen, for even back here, his name had become well known. What people hadn't realized was that the Smoke Jensen they had read and heard about was the same Kirby Jensen who had once been a schoolboy here.

The Reverend E. D. Owen asked if he might conduct graveside services and Smoke said it would be all right. As the reverend spoke of the good lives Emmett and Pearl lived, and how they are now reunited in the promised land, Smoke recalled the initial burial of his father, who had been buried with nobody present, and his mother . . . attended only by his sister and him. He recalled her burial in a feeding-trough-cum-coffin, its top closed by using a door from the tack room.

"All right, let's go," Janey said.

"Hold on a moment," Kirby said. "Don't you think we ought to say a few words?"

"What for? There ain't neither one of us preachers."

"No, but she was our ma. Seems to me like the least we could do is say a few words over her grave."

"You're right," Janey said. "I'm sorry. Go ahead, say somethin'."

Kirby had been wearing a hat to protect him from the sun, and now he took it off and held it in front of him as he stood there, looking down at the grave.

"You was a good ma," he said. "You done what you could with us, and I appreciate it, an' loved you for it. I know that I didn't tell you that I loved you as much as I should've, but I never was much for speakin' a lot of words. I reckon I just thought that you always knew."

After thinking of that awful day, so long ago, Smoke brought his mind back to the present, and looked around at the people gathered at the burial of Emmett and Pearl Jensen today. He felt a sense of great personal satisfaction that he was able to bring this about, and he glanced over at the preacher, who was just concluding the graveside services.

"'Earth to earth, ashes to ashes, dust to dust; looking for the general Resurrection in the last day, and the life of the world to come.'"

After the words were spoken, and the graves were being closed, citizens of the town came by to express their condolences as if his parents had died last week, instead of more than twenty years ago.

Sam Byrd made the announcement that no funeral was complete without a dinner, and he had arranged for a repast to be held at Fellowship Church of Galena. Although Sam made all the arrangements, people from all over town had brought food, so there was plenty to eat for everyone.

Several people brought books for him to sign, and that always made Smoke a little uneasy.

"You know that I didn't write these books," Smoke said. "Not only did I not write them, I didn't even have any of these experiences that the stories portray. These are just made-up stories, using my name."

"But it is your name," one of the petitioners said. "And you are from Galena. I'd be just real proud if you would sign the book for me."

"Sign the books, Smoke. What harm can it do?" Sally said.

With a surrendering sigh, Smoke signed books, and fielded questions for the rest of the afternoon. Some of the questions were legitimate, as to where he went when he and his father left home, but many were about some of the experiences written about him in the books. Finally Sally rescued him.

"I need some help," she said.

Smoke smiled, gratefully. "I'll be right there," he said as he excused himself from those who had gathered around him.

"Thanks," he said as they walked away from the group. "Or, do you really need help?"

"Not exactly, but Sam is back in the pastor's office, and he has a telegram I think you should see."

"Telegram?"

"From his father," Sally said.

"Hello, Kirby, come on in," Sam said when Smoke stepped to the office door. "I asked Reverend Owen if we could use his office to conduct some business. After our discussion the other night, I telegraphed my pa. I just got this back and thought you might like to see it." He handed the telegram to Smoke.

KIRBY I WILL PURCHASE 200 HORSES
FROM YOU AT FAIR MARKET VALUE IF
YOU WILL DELIVER THEM TO ME AT MY
RANCH EL BUCLE AMPLIA IN NUECES
COUNTY TEXAS STOP RESPOND
SOONEST STOP TOM BYRD

Smoke handed the telegram to Sally. "What about it, Sally? Do you think Cal and Pearlie would like to go to Texas?"

"I think we would all love to go to Texas," Sally replied.

It didn't escape Smoke's notice that she had included herself in the operation.

"Thanks, Sam," Smoke said. "I'll go down to the telegraph office right now and respond."

Half an hour later, Smoke passed his message across the counter to the telegrapher.

WILL BE THERE AS SOON AS POSSIBLE WITH 200 OF THE FINEST MOUNTS IN THE COUNTRY

Chapter Five

Sally opened her eyes and looked through the window of the railroad car and smiled with pleasure. The dawn sky was streaked with various shades of red, gold, and purple, and though she had enjoyed their trip to Missouri, she was pleased to be coming back home. She lay there listening to the rhythmic clack the wheels made on the tracks and enjoying the patterns and colors of the breathtakingly beautiful, ever-changing sky.

"Smoke?"

"You mean you're finally awake?" Smoke replied.

"Yes." Sally stretched. "I love sleeping on a train."

"Enjoy it while you can," Smoke said. "In a couple more days, you'll be sleeping in a wagon every night for about a month."

Sally smiled. "That can be nice too."

"We'll be pulling into Big Rock in less than half an hour. We'd better get dressed."

"You think Pearlie and Cal will be there to meet us? We didn't hear back from the telegram we sent."

"No good way for them to reply, but I expect they'll be there. I told them I'd buy breakfast at Lambert's."

As they approached Big Rock, Sally gazed out the window at the buildings along Front Street—Earl's Blacksmith, the sheriff's office, the newspaper, Longmont's Saloon, and Murchison's Leather Goods—before the train rattled to a halt at the depot. Here, the station platform stacked with crates and boxes and, beyond that, the nearly one hundred buildings that made up the little town of Big Rock. This was nothing like the sophisticated cities of Sally's youth, but there was no way she would trade what she had now with what she knew then.

The depot was a flurry of activity and noise. On the platform, men yelled at each other as a steel-wheeled car was rolled up to the baggage car to load and unload suitcases, crates, and mailbags. Here, also, the train took on water, precipitating a great deal of banging and clanging of tank covers and waterspouts as the water tank was filled. The fireman kept the fire stoked and the steam going, and the rhythmic opening and closing of the valves as the pressure repeatedly built up and then vented away sounded remarkably like the laborious breathing of some great beast of burden.

In addition to those people manning the depot and the train and the passengers arriving and departing—plus those meeting them or sending them off—dozens of townspeople, to whom the arrival of the train was a major event, crowded the depot.

"There they are!" Sally said, pointing to Pearlie and Cal, both of whom were leaning against the front of the depot with their arms crossed across their chest.

When Smoke and Sally stepped down, the two young cowboys smiled, and started toward them.

"Did you miss us?" Sally asked, hugging them both.

"We sure did," Pearlie said.

"But not until he ran out of the bear claws you left for us," Cal said.

"We wouldn't've run out as fast if you hadn't et 'em all," Pearlie said.

Norman Lambert, called "Hogjaw" by his friends, had a gimmick. As soon as a customer came into his café, he would throw at them, biscuits for the breakfast meal, rolls for lunch and dinner, or as the locals called it, dinner and supper.

Pearlie caught the first biscuit and had it half eaten by the time the four of them were seated.

Over breakfast, Smoke explained his plan of driving two hundred horses down to Texas to be sold to Tom Byrd.

"Can you trust this fella?" Cal asked. "What I mean is, what if we get down there and he changes his mind, or starts quibbling over the cost. That would be a long trip for nothin', wouldn't it?"

"I suppose it would, but I've sold him livestock before, and he paid as agreed."

"Oh, I didn't know that. I guess it'll be all right then."

"I guess so," Smoke replied with a grin.

Sally laughed out loud. "Are you going to tell him, or am I?"

"Tell him what?"

"Tell him what livestock you sold."

"Go ahead and tell him," Smoke said. "You know you're dying to."

"He sold him two mules. Ange and Rhoda."

"But he paid you, right?" Pearlie asked.

"Yeah," Smoke said with a chuckle. "He paid me seventy dollars."

"That's about what one horse cost, and we're takin' 'im two hundred," Pearlie said.

"Because he is buying so many, I'm going to let him have them at sixty dollars a head."

"Still, that's." Pearlie closed his eyes and started figuring.

"Twelve thousand dollars," Cal said, quickly.

"Show-off. I was cipherin' up to it."

"When do we leave?" Cal asked.

"As soon as we can get our stock gathered, and our chuck and hoodlum wagons ready. I'd say we should be ready by Monday morning."

"You mean we're not going to take 'em by train?" Cal asked. "That would be a lot faster."

"I expect it would, seeing that it's three days by train, and at least thirty days by trail drive. But, it would take at least thirty-five cars, and that would cost seventy-two hundred dollars. We can drive them down for less than twenty-two hundred, and that includes paying forty and found for the wranglers."

"Yeah, I see what you mean. How many men do you think we'll need?" Pearlie asked.

"I'd say at least four more, beside us. That would give us five men by day, and two riding nighthawk."

"Who are you going to get to drive the wagons?" Cal wanted to know.

"Sally is going to drive the chuck wagon," Smoke said.

"That means you'll be doin' the cookin', don't it?" Cal asked with a wide grin.

"Doesn't it," Sally corrected, always the teacher. "And yes, I will be driving the chuck wagon."

"That'll be good, you doin' the cookin'. At least I know we'll eat real good."

"You'll eat well," Sally said.

"Yes, ma'am, that's what I'm countin' on."

Sally sighed. "Never mind."

"Who'll be drivin' the hoodlum wagon?" Pearlie asked.

"I haven't decided on who to ask to drive the hoodlum wagon," Smoke said.

"What about having Old Mo drive it?" Pearlie suggested.

"He's too old," Cal said. "Why, he must be near seventy."

"You want to tell him that?" Smoke asked.

"What? You want me to tell that old man that he's too old? No, sir, I ain't about to do that."

Smoke chuckled. "I didn't think so. I think Mo will be perfect for the job."

Old Mo's real name was Arnold Morris, and he lived in one of the line shacks on Sugarloaf Ranch. Mostly retired, he earned his keep by riding fence line. He had come west in 1846, and since that time had supported himself in various occupations. He had trapped beaver, hunted buffalo for the expanding railroads, scouted for the army, rode the outlaw trail for a while, and wore a deputy's badge. More recently he had been a cowboy and a horse wrangler. He was a taciturn man who spoke little. Everyone referred to him as Old Mo, but when they were talking face-to-face with him, they called him Mo.

"May as well," Old Mo replied when Smoke asked if he would like to come along. "Ain't never been to Texas."

Smoke put the word out among his hands that he was looking for four men to go with them on the drive down to Texas. He got four eager volunteers.

At twenty, Walt Bizzel was the youngest. He was also the fastest, having won the annual Fourth of July Big Rock footrace the last two years.

Don Pratt was only a little older. He was starting out on the wrong path, until Sheriff Monty Carson took a hand. Instead of putting him in jail, he brought him out to Sugarloaf to see if Smoke would take him on. Smoke did, and Don had been a good hand ever since.

Fred Stone and Vernon Mathis were former soldiers who had served their time honorably, and when discharged, decided to stay in the West, winding up at Sugarloaf Ranch, working for Smoke.

"You're all going to get your regular pay," Smoke said. "And a hundred dollars apiece for making the drive."

"Yahoo!" Walt said.

"Now, before we go any further, I need to ask all of

you: Is there any reason why you can't go to Texas? Is there any paper out on any of you that some aggressive Texas sheriff might know about and pay us a visit?"

"I never done none of my, uh, business down in Texas," Don said.

Old Mo didn't answer, but he had already told Smoke that he had never been there before.

"All right, get everything you need to take and load it into the hoodlum wagon. Choose three riding horses you are comfortable with. You've got the weekend off, but be ready to leave Monday morning."

"Uh, can we have some of the money now so's we can go into town and buy a few things we might need?" Don asked.

"I'll give you fifty dollars now, and the other fifty when we deliver the livestock."

The four young men smiled; Old Mo simply nodded.

"I don't know about you boys, but I'm goin' into town," Walt said.

Webb, Texas

It was a Sunday morning and most of those who weren't sleeping off a Saturday-night drunk were gathered in the Fellowship Church. Nobody knew what denomination the church was, there were only sixty-eight people in the entire town, not enough to argue over such details.

The little community of Webb was about ten miles north of the Mexican border, and T. B. Keno and his army of bandits approached the town from the south. When he held up his hand to stop his men, they

could hear the congregation singing through the
open windows of the church:

> *O God, our help in ages past,*
> *Our hope for years to come,*
> *Our shelter from the stormy blast,*
> *And our eternal home.*

"There is no bank in this town, *Coronel*. What have
we come to steal?"

"Whiskey," Keno replied with a broad smile.

Motioning his men forward, they rode on into
town, then stopped in the square. There were only
four business buildings in town, the saloon, a mercantile store, a feed and seed store, and a blacksmith's
shop.

"Go into the saloon and the store," Keno ordered
some of the men. "Take all that you can carry. There
is no hurry, we will keep the people busy."

As eight men ran into the saloon and the mercantile, Keno took the rest of his brigade down to the
church, which sat at the end of the street. He spread
them around all four sides of the church, and once
they were all in position, he gave the order to fire.

Inside the church, the forty-nine people who had
actually attended services this morning were so engaged in singing the hymn that none were aware
that the church had been surrounded. Then, over
the sound of the organ, and the forty-nine voices,
came the explosive roar of gunfire, several guns firing
at the same time. The windows came crashing down

as bullets whipped across the nave, plunging into bodies.

The organist was one of the first hit, and she fell across the keyboard, causing one last, loud, discordant note to compete with the sound of shooting and screaming.

"Get down!"

The preacher was a veteran of the Civil War, and he had the presence of mind to look after his flock. "Everyone, down on the floor!"

The preacher's warning shout saved many others, but not him. In order to make certain that everyone got down, he remained on his feet a moment too long, and a bullet hit him in the side of his head.

Not one parishioner had a gun with him. This was, after all, a church service, and why would anyone need a gun during a church service?

After several seconds of shooting, the front doors opened, and six armed men came in. There was silence now, except for the moans of the wounded, and the cries of the bereaved.

"Good morning, my friends," Keno said in heavily accented English. "I do hope you haven't taken up the collection yet. Because that's what we are going to do. I'm going to pass the plate around, and I do want you to be generous."

"Who are you?" someone asked.

"*Soy el Coronel Taurino Bustamante Keno.* Learn this name, for one day I will be president of Mexico."

As the plate was passed, the living and the injured began to put money in it, passing it over the bodies of those who had been killed.

"Do not pass by the dead. They too must contribute. Take the money from their pockets."

When all the money was collected, Keno walked to the front of the church, and crossed himself. Then he turned with a demonic smile on his face.

"Remember the words of the Lord, how He said it is more blessed to give than to receive," he said.

"*Coronel,* the men have gathered," one of Keno's men said, stepping in through the front door.

"Then we must go. *Adios.*"

Keno stepped out through the front door and a second later there were three flaming torches tossed inside. Those who were still alive shouted in alarm and some of the uninjured moved quickly to extinguish the blazes.

Chapter Six

Sugarloaf Ranch

Sally prepared an early breakfast on Monday morning and the drive got under way as soon as everyone had eaten. They drove the horses right through the middle of Big Rock, and because most of the citizens of the town were aware of the drive, they had turned out to watch. The horses were well under control, but there were quite a few of them, so they made quite a sight as they practically filled the street from side to side.

Most of the citizens were standing on the boardwalks, and they shouted good-natured jabs at the company as they passed through.

"Look who's driving the chuck wagon! Hello, Miz Sally. Don't you go lettin' any o' them boys go hungry, now."

"Ha! There's Old Mo drivin' the hoodlum wagon. Old Mo, ain't you little old for this?"

Neither Sally nor Old Mo replied to any of the shouts, but several of the wranglers called back, and the good-natured ribbing continued until they were clear of the town.

The hoodlum wagon carried extra saddles and tack, canvas, ammunition, blankets, and tools. As soon as they were out of town, the chuck wagon and hoodlum wagon went on ahead of the herd.

While on the move, one of the cowboys would be riding as point man ahead of the herd, scouting for water and graze. Flankers rode on either side of the herd, keeping them moving, while one man rode drag, meaning the rear. This was the least desirable position because the cowboy who rode drag had to swallow all the dust.

It was up to Sally and Old Mo to determine where they would spend the night, and they did so, making forty miles on the first day, and finding a place alongside Elk Creek. Here, they would set up camp and get supper started for the wranglers.

Although Old Mo didn't do any of the cooking, he did help by gathering wood and starting the fire and bringing water from a nearby creek to keep the water barrel filled.

Supper was cooked over an open fire and the food was served from the tailgate. "My oh my, Miz Jensen, iffen you're goin' to cook like that for this entire drive, I'm goin' to get so fat none of my horses will be able to carry me," Walt said.

"I'm glad you appreciate my cooking," Sally said.

"It's a lot better 'n what Muley can do," Walt said, referring to the cook back at the ranch.

"All right, boys, time to put out the nighthawks,"

Smoke said. "Pearlie, you and I will take it until midnight. Any volunteers for midnight till dawn?"

"I'll do it," Cal said. "Walt, you want to take it with me?"

"All right," Walt replied.

Smoke didn't have to take nighthawk; he was the boss and he could just order it done. But he didn't mind it that much because it was quiet and he would be alone, since Pearlie would be on the other side of the herd. And the first half of nighthawk, until midnight, was always the easiest shift.

As Smoke rode around the horses, most of whom were asleep while standing in place, he felt a sense of peace with himself. He had gotten his mother and father buried together, he knew, now, that Janey had straightened out and was living a good life before she died, and there were no unfinished tasks hanging over him. The night breeze was refreshing, and the sounds of the night creatures, relaxing. He wouldn't trade this for anything in the world.

"Everything quiet?" Sally asked just after midnight, as Smoke bedded down beside her.

"Sorry, I didn't mean to wake you."

"You didn't. I was already awake."

"That's not good, Sally, you need your sleep. You have to get up before any of us to fix breakfast."

"I guess there was just too much on my mind for this first day."

"Everything is quiet," Smoke said. He leaned over to kiss her. "Go to sleep now."

* * *

The next morning breakfast was cooked and served from the tailgate of the wagon, just as supper had been the night before. Sally made several extra biscuits and cooked extra bacon. The men grabbed two biscuit and bacon sandwiches apiece, wrapped them up in cloth, and stuck them down into their saddlebags. That would be their lunch.

That established the pattern for the next several days, with an ample breakfast and supper being served in camp, while lunch was generally taken in the saddle.

After breakfast on each day of the drive, Sally and Old Mo would load up their respective wagons and go on ahead of the wranglers by approximately forty miles, covering the distance in about eight hours. There they would search out a place that provided forage and water for the horses, as well as a place that was suitable for the night's encampment.

"You don't talk much, do you, Mr. Morris?" Sally asked one afternoon as the two of them sat waiting for the herd to catch up.

"Talkin' ain't my strongest thing," Old Mo said.

"You knew Smoke's friend Preacher, didn't you?"

"I knowed Preacher. Can't say me 'n' him was ever close, 'cause we warn't. But I knowed him all right. I knowed him, Grizzly Adams, Kit Carson, Jim Bridger, and lots more. They was all decent men, good men, all of 'em."

"How come a handsome man like you has never married?" Sally asked, smiling to show that she was teasing.

"I was married oncet. Married, 'n' had me a boy."

Old Mo's answer surprised Sally.

"You were? I've never heard that. Was it to a beautiful Indian maiden? I know that a lot of you oldtimers did take Indian wives. Preacher did."

"No, Sara Sue was a white woman. She died in 1846."

"Oh," Sally said, sorry now that she had steered the conversation into what could be unpleasant memories. "I'm sorry that I brought it up."

"No need to be sorry. It ain't like I don't remember unless someone reminds me. It's purty much always on my mind. What Sara Sue done was, she starved to death. Her 'n' my boy both."

"Good heavens! Starved to death?"

"Was a lot of 'em starved to death that winter. Me, Sara Sue, and little Johnny come west with a wagon party in 1846. What happened was the wagons got snowbound in the Truckee Pass up in the Sierra Nevada mountains. We couldn't go ahead 'n' we couldn't come back. And all the while we was stuck there, the snow just kept on a-fallin'. I ain't never seen as much snow before, 'n' I ain't never seen so much since. We got stuck there 'n' soon, we run out of food. Then folks started into dyin' from starvation.

"We had started out for California to find us some land to farm. But, by the time I got out of that there pass, I wasn't lookin' to farm no more. I'd pure lost my taste for it. And truth to tell, I had near 'bout lost my taste for livin'."

"You're . . . you're talking about the Donner party expedition, aren't you, Mr. Morris?"

Old Mo nodded for an answer.

Sally wished she had not opened this conversation. She knew about the Donner party, and the extreme conditions they had faced. She reached over to put her hand on Old Mo's shoulder. "I'm sorry," she said quietly. "I'm terribly sorry."

"Until you've been there, you don't never have no idea what a person will do to survive," Old Mo said.

They were both silent for a long moment before Old Mo spoke again. "I'll, uh, go get us some more wood."

Old Mo got up then, and walked toward a scraggly line of trees. Sally felt her eyes well with tears, and she felt a lump in her throat. She knew that the survivors were forced into cannibalism in order to survive. And she wondered, but would never ask, if Old Mo had been faced with that terrible choice.

"Smoke, did you know that Mr. Morris was a part of the Donner party when they got snowed in, in the pass?"

"I knew."

"Do you think, Lord, I hate to even ask this question, but I must. Do you think . . ."

"Do I think it became necessary for Old Mo to eat his own wife and child to survive?"

"Thanks for asking the question for me, so I wouldn't have to."

"I've wondered about that myself," Smoke said. "He has never said one way or the other. But, he may have. I know that something haunts him."

"If we were ever in a situation like that, and I had died, and the only way you could save yourself, I would want you to do that."

Smoke shook his head. "No, there is no way I could ever do that. Don't even think such a thing."

"Why not?"

"Do you have to ask?"

"Think about it, Smoke," Sally said. "If you had to do something like that, I would be a part of you, forever."

Smoke was quiet for a long moment, and when he did speak, it wasn't a direct reply.

"Good night, Sally. I love you."

Sally knew that it was a painful and difficult subject, so she didn't pursue it.

"Good night."

The Wide Loop

Tom Byrd read the newspaper article, then shook his head, and held the paper up toward his wife. "Did you read this, Hazel? That damn Keno attacked a small town and killed twenty-seven people!"

"I read it," she said.

"He attacks, then he goes back into Mexico, where he's safe. Something needs to be done about that. I don't know why the army, or the Texas Rangers, or somebody, doesn't go after him."

"Because we can't cross the border," Hazel said.

"Why not? That son of a bitch did."

"Because it would start another war with Mexico."

"So, what if it did? We kicked their ass last time. We can do it again."

"Don't get yourself all worked up over it. Think about something else. I'm looking forward to seeing Kirby Jensen again. He was always such a nice boy."

"Hardly a boy now, Hazel. He's older than our Sam. And a lot older than Katrina, who is a grown woman now."

"I do wish she would find herself a nice young man, though. She needs to be married and starting a family."

"You know the school board won't let her teach if she is married."

"She doesn't have to teach forever."

"Yeah, well, let her do it for as long as she wants. Besides, if she ever does get married, I'm going to be very particular about the man she chooses."

"You just said it, Tom. The man *she* chooses, not you. I think Katrina is intelligent enough to make her own choice. Don't you?"

"She can make her own choice. As long as I approve of him."

Hazel laughed. "Tom, you are impossible. I don't know how I have lived with you all these years."

Ciudad Victoria

Captain Juan Cortina of the Mexican *Federales* studied the report in front of him. Taurino Bustamante Keno had raided across the border into Texas again, and the Texas Rangers had complained.

Keno called himself a colonel, and professed to be raising an army to fight a revolution against the government of Manuel González. González was a popular president though, and Cortina was certain that there would be no revolution. Keno was just using that to justify his raids, not only on Mexican villages, but now in Texas as well.

"Gomez," Cortina called to his lieutenant.

"*Sí, Capitán?*"

"Where is Keno? What does our latest report say?"

"He is near Nuevo Pacifico, *Capitán*."

"How many men does he have?"

"It is said that Coronel Keno has at least seventy, and maybe even one hundred soldiers."

"No!" Cortina said, angrily, bringing his fist down onto his desk. "He is not a *coronel*, and they are not soldiers! They are bandits!"

"*Sí, Capitán*, they are bandits. But he has fifty, and we have five."

Cortina pinched the bridge of his nose and shook his head. "It is impossible," he said. "The commandant wants me to go after Keno but how can I do so with but five men? I will send a letter, asking that the commandant give me more men." He smiled. "With more men I will be promoted. And so will you, Gomez."

Gomez smiled as well. "*Sí, Capitán*. That will be very good."

At that very moment, in Nuevo Pacifico, Keno and his officers were being entertained by the *alcalde*, or mayor, of the town. They were seated around a long table, which was filled with food and drink, provided by the town. The citizens of the town didn't provide the food and drink out of honor, or respect, but out of fear.

Nuevo Pacifico was Keno's headquarters, and because of that, except for the tributes, which he called a "tax" he didn't bother the town that much. He also felt perfectly safe here. The local *policía* didn't bother him, and the *Federales* lacked the manpower to challenge him.

"This is a fine city, *Alcalde* Hernandez," Keno said. "After the revolution, when I declare myself President for Life, I will make Nuevo Pacifico the capital of Mexico."

The mayor smiled, broadly.

Keno signaled to one of his men, who brought a cloth bag to him. When the bag was delivered, Keno emptied its contents onto the table. "Here are ten thousand pesos," Keno said, waving his hand toward the money. "Have the citizens of the town pass by in front of me, and I will give them all money."

"That is most generous of you, Coronel Keno!" Hernandez said.

"I am a generous man," Keno said. "And I want my people to love me."

Chapter Seven

Smoke and his company herded through Colorado, following the Canadian River down into New Mexico where they camped outside the small settlement of Liberty. Old Mo and Don Pratt went into town for supplies.

"You think maybe we could have us a beer or two while the storekeep is gettin' our supplies together?" Pratt asked.

"I reckon we can if we don't get drunk," Old Mo said. Although Old Mo had no particular authority over the others, unlike Pearlie, who was the trail boss, and Cal, who was Pearlie's assistant, the other men often deferred to Old Mo because of his age.

The two men went into the Freedom Saloon, ordered a beer apiece, then found a table. They drank their beer, then Old Mo sent Pratt down to the mercantile to check on their order.

Pratt hadn't been gone two minutes when six men came in. Old Mo had just lifted his glass to his mouth, when he realized that he knew one of them. It was

Edgar Tebo, a man Old Mo had ridden with back in his days on the outlaw trail.

It had been seven years since Old Mo last saw Tebo, and now as he saw the man from his past, the memory came flooding back.

Morris pulled the slicker about him and hunkered down in his saddle. The rain was cold and contained within it little bits of ice that whipped against his face. He and two others had been recruited to rob a train.

"It's carryin' sixty thousand dollars," Tebo said. "Boys, we make this haul, we'll be rich!"

"I don't know, Eddie, I've pulled some other jobs with you . . . holdin' up a few stagecoaches, rustlin' some cattle, even robbin' a bank," Morris said. "But robbin' a train? That's somethin' totally different."

"It ain't like trains ain't never been robbed before," Tebo said.

"Maybe so, but it ain't nothin' we've ever done before."

Morris sat there in the cold rain, wondering why he had let Tebo talk him into this adventure.

"Well, boys, we got ever'thing ready for the fire, and I seen the light way down the track. It'll be here in no more 'n a couple of minutes. Make sure all your guns is loaded and be ready to do what I tell you."

By now Morris could hear the train as it approached. The puffing of the steam and the whistle cut through the night. Then as the train drew closer, he could see the headlamp casting a long spear in front and catching the drops of rain in its beam.

"Pete, get the fire lit now!"

Morris saw little flames flicker and grow into a bigger fire. Pete came running back down the berm, then mounted the horse Morris was holding for him.

The burning wood was in the middle of the tracks and Morris could tell when the engineer saw it because he heard the exact moment that the engineer put on the brakes and the train started slowing.

"All right, boys, get them guns out," Tebo said.

When the train stopped, Tebo leapt from his horse onto the locomotive deck, and pointed his pistol at the firemen and engineer. Pete and Earl approached the express car. Morris remained back, to make certain that nobody climbed down from any of the passenger cars to cause a problem.

Pete banged loudly on the door with the butt of his pistol.

"If you don't open the door now we're going to kill the engineer and the firemen. Open that door and toss down the money bags."

The door opened. Then three men suddenly appeared in the open door with double-barreled shotguns. They opened fire and Pete and Earl were shot out of their saddles.

"What the hell happened?" Tebo shouted.

"Messenger guards!" Morris shouted back. "They kilt Pete and Earl!"

"Get out of here!" Tebo shouted. "Get out now!"

Morris turned his horse and spurred it into a gallop.

That was Old Mo's last experience on the outlaw trail. It was also, until he saw him come into the saloon a moment ago, the last time he had seen Edgar Tebo.

Tebo recognized Old Mo as quickly as Old Mo had recognized him, and he came over to the table.

"I'll be damn, Morris, I thought you was dead."

"Hello, Tebo."

"What are you doin' down in these parts? I thought you pretty much stayed up in Colorado."

"There's a man down a ways farther owes me fifty

dollars," Old Mo said, thinking it best that he not tell the truth.

"And you come this far, just for fifty dollars."

"When you don't have much to begin with, fifty dollars is a lot of money."

Tebo turned to the others who had come into the saloon with him. "Boys, come over here, I've got someone I want you to meet. Fellers, this here is Morris. Never did learn his first name. Don't even know if Morris is his real name."

"Morris will do," Old Mo said.

"Me 'n' Morris, and some other fellers did a few jobs up in Wyoming a few years back. I kinda lost track of 'im since then, though."

"I've been keepin' myself pretty much out of sight," Old Mo said.

"Me 'n' these boys have just come up with a plan that's goin' to make us a lot of money tonight. It's out there right now, just waitin' for us. Forget about that fifty dollars, your share of this deal could earn you five hunnert dollars. Five hunnert easy dollars. What do you say; you want to come in with us?"

"Stealin' ain't ever easy," Old Mo said.

"What makes you think this has anythin' to do with stealin'?"

"I don't figure you're goin' to pay me five hunnert dollars to shovel horse shit," Old Mo said.

Tebo laughed. "Well, you're right, we are goin' to do a little stealin'. So, what do you say? Are you in on it with us?"

Old Mo shook his head. "Don't know as I do. I mean, rememberin' the last job that we done together. Or at least, we tried to do. As you might recall, it didn't turn out all that good. Especially for Pete 'n' Earl."

"Yeah, well, that was different. Turns out they was waitin' on us. But what I got in mind now is goin' to be real easy. Just a matter of movin' a little livestock, is all. What do you say?"

"I'm old and plumb wore out," Old Mo said. "You don't want me. I wouldn't be no good to you."

"Yeah? Well, don't say I didn't give you the chance to come in with us."

"I guess I'd better get on my way," Old Mo said. "I just stopped in 'cause I was thirsty. I got more ridin' to do yet, tonight."

Old Mo left the saloon and reached the mercantile just as Pratt was putting the purchases in the back of the hoodlum wagon.

"What are you doin' here?" Pratt asked. "Ain't we goin' to have one more beer?"

"No time for that," Old Mo replied.

"Why not?"

"On account of I've got a feelin' they's some fellas that's goin' to try and rustle the horses tonight. We got to get back in time to get ready for 'em."

"His name is Edgar Tebo," Old Mo told Smoke. "I'm sorry to say that me 'n' him rode together some time back when I was . . . uh . . ."

"No need to apologize or explain," Smoke said. "You think he has our horses in mind?"

"Yeah, I do. He said my share would be five hunnert dollars, and he said it was a plan he had in mind for tonight. They was at least six of 'em that come into the saloon. That's about what it would take to rustle the horses, then herd them off."

"You're a good man, Mo," Smoke said, reaching out to squeeze Old Mo on the shoulder.

"What are we goin' to do, Smoke?" Pearlie asked.

"We're going to get ready for them. With the herd up against the Canadian River, they're not going to be coming from the north. There are mountains to the east, and there is desert to the west. The reason they're in Liberty is because that's the only way they can approach. Let's find some places here to wait for them—rocks, a ravine, anywhere you can find some cover. Pearlie, you take the left side over there, Cal, you take the right. The rest of you spread out between the two of them."

"Smoke, I don't have any love for Tebo, that's for sure. But there was a time when me 'n' him rode together. 'N' while I don't want to see him get none of your horses, the truth is I'd just as soon not . . . uh . . ."

"I know what you are saying, and I respect that. Why don't you stay back by the wagons with Sally. Also, get a campfire going."

Old Mo nodded, but didn't speak.

"A campfire? Why would you want a campfire going?" Mathis asked.

"It'll do two things," Smoke said. "If they see the campfire, they won't have any idea that we are expecting them. Also, they'll be expecting us to be around the campfire, and that will give us an advantage in position."

"Damn, boss, you shoulda been an army general," Bizzel said.

Smoke smiled. "For this army, I am a general."

"Where you goin' to be, Smoke?" Pearlie asked.

"I'm going to be wandering around to wherever I figure I can do the most good. Just make sure none of you shoot me."

As the men were getting into position, Smoke stepped back to the wagons and spoke to Sally. "After you get the fire going, move around enough stuff in the wagons so that the two of you can get inside, out of the line of fire and out of sight."

"I'll do that," Sally said. "But I'll have my rifle with me."

"I expect you to."

It was dark but not entirely quiet. A coyote howled and an owl hooted. There was the scratch of hooves on the ground and the creak of riders in saddle leather. Eddie Tebo stared down toward the river. He couldn't actually see the individual horses, but he could tell they were there, because the herd made a large, dark mass against the soft glow of the river. He had seen the horses approaching two days ago, and he knew they would be taking advantage of the town, and here, by the river, would be the best place for them to camp. Since that time he had rounded up five other men, sure that would be enough.

He could see the campfire and he chuckled. "Boys, we've caught 'em by total surprise," he said.

"Didn't you say there was a woman with 'em?" one of the other men asked.

"Yeah, when I went out to scout 'em this afternoon, I seen a woman with 'em," a man named Rogers said.

"Well, look here. Let's try 'n' not kill the woman,"

one of the others said. "I can have more fun with her iffen she's alive."

"Only if you beat me to her," Rogers added, and they all laughed.

"Don't be worryin' none about the woman," Tebo said. "After we pull this job off, we'll have enough money to buy ever' whore in New Mexico. When I give the word, I want ever'one to start shootin' toward the campfire. I expect they'll all be a-sleepin' around it, and we'll more 'n likely kill some of 'em, and scare the rest of 'em off without anyone ever takin' a shot back in our direction. But, don't shoot until we get closer and I give the word."

"Right," one of his men agreed.

"And from here on, keep quiet," Tebo said. "No sense in lettin' 'em know we're here."

Smoke already knew that they were there. He had ridden forward to stand lookout, and when he saw the riders approaching, he rode quickly back to the others, to pass the word that the rustlers were coming.

"When they get closer I'm going to call out to them," Smoke said. "I'm going to give them a chance to ride away, but if they start shooting, be ready to return fire."

After giving the instructions, Smoke took up his own position and waited. They were still too far away and it was too dark to make them out well enough for a shot, or even to determine exactly how many there were. Then, finally, they drew close enough for him to make them out. There were six of them.

"Where are you men headed?" Smoke called out.

"What the hell?" a gruff voice returned from the dark. "Tebo, you said we'd surprise 'em."

"As you can see, you didn't surprise us. Now I'm going to have to ask you boys to turn around and ride on back. Leave now, and nobody will get hurt. If you don't leave now some of you, maybe all of you, are going to wind up dead. There's nothing here for you," Smoke said.

"The hell there ain't! Fire!" one of the riders barked.

With the muzzle-flashes from their shooting, Smoke had a target. He selected one, squeezing off a round, firing just to the right and slightly below one of the flashes.

That was the signal for Pearlie and the others to open fire, and instantly thereafter the night was lit up by the many flame patterns of the rifles and pistols. Gunshots roared, and reverberated back from the nearby mountain range.

"They been waitin' for us with a whole army!" one of the attackers shouted in a frightened voice. "We got to get the hell out of here!"

Smoke heard the sound of hoofbeats as the would-be rustlers turned their horses and began beating a retreat. The defenders fired three or four more times but they were just shooting in the dark with no idea as to where their targets were. It didn't really matter. The idea now was simply to run them off and that they had done.

"All right!" Smoke shouted. "Hold your fire, save your ammunition! They're gone!"

After the rustlers left, Smoke and the others

walked through the area, and they found three bodies.

"What are we goin' to do with 'em?" Pearlie asked.

"We'll take them into town tomorrow and leave them with the sheriff," Smoke said. "He'll know what to do with them. In the meantime, I expect we had better keep a guard out here, in addition to our nighthawk riders, just in case they decide to come back."

"They won't be coming back," Old Mo said.

After the shooting died down he had come up from the wagons, and was now standing over one of the bodies, looking down at it.

"How do you know?"

"This here is Eddie Tebo. He's the one got 'em all together in the first place, and they ain't likely to come back without 'im."

The men dragged the three bodies back to the site of the campfire, then they sat around the fire, talking in excited tones, about what had just happened.

"Fred, Vernon, you was both in the army," Don Pratt said. "Was what we just done like a real battle?"

"Only battles me 'n' Vernon was ever in was with Injuns," Fred said. "And was most always in the daytime."

The conversation continued, with the conspicuous absence of Old Mo. Old Mo was out in the dark, looking down at the three bodies.

"Smoke, I'm worried about Mr. Morris," Sally said.

"Why?"

"He said he had been put in a position where he had to betray one friend or another, and no matter how it wound up, he could only lose. What was he talking about?"

"He and Tebo were friends, once," Smoke said. "I think Mo knew that by telling me about the plan to steal the horses, it could well mean Tebo was going to be killed. But he told me anyway."

"Oh, then I can see what was bothering him."

Old Mo came back out of the darkness, then started toward the hoodlum wagon.

"Mr. Morris, are you all right?" Sally called after him.

Old Mo stopped, and looked back toward Smoke and Sally. He nodded his head. "Yes, ma'am, I'm all right," he said. "It was a hard thing for me to do. But I done what was right, an' that's all that matters."

"You did indeed do the right thing," Smoke said.

Old Mo nodded, then climbed into the hoodlum wagon to go to bed.

Chapter Eight

The next morning Old Mo drove the hoodlum wagon into town with the three bodies thrown in the back. Smoke, Sally, Pearlie, and Cal rode into town with him. Smoke went in so he could explain the incident to the sheriff, but also just so Sally could have a look around town. They had passed through several towns since leaving Big Rock, but this was the first time Sally had left the herd since they'd gotten under way several days earlier.

There was no canvas over the wagon so the three bodies were clearly visible, and that attracted the attention of several of the townspeople. By the time Old Mo stopped in front of the sheriff's office, word had already reached him that a wagon carrying three bodies was coming into town.

The sheriff bit off a chew of tobacco as Pearlie and Cal took the bodies from the back of the wagon and laid them out on the ground, faceup.

"Did you just find 'em, or did you kill 'em?" the sheriff asked.

"We killed them," Smoke said.

"I expect you had a good reason, or you wouldn'ta brought 'em in here."

"I'm taking a herd of horses down to Texas. These men, and some others, tried to steal them."

"Damn," someone said, pointing to the first body. "That's Arnie Tate. I thought he was in prison."

"That's Jake Loomis," another said, pointing out the second body. "It don't surprise me none to see him wind up like this."

"Anybody know this man?" the sheriff asked, pointing to the third body.

"That would be Edgar Tebo," Old Mo said.

"Edgar Tebo? Are you sure? The reason I ask is, I just got paper on Tebo. He robbed a store up in Salcedo, kilt the storekeep and his wife."

"How do you know Tebo was the one who done it?" Old Mo asked.

"They was a handyman in the back of the store and he seen the whole thing," the sheriff said. "'Course, we got no way of provin' that this here feller is Tebo, 'ceptin' your word on it."

"Does the paper say that Tebo is missin' his big toe on his right foot?" Old Mo asked.

"I don't know, let me check."

The sheriff stepped back into his office for a moment and as he did so, Old Mo pulled the boot off Tebo's right foot. Tebo wasn't wearing a sock, and there were a few sounds of surprise when the people who had been drawn to the macabre scene saw that the outlaw was indeed missing his big toe.

"Yeah," the sheriff said, coming back out. "It does say that."

"How much is the reward?" Smoke asked.

"One thousand dollars."

Smoke smiled at Old Mo. "Looks like you're a thousand dollars richer."

Old Mo shook his head. "I wasn't even up there shootin' at 'em, if you remember. I was back with the wagons."

"But you're the one that warned us about him, and you're the one that identified him."

"Tell you what. Divide it up among all the men, 'n' I'll just take my share," Old Mo said. Then he smiled. "But, if you'll lend me five dollars till I get my share, I'll be able to have me a fine time in town tonight."

Smoke laughed. "You've got a deal."

"What's your name?" the sheriff asked.

"This is Smoke Jensen," Pearlie said, answering the sheriff's question.

"Smoke Jensen?" somebody in the crowd said. "Lord Almighty, what's someone like Smoke Jensen doin' in Liberty?"

"You heard 'im. He's takin' some horses down to Texas."

"I've heard of you," the sheriff said, suspiciously.

"Yes, a lot of people have," Smoke said. "I'd just as soon people not have heard of me, but it's too late to put the horse back in the barn now."

"Well, Mr. Jensen, I'll say this. I ain't never heard nothin' bad about you. I'll have the money for you tomorrow," the sheriff said, "soon as I get word back from the capital."

"Thank you," Smoke said. "Do you need me to sign anything about this?" He took in the bodies with a sweep of his hand.

"No, seems pretty open-and-shut to me," the sheriff said. "Will you be staying in town tonight?"

"Yes, the herd is well guarded, so we will spend the night in town."

"Hope you enjoy it."

"I'm sure we will, thanks."

After taking care of the horses and wagon, Smoke and Sally took a stroll around town just to see what the town was like. Sally stepped into a dress store, not that she wanted to buy a dress, which certainly wasn't appropriate for now, but just to have a look around. Smoke stood at the window just looking out over the street while Sally was talking to the clerk.

For such a small town it seemed to be quite busy with people walking back and forth on the boardwalks, and with wagons and buckboards moving up and down the street. A sign was stretched across the street advertising an upcoming election.

Smoke turned toward Sally. "Are you going to be much longer?"

"What is your hurry, Smoke? We don't have anything else to do in this town."

"I thought we could get a good supper, then find a hotel room, and sleep comfortably tonight."

"All right, I was just looking anyway." Then to the clerk, Sally added, "You have some very beautiful things here. Thank you very much for letting me look around."

As it turned out there was quite a nice dining room in the hotel, and Smoke and Sally enjoyed a good dinner. It was particularly enjoyable to Sally because it was one that she didn't have to cook over an open fire.

"What do you think Mr. Morris meant by having a fine time in town tonight?" Sally asked Smoke later, after supper, when they were in their hotel room.

"What do you think he meant?"

"I don't know, that's why I asked you. I mean he's too old for . . . *that*, isn't he?"

"What do you mean by *that*?" Smoke asked.

"Oh, you!" Sally said with an embarrassed laugh. She hit him on the shoulder. "Never mind."

"On the other hand," Smoke added, reaching for her with a big smile. "I'm not too old."

"Oh, my," Sally said. "I guess you really aren't."

"I'll let you know when I am too old," Smoke said. "But I don't think that will be for quite a while yet."

Old Mo's idea of a fine time started with supper at a place called The Big O. With five dollars in his pocket, he was able to examine the menu for something that he actually wanted to eat, as opposed to looking at it with an eye as to what everything cost. He saw that the restaurant featured chicken and dumplings, and seeing that, it brought back memories from a long time ago. Old Mo had been born and raised in Missouri, and his mother had made chicken and dumplings quite frequently. His wife, when learning how much Old Mo enjoyed the dish, learned to fix them as well.

For a long time after that awful winter, Old Mo

would not eat chicken and dumplings because it brought back the unpleasant memories of having lost his wife and child in the cold and snow of what was now being called Donner Pass. Now he would have chicken and dumplings anytime the opportunity presented itself.

As he waited for his meal to be served he recalled the first time his wife had ever tried to make the meal.

"All, Arnie, I have ruined them all. They're all so soggy, and joined together, in big clumps. I am so sorry."

Old Mo chuckled quietly as he recalled that first meal. It had been very hard to eat her dumplings that day, but he would give anything in world if he had the opportunity to eat them again.

After supper he went down to the Freedom Saloon where he saw Cal and Pearlie sitting at a table.

He started to join them at the table, but saw three girls standing at the other end of the bar. One had red hair, one was a blonde, and one was a brunette. The color of their hair didn't seem natural, but he was sure they had worked it out among themselves to appeal to every predilection. He motioned to them.

"Ladies, I got me a big thirst, and I don't like to drink alone. I want you to join me 'n' my friends at the table."

"Which one of us do you want, honey?" the blonde asked.

"Why, I want all three of you," he said.

The redhead laughed. "Woo wee, honey, you must be some kind of man if you want all three of us."

Old Mo chuckled. "I ain't goin' to bed you, darlin's. I'm just goin' to drink with you."

Old Mo and the three girls walked over to Pearlie and Cal's table.

"You don't mind if me 'n' my lady friends here join you two boys, do you?" Old Mo asked.

"Why, we don't mind at all," Pearlie replied with a broad smile. "Let me get a couple of extra chairs for our guests."

"Oh, my!" the brunette said. "Why, this is just like a party."

"You two take your pick among them two. This gentleman is mine," the redhead said, grabbing Old Mo's upper arm with both hands.

"Where you been?" Pearlie asked, as Old Mo and the three girls sat down.

"I got me some supper," Old Mo said.

"We had supper here. Beans, bacon, and a couple of biscuits," Cal said. "It wasn't as good as what Miz Sally cooks, but it was pretty good."

"I had chicken 'n' dumplings and it was fine." Old Mo said. "Now I want a couple of drinks just to round the night out."

"Honey, is that really how you want to round the night out?" the redhead asked.

Old Mo laughed. "Honey, I'm just real flattered at your confidence in me, but I'm of an age where I know my limitation," Old Mo said.

On the other side of the room a man sat glaring at the table where Old Mo and the others were sitting. He had no idea who they might be but he knew they were not local people, so as far as he was concerned, they had no business taking up time with the girls. He was especially irritated that the redhead was with them. Long ago, he had picked Emerald out as his personal favorite.

"Look at Emerald over there," he said to the two men who were at the table with him.

"What about her?" one of the others asked

"What do you mean, what about her? Look at who Emerald is sittin' with. Hell, he's older 'n dirt, old enough to be her grandpa, and there he is, sittin' right there, next to my girl as big as you please. He ain't got no right to do that."

One of the other men laughed. "What do you mean 'your girl'? Come on, Pogue, you know that Emerald is the girl to anyone who has the money for her. Abby and Judy as well. That's how they make their living."

"Well, I've got the money for her and she knows that. So what is she doin' over there with that old man? He's so old that I bet he farts dust."

"Seems to me like I remember Emerald tellin' you she didn't want nothin' to do with you no more."

"She was just mad. She didn't mean it."

"She sounded pretty certain to me."

"Well, she's got no business bein' over there with that old man."

"Maybe she thinks that old man is better-looking than you are, Pogue."

The others at the table laughed.

There was some reason for the man making such a remark. Pogue was a particularly unattractive man.

He was in his midtwenties, relatively tall, with three missing teeth in front, and a scar on his cheek. He had a flattened nose, and beady eyes that seemed to have a difficult time finding their position in the socket.

"Well, I ain't goin' to put up with it."

"What do you plan to do about it?"

"You just watch. Hey, Emerald," he called across the room. "What are doing over there, sittin' beside that old fart?"

Emerald didn't respond.

"I asked you a question," Pogue said. "What are you doin' with an old man like that? You know damn well he can't do anything for you."

"Leave 'er be, Pogue," one of the others in the saloon said. "She ain't doin' nothin' other 'n what she's s'posed to be doin'. She's sittin' with someone while they drink."

"Nah, I don't aim to let my girl sit there with that damn old fool. Emerald, you come over and sit by me. I'll buy you a drink."

"Do you want to go over and sit with him?" Old Mo asked.

"No, I wouldn't want to be with him, even if you weren't here. But he's an evil man. I'm afraid of what he might do."

"Don't be afraid. He isn't goin' to do anything," Old Mo said.

"Did you hear me, woman? I told you to get over here, now!"

"The lady chooses not to join you," Old Mo said.

"You know what? I'm comin' over there to get her,

and if you get in the way, I'm goin' to kick your ass!" Pogue said.

Pogue went over to the table, then grabbed Emerald and tried to pull her up from the chair.

"No! Leave me alone!" Emerald said.

Old Mo started to stand, and Pearlie reached out for him. "Why don't you let me handle this, Mo?"

"I'll take care of it," Old Mo said.

"Ha! You'll take care of it?" Pogue said. "What do you think you can . . ."

That was as far as Pogue got. Taking advantage of the fact that Pogue had both his hands on Emerald, Old Mo hit him with a roundhouse right that dropped the belligerent young man to the floor, out cold.

"I'll be damn!" someone said. "Did you see that?"

Everyone saw it, and they looked on in silent awe as Old Mo sat back down. Emerald and the other two girls were looking at him with their mouths wide open. Even Pearlie and Cal had surprised expressions on their faces.

"I expect you boys had better drag your friend back before he comes to. Otherwise, I'll knock his damn head off," Old Mo said.

The men who had been sitting at the table with Pogue, and with expressions of shock still on their faces, came over to drag their friend back away from Old Mo's table.

"Why don't you ladies go get us all another round of drinks?" Old Mo asked.

Still awestruck, the three women started toward the bar.

"Mo, how the hell did you do that?" Cal asked.

Mo uncurled his right fist. It had been wrapped around a lead cylinder about the width of his hand.

"I had a little adjustment for age," he replied with a smile.

Pearlie and Cal both laughed out loud.

"Cal, you're the youngest. Pay attention. I think Old Mo . . . I mean *Mister* Morris, could teach us a thing or two."

The girls returned with the drinks then, and when they were all seated, Emerald proposed a toast.

"I just heard that you broke Pogue's jaw," she said. A huge smile spread across her face. "That means I won't have to be listening to him for a while. Here's to you."

All lifted their glasses to Old Mo, who took it all in as if it were his due.

The next morning when the sheriff gave Smoke the one thousand dollars, Pearlie spoke up.

"Smoke, me 'n' Cal's talked this over. We both make more money than any of the other boys, and we've been with you for the longest, so, truth is, we don't need any of the money. This way, if you just divide it up between Old Mo and the other four men, why, they'd have two hundred dollars apiece. And that would be real good money for them."

"You're sure you want to do this? Both of you?"

"We're sure," Cal said.

"That's a very decent thing for you to do," Smoke said. "I'm proud of you. Both of you."

"I'm proud of you too," Sally said. "And just to

show you how proud I am, I'll make some bear claws tonight."

"For ever'body? Or just for me 'n' Cal?" Pearlie asked.

"For everybody, of course," Sally replied. "You didn't really expect I would make them just for you two, did you?"

"Well, you did say you was proud of us," Pearlie said. "And I figured it wouldn't hurt to try."

Sally laughed. "You two are impossible."

Chapter Nine

Rick Isback grew up in Hell's Kitchen in New York. One day, in an argument with someone who was older and bigger, he grabbed a shotgun and blew a large hole in the belly of the man who was bothering him. His adversary, who hadn't expected such a thing, looked at Isback with an expression of shock on his face, holding his guts in his hand as he died.

Isback's claim of self-defense held up, so he didn't go to prison. But he learned two things from that incident. He learned that it didn't bother him to kill someone, and he also learned that he could employ that willingness to kill to his advantage. Overnight he changed from someone that others had always picked on, to someone that others feared. And he greatly enjoyed the power of seeing others cower before him.

He was soon able to put that newfound skill to good use, working for a gang of New York outlaws who were willing to pay him to kill people with whom they were having an issue.

Isback made good money being a killer, and he liked to spend the money on clothes. He enjoyed dressing well, and because of his attire, a tailored jacket, silk shirts, colorful cravats, and well-cut trousers often stuffed into the top of highly polished boots, he always stood out in any crowd.

He continued to kill for hire for almost a year, until one day one of the men he had been hired to kill was a New York City police captain. One didn't kill police officers with impunity, especially high-ranking police officers. After that incident, it was no longer safe for Isback to remain in New York. When he went to the criminal element he worked for and asked for enough money to allow him to leave town, they refused his request.

Isback killed the leader of that gang, and now he was wanted by both sides, the police, and the outlaws. He fled the city just before the law caught up with him.

When he first arrived in the West he was mocked for being a tenderfoot from the East, partly because of the way he was dressed. Isback killed one of the men mocking him, earning the respect, and the fear, of the others. No one mocked him again.

Shortly after that incident he discovered a trade that would allow him to continue to do what he was doing in New York. He became a bounty hunter, specializing only in the most desperately wanted men, the "dead or alive" cases. This way he could kill without compunction . . . and without fear of punishment, while also being paid for it. It was as if the vocation had been developed especially for him. He continued to dress in fine clothes, choosing that as his trademark.

Isback developed a great pride in his craft and, like

any craftsman, had the desire to be regarded as the best. To that end, he developed the skill of the quick draw. Although the speed with which one could draw his gun was important, Isback learned early in his career that more important than speed was the willingness to kill. And Isback was not only willing, he was eager to do so.

Although Isback was developing quite a name for himself, he was soon aware there was another name, more revered, and more respected. That name was Smoke Jensen, and Isback decided that the only way he could ascend to that pinnacle was to kill Smoke Jensen. But he couldn't just kill him. He would have to kill him in a way that would elevate his name above Jensen's.

It took very little effort to learn where Smoke Jensen lived, so he bought a train ticket to Big Rock, Colorado.

After getting off the train in Big Rock, Isback took a walk around town, winding up in the Brown Dirt Saloon. He bought a beer, and as the bartender set the mug in front of him, he inquired about Smoke Jensen.

"I've been looking for an old friend of mine, Smoke Jensen, and I was told he lived here, in Big Rock."

"Not in town, he don't," the bartender replied. "He's got him a ranch about seven miles west of here. Big spread called Sugarloaf."

"Ahh, thanks. I'm glad I finally found him. I think I'll just run out there and see him."

"No, sir, you won't see him if you go out there now," the bartender said. "He's gone down to Texas."

"He's moved there?" Isback asked.

"No, he ain't moved there. He's took some horses there."

"Texas is a big state," Isback said with an easy smile. "Where in Texas did he go?"

"I don't rightly know where at it was that he went. But they was an article about it in the *Big Rock Journal.* I reckon if you'd go down to the newspaper office, they'd have a copy so's you could find out just where it was that he took them horses."

"Thanks," Isback said.

"San Vicente? Where is that?" Isback asked.

Blanton, the publisher of the *Big Rock Journal,* chuckled. "I didn't know myself where it was, so I got me a map and looked it up. It's way down in southwest Texas, right there on the Rio Grande River."

Isback had intended to check into the hotel but chose, instead, to go back to the depot, where he bought a train ticket to San Vicente, Texas.

Smoke and the others continued to push the two hundred horses southward. The drum of horses' hooves, their occasional whicker and whinny, the scream of an eagle, and the bark of a coyote provided a welcome and familiar concert to accompany their passage. They drove the herd through land that was mostly red or brown, and with very few houses, or even ranches to break up the vistas. The horizons were studded with red mesas and cliff walls, and in the distance they saw shadowy purple mountains.

When night came, the stars and moon shed so much light that they could see almost as clearly as at midday.

Rising at dawn each day, they watched the red sun lift above the eastern horizon as they moved deeper and ever deeper into Texas. Then at day's end, and with curling blue smoke rising from the fire, they had a supper that testified to Sally's skill at cooking under the most difficult of conditions.

Thirty-seven days after leaving Sugarloaf Ranch, they found themselves just outside the small village of San Vicente. Hot and dusty, the town was little more than a two-block-long main street with flyblown adobe buildings on either side.

"Are we goin' to get to go into town, boss?" Walt Bizzel asked.

"I tell you what," Smoke said, producing a deck of cards. "You boys draw from the deck; whoever gets the lowest two cards will have to stay with the herd tonight. Whoever has to stay tonight can go into town tomorrow."

"You only need to draw one card, Smoke," Old Mo said. "I don't have any need to go into town. I'll stay."

"I'll stay too," Fred Stone offered.

"Yahoo! All right, boys, let's go into town!" Walt said.

Smoke and Sally checked into the Marshal House Hotel, and Smoke arranged to have a tub and hot water brought up to their room. Pearlie, Cal, Don

Pratt, Walt Bizzel, and Vernon Mathis had other ideas.

"Want to get a couple of beers?" Pearlie asked.

"No, sir, not yet. 'Bout the only thing I want to do now, is get me somethin' to eat that wasn't cooked out on the range," Walt said.

"Whoa, don't you let Miz Sally hear you sayin' that," Pearlie said. "I thought she done a fine job of cookin'."

"I reckon she did at that," Walt replied. "What I meant to say is, I'd like to have me somethin' I can eat without sittin' on my own haunches."

"Well, I can go along with that," Pearlie agreed.

"You fellas go eat if you want to," Don said. "I'm goin' to get me somethin' to drink."

Supper turned out to be steak and beans, with the beans being liberally seasoned with hot peppers. They washed the meal down with sweetened tea.

"Those beans'll set you afire," Cal said. "But damn me if they aren't about the tastiest things I've put in my mouth in quite a while."

"Yeah? Well, as fast as you ate 'em, how would you know what they taste like?" Pearlie teased. "You ready for them beers now?"

"Sounds like a good idea to me. Maybe somethin' even a little stronger 'n beer."

"Yeah, a beer sounds good," Walt said.

"I don't know about you, Walt," Pearlie teased.

"What is it you don't know about me?"

"I don't know if me 'n' Cal ought to be lettin' a boy drink."

"I've done a man's job these last few weeks, ain't I?" Walt asked, bristling.

Pearlie laughed, and reached out to put his hand on Walt's shoulder. "I was teasin' you, Walt. And you've done more than a man's job. Matter of fact, I'll buy you your first drink."

"Thanks," Walt said with a broad smile.

The Lone Star Saloon was filled with tobacco smoke and scented with the aroma of beer and various alcoholic spirits. The drinking men, wearing wide-brimmed or high-crowned hats, sat at tables, either playing cards or engaged in animated conversation. Half a dozen painted women, their hair adorned with feathers, ribbons, or sparkling glass jewelry, paraded around, their low-cut, silk dresses rustling. Another dozen drinkers were at the bar, their spurred, high-heeled boots resting on a brass rail. Highly polished brass spittoons were placed at strategic places around the bar, though stains and bits of chewed tobacco were so prevalent in the sawdust on the floor that the spittoons seemed to serve a purpose which was more decorative than functional.

When Pearlie, Cal, and Walt walked into the saloon, they stepped up to the bar.

"What'll it be, gents?" the barkeep asked as he moved down to greet them when they stepped up to the bar. He wiped up a spill with a wet, smelly rag.

"You got any good whiskey?" Cal asked.

"Got some Old Overholt."

"That'll do," Cal said.

"Yeah, me too," Pearlie added. "Walt?"

"I think I'll stick with beer," Walt replied.

Pearlie nodded. "Good for you."

The bartender left to pour the drinks.

"Lookie over there, Pearlie," Cal said, pointing to

one of the painted women. "I do believe that girl's in love with you. Don't you want to buy her a drink?"

"Right now, I just want to drink my whiskey."

"You're goin' to break her heart," Cal teased.

There were several large jars of pickled eggs and pickled pigs' feet on the bar and Cal used the wooden spoons that were down in the jars to take out a couple of eggs and handful of pigs' feet.

"Damn, Cal, we just got up from the supper table. Ain't there no bottom to your stomach? Don't you never stop eatin'?"

"This ain't eatin'. This is just snackin'."

"That'll be two bits apiece for the whisky, and a nickel for the beer," the bartender said, returning with the three drinks.

Pearlie and Cal paid, then the three men took their drinks over to the table where Don Pratt and Vernon Mathis were sitting.

The saloon had an upstairs section at the back, with a stairway going up to a second-floor landing. When the men glanced up, they could see rooms opening off the second-floor landing. The saloon girl Cal had pointed out to Pearlie a moment earlier was now taking someone up the stairs with her.

"There goes your girl, Pearlie. You didn't act soon enough, and now that cowboy is beatin' your time."

"Damn, that girl sure got over her broken heart fast," Pearlie said.

The upstairs area didn't extend all the way to the front of the building. The main room of the saloon was big, with exposed rafters below the high, peaked ceiling. There were nearly a dozen tables full of drinking customers, though there were card games in session at three of them.

The piano player wore a small, round derby hat and kept his sleeves up with garter belts. He was pounding out a song, though the music was practically lost amidst the noise of a dozen or more conversations.

A very pretty woman, dressed just as the other girls were, stepped over to the piano player, said something to him, and he stopped in the middle of his song to play a very loud fanfare. The fanfare got not only the attention of Pearlie, Cal, Walt, Don, and Vernon. It also got the attention of everyone else in the room.

The woman held up a deck of cards. "Gentlemen," she called. "For those of you that don't know me, my name is Bridget. And I'm looking for three men who aren't afraid to play cards with a woman. I'll be at that table right over there."

"Ha!" one of the saloon patrons called. "You'd better get the ones who don't know you, Bridget. 'Cause ever'one that knows you, knows better than to play you."

"You aren't sayin' I cheat, are you, Briggs?"

"No, no, I ain't sayin' you cheat," Briggs replied, stuttering at the accusation. I'm just saying that you're good, darlin'. Too damn good for me to ever play with you again."

"I'll play with you," Pearlie said, standing then.

"Pearlie, you sure you want to do this?" Cal asked.

"You don't think I'm good enough?"

"I don't know. I've seen you play, and I've played with you. You're good, I know that. But we don't know how good this woman is."

"Well, I'm about to find out, and I'll let you know after the game is over."

By the time Pearlie reached the table, two other players had arrived.

"Gentlemen, new game, new deck," Bridget said. She picked up a box, broke the seal, then dumped the cards onto the table. They were clean, stiff, and shining. She pulled out the joker then began shuffling the deck. The stiff, new pasteboards clicked sharply. Her hands moved swiftly, folding the cards in and out until the law of random numbers became king. She shoved the deck across the table.

"Would you like to cut, handsome?" she asked Pearlie. Leaning over the table, she showed a generous amount of cleavage.

Pearlie cut the deck, then pushed them back. He tried to focus on her hands, though it was difficult to do so because she kept finding ways to position herself to draw his eyes toward her more interesting parts. When he looked around the table, he saw that the other players were having the same problem.

"Well now, gentlemen, you fellows aren't having a difficult time concentrating, are you?" Bridget teased.

"What would make you think something like that?" Pearlie asked, still staring at her cleavage.

"The game is five-card . . ." Bridget started, then she paused and looked directly at Pearlie before she said the next word. "*Stud,*" she added pointedly.

"Fine," Pearlie answered.

Chapter Ten

Pearlie won five dollars on the first hand, and a couple of hands later he was ahead by a little over fifteen, second only to Bridget. The other players were taking Bridget's and Pearlie's good luck in stride, but one of the players began complaining.

"Somethin' kinda fishy is goin' on here," he said.

"Oh? And just what would that be, Mr. Parker?" Bridget asked.

Parker looked at Bridget, then nodded toward Pearlie. "You're dealin' him winnin' hands," he said.

"How can you say that?" Bridget asked. "The deal has passed around the table and this gentleman, and I, have been winning, no matter who is dealing. Do you think I'm cheating, Mr. Parker?"

"No, ever'body knows you are good at poker. But they don't nobody know this man, and I don't believe all his winnin' is just dumb luck."

"There's some luck to it," Pearlie said. "But you have to know how to play with the luck. You need to know how to fold when luck gives you a bad hand, and hold when you get a good hand. I've been watchin' you, mister, and you haven't learned that. You think you can bluff or buy a pot, when you don't have the cards to back you up."

"I tell you what," Parker said. "How much have you won tonight?"

Pearlie looked down at the table. "It looks like I've won about fifteen dollars."

"Then what do you say about me 'n' you havin' us a little two-hand game here? Showdown for twenty-five dollars."

"Showdown?" Pearlie chuckled. "Well, there's no skill in showdown, but if that's what you want, I'm willin'."

Parker reached for the cards but Pearlie stuck his hand out to stop him. "You don't think I'm going to let you deal, do you? We'll let the lady deal."

"Huh, uh," Parker said, shaking his head. "Like I said, she's been dealin' you winnin' cards all night. We'll let Hendrix here, deal."

"Is Mr. Hendrix a friend of yours?" Pearlie asked.

"What if he is?"

"I'd rather get someone who doesn't know either one of us."

"I don't know either one of you," one of the men who had been watching the game said. "If you fellas will trust me, I'll deal the hand for you."

Pearlie looked at Bridget, and she nodded.

"All right," Pearlie agreed.

"That's fine by me," Parker said.

The new man dealt five cards to each of them. Pearlie took the pot with a pair of sevens.

Parker laughed. "Not exactly a big hand, was it? How about another?"

Pearlie won that hand with a jack high.

"Want another one?" Pearlie asked.

"Yes," Parker replied. "You can't possibly win three in a row."

Pearlie did win the third, with a pair of tens, and Parker threw his cards on the table in disgust. He slid the rest of his money to the center of the table. "I've only got twenty-six dollars left," he said. "I'll bet it all on high card."

Pearlie covered the bet, then the dealer fanned the cards out.

"You draw first," Parker said.

Pearlie started to reach for a card, but just as he touched it, Parker stopped him. "No, I changed my mind," he said. "I'll draw first." Parker smiled triumphantly, then flipped over the card Pearlie was about to draw. It was a queen of diamonds.

"Well now, what do you think about that?" he asked triumphantly. "It looks like I caught you at your own game, don't it?"

Pearlie drew a king of clubs.

"What?" Parker shouted in anger. "You son of a bitch! How did you do that?"

"Well, since there is absolutely no skill involved in drawing for a high card, I have to confess that it was luck," Pearlie replied, smiling as he reached for the money.

Parker stuck his hand down into his pocket, then pulled out a pepperbox, a small, palm-sized pistol.

"Mister, I ain't givin' up my money to a cheater," Parker said. "I'll thank you to slide that money back across the table."

"Mr. Parker, now you tell me just how you think he

could have been cheating at high card?" Bridget asked.

"I don't know, I ain't figured that out yet," Parker said. "But it don't matter none now, anyhow. I'm about to get my money back."

"That's no way to get your money back," Pearlie said.

"Yeah? Well, it seems like a pretty good way to me, seein' as I'm holdin' a gun on you," Parker said.

"And I'm holdin' one on you," Cal said, stepping up to the table at that moment. He had his pistol out and was pointing it directly at Pearlie.

"What? Who the hell are you? What business you got buttin' in on this?"

"You said you were about to shoot Pearlie."

"Who's Pearlie?" Parker asked, confused by the comment.

"That would be me," Pearlie said.

"Pearlie is my friend."

"Is he? Well, I'm tellin' you right now, that your friend is about to get hisself kilt, if you don't put that gun down," Parker said.

"If you shoot him, I'll shoot you."

"Did you hear me?" Parker said. "Are you stupid? I said I'm going to shoot your friend if you don't put that gun down."

"Go ahead," Cal said.

"What?"

"I said go ahead. Pearlie ain't my only friend. I've got other friends. On the other hand, you don't have another life. Also, I notice that your gun isn't cocked yet." Cal cocked his own pistol, the hammer making a distinct sound in a saloon that had now gone so quiet that the loudest sound was the rhythmic tick of the clock standing against the back wall.

"But as you can see, my gun is. And I see your thumb so much as quiver, I'll shoot."

"You would risk your friend's life like that?" Parker asked, incredulous at Cal's words.

"I'm riskin' his life, not mine," Cal said. He smiled. "It's not like what you are doing. You are riskin' your own life. But go ahead, Mr.—Parker, is it? Do whatever you think you have to do. Shoot Pearlie if you think that's necessary. Then I'll shoot you."

Parker stood there for a moment longer as it slowly dawned on him that he had the worst position in this triangle. Then, with a trembling hand, Parker put the pistol down on the table. Pearlie reached and picked it up, then handed it to Bridget. Bridget took it from Pearlie by using only her thumb and forefinger.

"Break it open and empty the charges," he said.

Carefully, Bridget pushed the hinged barrel down, then shook out all the cartridges.

"What do you mean, you have other friends?" Pearlie asked.

"I do, Pearlie," Cal said. "Hell, you know that. I have lots of other friends. I mean, look over at that table. There's three of 'em sittin' right there."

Bridget laughed.

"Mr. Parker, was this twenty-six dollars really the last of your money?" Bridget asked.

"Yes," Parker said, quietly.

"Shame on you, Mr. Parker," Bridget said. "You would gamble away all of your money, when you've got a wife and kid at home?"

"You've got a wife and kid?" Pearlie asked.

Parker didn't reply, but he looked down toward the floor in shame.

Pearlie slid the twenty-six dollars back across the table. "I don't want to take all your money, Parker. And I also don't want to play cards with you anymore. Take your money, and go home."

Parker blinked a few times, bit his lower lip, then nodded.

"Thanks," he mumbled as he picked up the money. Turning, he left without another word being spoken.

"Mr. Pearlie, that is about the most decent thing I've ever seen anyone do," Bridget said, beaming at him. "You are welcome at my table anytime."

"Thanks," Pearlie said. Glancing toward the clock, he saw that it was nearly ten. "But I guess it's time for my friends and me to go now."

Nuevo Pacifico, Mexico

Keno sat a table in the cantina, drinking tequila and watching one of the girls dance for him. She had been dancing for several minutes, and both she and the guitar player were getting tired, but Keno told them that he'd say when they could finish.

Just when the musician and dancer were on the edge of total exhaustion, Vargas, one of Keno's men, came in.

"*Coronel,* I have news that you will like," he said.

Keno picked up his pistol and fired it straight up, punching a hole through the roof of the cantina. At the shot, the dancer screamed and fell to her knees, bending over and covering her face with her arms. The guitarist stopped in mid-chord.

"That is enough," Keno said. He tossed a hundred pesos onto the floor. "This is for you," he said. "You see, when you are good to me, I can be very good to you."

"*Gracias, señor,*" both said, hurrying to scoop up the money.

"Now, what news do you bring me?"

"In the town of San Vicente, in Texas, there is a herd of two hundred horses. Only a few men are keeping watch on the horses."

"Why are the horses there?" Keno asked.

"They are to be delivered to The Wide Loop, the *rancho* of Señor Tom Byrd. He is to use them as mounts for his *vaqueros.*"

"If the herd is that large, the horses will not be broken," Keno said.

"But they will still be very valuable, will they not?"

"*Sí,* but they will be more valuable when they are broken. We will keep our eyes on these horses, and after they are broken, we will take them," Keno said. "Go and keep an eye on them. When all the horses are broke, come and tell me."

San Vicente

It was only a mile outside of town before Pearlie, Cal, Walt, Don, and Vernon came across the herd of horses they had moved all the way from Colorado. For now, the horses were being watched over by only two men, Old Mo and Fred Stone. A campfire was burning low, and the blue metal coffeepot was suspended from an iron, overhead frame. The pot was pushed to one side so that it would keep the coffee warm, but not too hot.

The five men dismounted, and Cal went straight to the chuck wagon to get a tin cup. Filling the cup with the hot, black brew, he had just taken his first sip when Old Mo rode up.

"I was hopin' someone would show up to spell us by midnight," Old Mo said.

"All quiet? Cal asked.

"All quiet," Old Mo replied.

"Walt, you want to take the watch with me?" Cal asked.

"For how long?"

"Until dawn."

"Damn," Walt said.

"No need to go all the way till dawn. Vernon and I will relieve you at four," Pearlie offered.

"There's a good friend for you," Cal said.

Pearlie looked at Cal. "Come to think of it I'm sure you can find someone else to do this for you," he added with a smile. "I mean, seeing as you have so many friends and all."

"You ain't goin' to ever let go of that, are you?" Cal asked.

Pearlie laughed out loud. "On the contrary, I think you were very smart. Parker wasn't sure whether to call your bluff or not. I know you weren't really goin' to let him shoot me."

"Are you sure?" Cal asked with an enigmatic smile.

Back in town, Smoke lay in bed, studying the moon pattern on the wall before him. Beside him, ' the rhythmic breathing of Sally told him that she was asleep.

This was the end of the long drive. Tom Byrd's ranch was only three miles from here. Tomorrow he would hire someone to ride out to the ranch to tell him that he had arrived so he could make arrangements to deliver the horses.

Smoke had come a long way since he left Missouri as a seventeen-year-old boy in 1865. No, he was seventeen all right, but he could hardly be called a boy. By that time he had already buried his mother, run the farm by himself, and gone to war with the Confederate guerrilla Asa Briggs. Since that time he had buried his first wife and child, taken revenge against the killers of his father and Nicole, his first wife, been mentored by an old mountain man named Preacher, and had mentored a young man who now called himself Matt Jensen. And of course he had also married Sally Reynolds, a schoolteacher from a wealthy Vermont family.

Smoke was now a wealthy man, one of the wealthiest in all of Colorado, and he had done it all by himself, without one penny of the Reynolds family's money.

Over the years though, Smoke had developed another legacy, one that he would not have sought, but one that he could not walk away from. Smoke had a reputation as being one of—if not *the*—fastest and most skilled gunfighters in the entire West.

Now he was about to reconnect with someone from his distant past. When he and Sally were in Missouri to rebury his parents, he had visited with Tom Byrd's son, Sam, and Sam's wife, Mollie. These were people he had known from his time before, but they had both been very young children when he left Missouri.

Tom Byrd, on the other hand, was as old as Smoke's father had been, and because the Byrd farm and the Jensen farm were adjacent, they visited, and worked together frequently. This would be his most direct connection with his past since he left home, and he was very much looking forward to it.

Chapter Eleven

When Pearlie came back into the camp from having taken the last relief of nighthawk, the sun was just rising. He walked over to the bedroll where Cal was sleeping and pushed his boot against Cal's stocking-covered foot, just hard enough to wake him up.

"What?" Cal asked. "What is it?"

"Let's go into town and get us a bath," Pearlie suggested.

"A bath? Are you serious? You woke me up for a bath?"

"Not just any bath," Pearlie said. "A hotel bath. You don't have to stay there, they've got bathing rooms out behind the place where you can take a bath for half a dollar. Don't you think a tub bath would be good, after bathin' in nothing but creeks, rivers, and streams for more 'n a month?"

"Yeah, I guess it would."

"And the hotel's got a dining room too. The best breakfast you can buy in a town is always in a hotel dining room."

"What makes you say that?"

"Well, think about it, Cal. Most of the people that eat in the hotel dining room are staying right there. You know that the hotel folks are going to want to feed those people a real good breakfast. If not, they'll be right there where they can complain about it."

Cal laughed. "You know what, Pearlie, sometimes when you don't make any sense at all, you make pretty good sense after all."

"What?" Pearlie asked, totally confused by Cal's rather convoluted answer.

"Never mind," Cal said. "Let me get my boots on and pull out a clean change of clothes and I'll be right with you."

Smoke and Sally were having breakfast in the hotel dining room when Pearlie and Cal came in later that same morning.

"Do you mind if we join you?" Pearlie asked.

"No, of course not," Sally replied. "Oh, my, don't you two boys look good. I see that you got all cleaned up," she added with a smile.

"I had to talk Cal into it. I swear, if I didn't tell 'im to do it, I don't think that boy would take a bath till we got back home."

"It ain't been much more 'n a month since my last one," Cal said

Smoke laughed. "You remind me of Preacher."

"Smoke, is Old Mo like Preacher?"

"I expect there's a lot of similarity between the two," Smoke agreed.

"We're near 'bout to the ranch where we're a-takin' the horses, ain't we?" Cal asked, then seeing

Sally's frown, he corrected himself. "What I mean is, aren't we?"

"Thank you, Cal," Sally said.

"We're not only close, we're here," Smoke said. "I thought that Sally and I would ride out to the ranch today to see Mr. Byrd."

"Would you mind if me 'n' Pearlie . . . uh . . . if Pearlie and I went out there with you?"

"Why, no, I wouldn't mind at all. But why on earth would you want to go?" Smoke asked.

"All Walt and the others want to do is get drunk, and take the women upstairs," Cal said. Then, realizing he had spoken in front of Sally, he put his hand over his mouth and looked at her, embarrassment showing in his face.

"Sorry, Miz Sally," he said contritely.

"No apology necessary, Cal. I'm proud of you for showing such forbearance."

"Yes, ma'am," Cal said. "Anyway, me 'n' Pearlie don't want to do all that, which is why we went to take us a bath, then come over to see you."

"Because we figured if we did ride out to the ranch with you to meet such an important man, then we ought to at least be clean," Pearlie added.

"Good thought," Smoke said. "Have you had your breakfast yet?"

"Uh . . ." Cal started.

Sally laughed. "Would you like to join us?"

"Yes, ma'am, we'd like that just fine," Pearlie replied.

"We'll go out to the ranch as soon as we eat."

* * *

Tom Byrd greeted Smoke effusively when he arrived. Though considerably older than he was the last time Smoke saw him, he would have recognized his former neighbor immediately.

"Mr. Byrd, I'd like you to meet my wife, Sally, my foreman and assistant foreman, Pearlie and Cal."

"You called me Mr. Byrd when you were a boy, Kirby. You're a grown man now. Why don't you call me Tom?"

"Tom," Smoke said with a smile and a nod.

"This is my wife, Hazel," he said, indicating the smiling, gray-haired woman standing next to him. "And I'm sure you remember my daughter, Katrina," he added, introducing the very pretty young woman who was standing between him and Mrs. Byrd.

"I remember a little girl named Katrina," Smoke said. "I don't remember a beautiful young woman."

Katrina smiled shyly.

"I'm Cal," Cal said, looking directly at Katrina. "Smoke is right. You're the prettiest woman I've ever seen."

"Smoke?" Tom said. "Is that what he called you?"

"Ever'one calls him Smoke," Pearlie said. "Fact is, I've known him for a lot of years now, and I've never heard anyone call him Kirby."

"Are you *the* Smoke Jensen?" Katrina asked. "The one the books are about?"

"What books?" Tom asked.

"Adventure stories," Katrina said. "All my boy students love to read them, and I encourage them, because I think reading anything at all, even adventure stories, is very good for them."

"That's him all right," Cal said. "Why, I reckon that, by now, nearly ever'one has heard of Smoke Jensen."

"My goodness," Tom said. "Who would have ever thought that the boy I knew would grow up to be so famous."

"Believe me, Tom, fame, if that is what you can call it, some might call it infamy, can be quite a burden. I'd just as soon lay it down, if I could."

"I can understand that," Tom said. "Fame lies uncomfortably on the shoulders of a good man. And if the man is anything like the boy I once knew, I would say that you are a good man."

"Mr. Byrd, he's the best man I've ever known," Cal said.

"That's good to hear, but it's no surprise," Tom said. "So, did all the horses get here all right?"

"At last count, we had lost only twelve of them," Smoke said. "Two dead, and ten must have drifted away from us. But I'll be sending most of my wranglers back home by train, so I'll be throwing in the remuda, which will bring the count back up to two hundred head."

"That's good. Oh, the two that died, it was nothing that could spread to the rest of the horses, is it?"

"Not unless lead poisoning can spread," Cal said.

"Lead poisoning?"

"We ran into some rustlers up in New Mexico," Smoke said. "There was some shooting, and two of the horses were hit."

"And three of the rustlers," Pearlie said, quickly.

"Their just reward, I'm sure," Tom said. "Where are the horses now?"

"We're holding them just outside of town," Smoke said.

"If you want to, you can bring them on to The Wide Loop today. Once they are here, my men will be responsible for them."

"Thanks. By the way, Tom, I'm curious about the name of your ranch. The Wide Loop?" Smoke asked.

Tom laughed. "Anytime someone gathers as large a herd as I have, inevitably, they are going to be accused of swinging a wide loop, so I just decided to name my ranch that."

"Part of the deal was to deliver you horses that are saddle-broken," Smoke said. "Pearlie and Cal are two of the best, so I thought Sally, Pearlie, and Cal would hang around until the mounts are all broken. That is, if you don't mind."

"I don't mind at all, and I appreciate the offer. I've got a pretty good man myself, so if you'd like, you can have him help with breaking the horses. Of course, Pearlie, you and Cal will be the lead broncobusters."

"That'll be fine, Mr. Byrd, and we'll welcome the help," Pearlie said.

"You will be staying for lunch, won't you?" Hazel asked. "We have a large smoked ham, which is really good with butter beans, collard greens, and corn bread. I think I can even talk our cook into making us some fried peach pies."

"Yes, ma'am, we'll stay!" Cal said enthusiastically, then when he realized he may have spoken out of turn he looked toward Smoke and Sally with an expression of embarrassment on his face.

"Uh, I mean, uh, if Smoke says we will."

The others laughed.

"We would be glad to stay for lunch," Smoke said.

"Tell me how you found Sam, Mollie, and our darling little granddaughter," Hazel said. "It has been so long since we have seen them, and I miss them so."

"Oh, they were most gracious to us," Sally said. "And the little girl Ellie Mae was such a delight. I know you must be very proud of all of them."

"Yes, I am. I am told that Ellie Mae wants to be a teacher just like her aunt."

"Yes, that is what she told us. And from speaking with her, I think she will make a very good teacher."

"Kirby, a letter that I got from Sam said that you had come back to Missouri to bury your parents in the local cemetery. I wish I could have been there for that. Your parents were wonderful people."

"Yes, it was just something I wanted to do."

"And the people of the town were wonderful about it," Sally said. "So many of them turned out, that you would hardly know it was a funeral for two people who had died over twenty years ago."

When they had taken their seats at the dining room table, Cal managed to arrange it so that he was directly across from Katrina. During the meal he found himself looking at her and realized that, in the space of a single meal, she could change from the coquettishness of a young girl to the more haunting promise of a young woman. He found her to be the most charming young woman he had ever met. Beautiful, yes, she was that. But it wasn't just her beauty that intrigued him. There was much more, there was a depth to her, and there was an unspoken connection between them, as if their very souls were singing in harmony.

Conversation went on at the table between Smoke and Tom, between Sally and Hazel, but Cal was aware of none of it. He tried not to stare, but he looked at Katrina as often as he could. And often he caught her looking at him, though, shyly, she always managed to look away before he could catch her eyes with his.

When the meal was finished, everyone else at the table got up but Cal and Katrina. They remained seated so long that it became obvious that the others were looking toward them.

"Oh," Cal said, standing quickly. "I'm sorry, I guess I wasn't paying much attention."

"Oh, you were paying attention all right," Pearlie said with a smile. "It's just a matter of what it was you were paying attention to."

"I, uh, don't know what you are talking about," Cal said, flustered.

"Tom, I thank you very much for your warm welcome," Smoke said. "But we need to get back into town. I'm going to send the others back on the afternoon train, then we'll drive the herd out here to your ranch."

"If you're going to send all your wranglers back first, will you need help bringing the herd out? Because, if so, I can send some men in with you."

"No, we can handle it all right. By now the horses are used to being driven, and they handle easily. We'll have them out here before nightfall."

"I'm looking forward to seeing them," Tom said.

Tom, Hazel, and Katrina came out onto the front porch to tell Smoke and the others good-bye. Before they rode off, Cal and Katrina exchanged a few more looks.

When they got back to town, Smoke bought train tickets for the men who would be going back to Sugarloaf. Old Mo had already said that he would like to stay here with them, if Smoke didn't mind. He wouldn't actually be breaking the horses, but he would be training them, once they were broken.

"Here are your tickets back to Sugarloaf. Try and stay out of trouble on your way back," he said, as he paid the men off and gave them the tickets.

"Why, boss, we'll be so good that folks will think we're angels that's come down to live with the common folk," Don said as, with waves and good-byes, the four started back to town to catch the train.

Chapter Twelve

When Rick Isback left the train in San Antonio, he learned that he would have a four-hour wait before the next train that would take him to San Vicente. He decided to spend that time in a saloon and, since this was his first time in San Antonio, he had no specific saloon in mind. He stepped into the Buckhorn Saloon, and was immediately amused by the number of antlers and horns that decorated the walls. Stepping up to the bar, he ordered a drink.

"Hey, Fancy Pants," someone said.

Isback didn't look around at the first call.

"You, Fancy Pants, are you deef?"

The bartender put a beer in front of Isback. Isback paid for the beer, then took a drink of it before he turned toward the man who had called out at him.

"Were you talking to me?" he asked in a calm voice.

"Yeah, I'm talkin' to you. You're the only one in here wearin' fancy pants, ain't you? Where'd you get that getup, anyhow? If you was a woman, folks would think you was a whore, with a getup like that."

Another man in the saloon laughed, then stepped up beside the first man.

"You know what, Toby, maybe he is a whore," the second man said. "I've heered tell that they was men that wasn't really men, if you know what I mean."

"Yeah, Murphy, I know what you mean. Is that what you are, Fancy Pants? Are you one of them men that likes to lie with other men?"

Isback took another swallow of his beer. "I'm sorry, but if you are looking for a man to have sex with, I'm afraid I can't accommodate you. If you two are so in-clined you might try one of the bathhouses, or, maybe, just do it with each other."

"What the hell, Toby! Did this son of a bitch just call us funny men?"

"Yeah," Toby said. "I think he just did."

Toby drew his pistol and pointed it at Isback. When Murphy saw that Isback made no reaction to the drawn pistol, he drew his as well.

"I tell you what I'm goin' to do, mister," Toby said. "I'm goin' to take your gun away from you, just to keep it honest. Then me 'n' Murphy is goin' to flip a coin, and whichever one of us wins, why, that's the one that's goin' to whip your fancy-dressed ass."

"You're going to take my gun?" Isback asked.

"That's right. Take it out now, hold it by the barrel, and bring it to me."

"Toby, what are you pickin' on this fella for?" the bartender asked. "He ain't done nothin' but come in here and order hisself a beer."

"He called me 'n' Murphy funny men," Toby said angrily. "You heard him."

"He said no such thing."

"I didn't use the word 'funny men,'" Isback said. "However, from the way these two were carrying on, I'm quite sure they are both sodomites."

"Sodomite? What does that mean?" Murphy asked.

Isback smiled, which surprised everyone, considering the situation he was in at the moment.

"It means just what you thought it meant," Isback said. "It means that I think you two men are probably the kind that prefers other men to women."

"See!" Toby said. "The son of a bitch said it again! There ain't goin' to be no flippin' a coin. I'm goin' to whup his ass myself. Now, give me that gun, mister."

"And if I don't?"

"I'm goin' to count to three," Toby said. "And if you ain't give me that gun by the time I get to three, I'm goin' to shoot you dead."

Isback started across the floor with his gun in his hand, the butt of it pointed toward the two men who were holding their pistols on him. But before he went half a step, he executed a sudden and perfect border roll. Now the business end of the gun was pointing toward Toby and Murphy, both of whom had let down their guard.

The quiet room was suddenly shattered with the roar of three pistols snapping firing caps and exploding powder almost simultaneously. The bar patrons yelled and dived, or scrambled for cover. White gun smoke billowed out in a cloud that filled the center of the room, momentarily obscuring everything.

As the smoke began to clear, Isback stared through

the white cloud, smiling broadly at the two men who had accosted him. Murphy was down, but Toby was still standing. He opened his mouth as if to speak, but the only sound he was able to make was a gagging rattle, way back in his throat. His eyes glazed over, and he pitched forward, his gun clattering to the floor.

Isback looked down at the two men for a long moment, a thin wisp of smoke drifting up from the barrel of the gun he still held.

"What happened? What's goin' on in there?" someone shouted from outside.

The sound of footfalls on the boardwalk could be heard, and several men pushed through the batwing doors. Once inside, they stood under the rising cloud of gun smoke to stare in wonderment at the two dead men on the floor. One of the new arrivals was a sheriff's deputy, and he saw Isback standing there, still holding the gun.

"The sheriff's deputy pointed at the two bodies on the floor. "Mister, I take it from the fact that you're standin' there holdin' a pistol, that this is your doin'. Is that right? Did you do this?"

"Yes," Isback answered. "I killed both of them. But it was a fair fight."

"What do you mean it was a fair fight? There's two of them, and only one of you. Are you tellin' me it was a two-to-one fair fight, and you beat both of 'em?" the sheriff's deputy asked, incredulously.

"That's right," Isback replied. "You can ask anyone."

The sheriff glanced toward the bartender. "Did you see this, Paul?"

"Yes, sir, I sure as hell seen it. Damndest thing I ever saw."

"Is this feller tellin' the truth? Was it a fair fight?"

"It was fair all right. Like I said, it was the damndest thing I done ever saw. Toby and Murphy both had their guns pointin' at this fella, and he was holdin' his gun by the barrel, butt first, as if he was goin' to give it to 'em."

"Wait a minute, he was giving his gun to them two?" He pointed to the two men on the floor.

"Yes, sir."

"Why was you givin' your gun to 'em?"

"Because they both had their guns pointed at me, and they asked for it."

"No, I mean why is it they was askin' for your gun in the first place?"

"Apparently, they took issue with the clothes I was wearing," Isback said. "It is my understanding that they wanted to take my pistol from me, then beat me up. I asked them what would they do if I didn't give them my pistol, and that one started counting. He said when he got to three he was going to shoot me."

"That's it, exactly, Deputy," one of the other saloon patrons said.

"So I shot them, before he reached three."

"How did you do that? Paul said you was holdin' the gun by the barrel."

"This way," Isback said. He held his pistol out toward the deputy, presenting the gun handle. But just as the deputy reached for it, Isback flipped the pistol around, doing it so fast that it was a blur.

"Damn!" the deputy said.

Isback didn't offer his pistol again, but he did put it back in his holster.

"Am I under arrest?" he asked.

"No, ever'body seems to agree with what you told me. I don't see no need to put you under arrest."

Isback smiled. "That's good, I wouldn't want to miss my train this evening. I have an appointment with a man named Smoke Jensen."

"Smoke Jensen?" the deputy replied, growing more animated. "You know Smoke Jensen?"

"You might say that we are colleagues, of a sort," Isback said.

"You don't say. My oh my. Your friend is one famous man, do you know that?"

"Yes, so I have heard," Isback replied.

"What's your name, mister?" the deputy asked. "Like I said, there ain't goin' to be no charges or nothin', but I'll need to put your name in the report."

"My name is Isback. Rick Isback."

Isback waited for the deputy's reaction of recognition, but there was none.

On the train that evening, as it pulled away from the depot in San Antonio, Isback thought about what happened this afternoon. There had been several witnesses to the event, and he knew that the story would be told, and retold, many times, gaining more notoriety with each retelling.

What they didn't realize was that his performance was just that, a performance, and it was much easier than it looked. Neither of the two cowboys had cocked their pistol, and it was immediately apparent that neither of them were gunmen. But, such events, spectacular as they were, would help to build his name.

The deputy had not recognized his name, though he had recognized Smoke Jensen's name.

That was all right. By this time one week from now, Smoke Jensen would be dead, and everyone would know the name of the man who killed him.

The Wide Loop

Pearlie, Cal, and Stan Hardegree, the ranch hand whose help Tom Byrd had offered, began breaking the horses the very next day after the herd was delivered to Tom Byrd's ranch. After a horse was broken, it would be turned into a different corral and there, Old Mo would start working with them. A good cow horse needed to neck-rein easily and consistently, and it needed to be able to walk, jog, lope, and gallop on a loose rein. The horse also had to be trained so that the rider could stop it by voice alone.

Because most cattle work involved the use of lassos, that was another, and very important, element of Old Mo's training. Knowing that horses are often startled by movements in the corner of their eye, he began working with them, getting them used to the rope.

Each of the three men who were breaking horses could break four horses in a day, which meant twelve per day. That figured to be a stay of from fifteen to twenty days for Smoke, Sally, Pearlie, Cal, and Old Mo. Smoke and Sally stayed in the guest room of the Big House; Pearlie, Cal, and Old Mo found room in the bunkhouse.

* * *

Word of the horse breaking moved all through town, so several, thinking that watching cowboys riding bucking horses made a good show, would go out to the ranch each day, just to watch.

Ramiro Vargas, who had been sent by Keno to monitor the progress of the horse breaking, went out to the ranch as well. There was nothing in Vargas's demeanor that would suggest to anyone that he was a soldier in Keno's *Ejército Mexicano de la Liberación*. On the contrary, he looked like a Mexican peasant trying to eke out a living by selling sopaipillas to the crowd who had come to watch the bronco busting.

In this guise, Vargas all but disappeared, and nobody paid him any attention at all. Because of that, no one was aware that he was keeping a very close account as to how many horses had been broken.

"They've got damn near fifty of 'em done, already," a cowboy said to the barber who was cutting his hair.

"That's quite a few," the barber replied.

"I reckon it is, but them three boys that's doin' all the bronco bustin' is good. They're real good. Sometimes you'd swear they was glued into the saddle. But I'll tell you who is the best."

"Who would that be? Stan Hardegree?"

"No, sir, not by a long shot. Now, don't get me wrong, the Hardegree boy is good all right. He's damn good. But he ain't the best."

Of the three broncobusters, Cal was recognized not only by the cowboy who was getting his hair cut, but by the other two riders as well, as the most skilled. Then, on the fifth day they encountered a horse that neither Pearlie, nor Hardegree, wanted anything to do with.

The job fell to Cal, and at two o'clock that afternoon, the entire ranch, including every ranch hand, Smoke, Sally, Tom Byrd and his wife, and Katrina—at least twenty people—were gathered around the breaking corral to watch Cal work.

The horse was tied to a pole in the center of the corral, not by Cal, but by one of the ranch hands. Not until the horse was already secured, did Cal approach him.

"Hello, horse," Cal said, quietly, soothingly, reaching up slowly to pet the horse gently on his neck. "Me 'n' you are goin' to be great friends." Cal chuckled. "I meant to say that you and I are going to be great friends, but don't you tell Miz Sally what I said. She would be upset, and friends don't tell on friends."

All the time he was talking, he continued to pet and stroke the horse.

"Would you like a carrot?" he asked, offering it to the horse.

The horse stared at him with suspicious eyes.

"Come on, let's be friends," Cal said, and he stuck one end of the carrot in his own mouth, then offered the other end to the horse. The horse took it.

"See, I knew we could be friends." Cal squeezed the horse's ear, gently, then he attached a lead line to the horse's halter.

"What do you say I untie you from that post, and let's take a little walk?"

Cal untied the horse, then led him around the corral, all the while talking quietly and soothingly to the animal, getting it used to responding to the tug on its reins.

Next, he put a saddle on the horse, and now it began to grow a bit more skittish. Then, with the saddle in place, he mounted the horse.

The horse immediately began to buck, but Cal stopped it, pulling the horse's head hard to the right until its nose touched its right foreleg. The horse couldn't buck in that position, all it could do was turn in a very tight circle.

Cal kept the horse in the circle for a moment, then he released the pressure on the reins. When he did the horse started to buck again, arching its back, leaping up and coming down on all four legs, then lowering its head and kicking up its hind legs.

Cal rode with the bucking horse, keeping his shoulder back and his feet well in the stirrups.

The cowboys and others who were watching shouted and cheered as Cal took everything the horse had to offer. Finally, when the horse realized that it would not be able to throw the rider from its back, it stopped bucking and galloped around the corral a few times. Cal bent low, leaning over the horse's neck and let it run full-out, finally slowing it to a trot, then to a gentle walk.

Those who had been watching him, now cheered and applauded, and Cal took off his hat, waved it at the crowed, and made the horse rear up on its hind legs.

Chapter Thirteen

Cal dismounted, patted the horse on the neck, gave him another carrot . . . then swung into the saddle again. He rode over to the fence where his audience had been standing, though some of them, including Katrina, were actually sitting on the top rail of the fence.

"Anybody else want to ride him now?" Cal said. "He's calm, he won't try and throw you."

"I'll ride him," Katrina offered.

"Honey, no," Hazel Byrd said. "It's too dangerous."

"Do you ride at all, Miss Byrd?" Cal asked.

"Yes, I ride."

"Then, come ahead."

"Honey, are you sure you want to do this?" Hazel asked.

"Mrs. Byrd, it'll be all right," Cal promised.

"You're sure?"

"Yes, ma'am, I'm certain."

Katrina climbed down from the fence and walked out to Cal and the horse.

"Give him a little pet on the neck," Cal said.

"Cal?" Smoke said, walking out to them. "Let Katrina ride double with you for a moment, then you can dismount and leave her in the saddle."

"Yes, that might be the best way to do it. Do you mind riding double with me, Miss Byrd?"

Katrina smiled. "Well, if we are going to ride double, don't you think you should call me Katrina?"

"All right, Katrina," Cal replied with a big smile. "I'll get on first, then bring you up in front of me."

With both Katrina and Cal in the saddle, they rode around the corral a couple of times, then Cal dismounted by shoving himself off over the haunch of the horse, leaving Katrina alone. She rode around several times, putting the animal through its turns, smiling, and petting it. She rode up to where her mother and father were sitting. Chairs had been brought out for them, and she stopped the horse, which obeyed her directions instantly.

"Papa, I don't want you to put this horse into the remuda. Sundance is going to be my personal horse."

"Sundance?"

"Yes, can't you see how the sun is dancing off his skin? Isn't he beautiful?"

Tom Byrd chuckled. "All right, Katrina. Sundance is your horse."

"You know what I think, Cal?" Pearlie asked later that day. "I think Miss Byrd has eyes for you."

"Ah, she was just happy to get the horse, is all."

"No, sir. You're the only one she's lookin' at."

"You really think so?"

"Yes, I really think so. And it didn't start just because of the horse. I saw the way the two of you were lookin' at each other across the table that first day we got here."

"Well, we were just . . . looking."

"Uh-huh. But I don't blame you. I mean, I'm not sure whether or not you've noticed, but she isn't all that bad-lookin'."

"Not bad-looking? Pearlie, what are you talking about? Why, she's about the most beautiful woman I've ever seen in my entire life!"

Pearlie chuckled. "So you *have* noticed," he said.

San Vicente

Back in town, Rick Isback stepped down from the train and stood on the depot platform for just a moment or two, looking around. There appeared to be only three streets to the town, all three running perpendicular to, and not parallel with, the railroad track. The center street appeared to be the only one with business establishments, the other two were residential.

From here, Isback could take in the entire town, able to see to its very limits. It had been several years since he left New York, but there was still a part of him that experienced shock when he encountered a place as small as San Vicente. Since coming west, though, he had known many towns like this: isolated, inbred, and stagnant.

As he was waiting for the luggage to be off-loaded, he stepped into the depot office and walked up to the ticket counter.

"Yes, sir, can I help you?"

"I've just arrived in town and I wonder if I might prevail upon you for a little information."

"Yes, sir, I'll be glad to, if I can."

"First, I would like your recommendation on where I might find lodging."

"Well, sir, that depends on how long you are plannin' on staying," the ticket agent replied. "If you're just goin' to be here for a day or two, I'd suggest the Marshal House Hotel."

"And if I'm going to stay longer?"

"Then you might want to try one of the boardin'-houses. Their rooms is nice, and your meals comes with your fee. Mrs. Pauline Foley runs the nicest one in town. That is, if you go by the eatin', 'cause folks say that her food is the best."

"What about the hotel? Does it have a dining room?"

"Yes, sir, it has a fine dinin' room. And we also got us a real good restaurant besides the one that's at the Marshal House. That would be the War Drum."

"Thank you," Isback said. "You've been most helpful."

"If you just come in on the train that's standin' here in the station, 'n' if you had any luggage with you, it'll more 'n likely be off-loaded by now," the ticket agent said.

"Again, I thank you, sir."

Stepping back outside, Isback picked up his leather case, then walked a short way down the center street to the hotel. At this point he wasn't sure how long he would be here, so he decided that staying in the hotel would be the easiest.

Isback walked past the buildings, subconsciously enumerating them as he passed. There was a rooming house, a livery, a smithy's, and a general store that said DRUGS, MEATS, GOODS on its high, false front. There was the War Drum Restaurant the clerk had told him about, and of course the ubiquitous saloon . . . this one called the Lone Star Saloon.

Across the street from the saloon was the jail. A few buildings away a door slammed while, just ahead of him, someone closed the upstairs window of the hotel. A sign on the apothecary creaked in the wind and flies buzzed loudly around the piles of horse manure that lay in the street.

Isback walked into the hotel and set his bag down in front of the check-in desk.

"I would like a room," he said.

"Yes, sir. Would you prefer to be upstairs, or down?"

"Upstairs, overlooking the street, if you don't mind."

"We've only got one upstairs room available that overlooks the street. It is our special room, and it is the most expensive room in the hotel. It will cost you a quarter a night more than any of the other rooms."

"Is it a nice room?"

"Yes, sir, you won't find a nicer room between here and Houston. Why just a few days ago Smoke Jensen 'n' his wife stayed in that room, and Mr. Jensen told me hisself, personal, that it was as fine a room as he's ever stayed in. And, I reckon you've heard of Smoke Jensen, haven't you?"

"Indeed, I have heard of him," Isback said. "I heard that he was in San Vicente, but you say he isn't staying here at the hotel anymore. Has he gone back to Colorado?"

"Oh, no, sir, he is still in town. Well, I say he is in town, but right now he is staying with Mr. Byrd out at his ranch, The Wide Loop. He recently delivered several horses, you see, and he is remaining with them until they are all broken."

"Does he ever come into town?" Isback asked as he wrote his name in the register.

"Yes, from time to time, he does. He has dined with us. And, I believe he has also dined at the War Drum, though why he would want to eat there, instead of with us, I don't know. How long will you be with us, Mr."—the clerk looked at the name—"Isback."

"I'm not sure," Isback replied. "Suppose we just take it one day at a time. And I will take the special room."

"Very good, sir," the hotel clerk said with a broad smile. "That will be one dollar per night."

Isback looked up. "That must be some special room," he said. "I can get a very good room in Denver, Cheyenne, or even San Francisco for that much money."

"Yes, sir, but they must compete with other hotels. You may have noticed that we are the only hotel in town."

"Yes, I noticed," Isback said.

After checking into his room, Isback left the hotel and walked down to the Lone Star Saloon. It wasn't quite dinnertime, so it was a little early for the saloon to be at its peak. It was about one-third full. The scarred piano sat, unused, in the back of the room. There were two saloon girls working the customers, but they were occupied by a table full of men.

"A whiskey," Isback ordered, sliding a piece of silver across the bar. The man behind the bar poured the whiskey, slid the glass across to him, and picked up the money.

With the drink in his hand, Isback turned his back to the bar and looked out over the saloon. Noticing him then, one of the two girls pulled herself away from the table and sidled up to the bar. She had bleached hair, was heavily painted, and had very tired eyes.

"My, you are quite a handsome gentleman," the girl said. "Would you buy a girl a drink?"

"Go peddle your wares somewhere else, miss, I'm not interested," Isback said.

For just a second the girl looked hurt by his response, but she had been in the business long enough to shake it off, so with a practiced smile, she turned away from him.

"Too bad," she said. "I can be very good company."

"When I am visiting with someone, I like to engage in intelligent conversation," Isback said.

The girl turned back. "Oh, and what do you consider intelligent conversation?"

"Read any good books lately?"

The girl smiled. "I read a lot. That's all I do in my off time."

"What have you read?"

"*A Tale of Two Cities*."

"How do I know you aren't just saying that?"

"'It was the best of times, it was the worst of times, it was the age of wisdom, it was the age of foolishness, it was the epoch of belief, it was the epoch of incredulity, it was the season of Light, it was the season of Darkness, it was the spring of hope, it was the winter of despair,'" she said.

"I'm impressed. What's your name?"

"Ida Rose."

Do you have a room, Ida Rose?"

The girl smiled. "I do."

Half an hour later, Ida Rose lay naked in her bed, whimpering quietly. She had bruises on both her breasts.

"You hurt me," she said. "You had no right to do that."

"In your profession, you can't tell me you've never encountered anyone who got a little carried away."

"You got more than a little carried away. You hurt me, and you hurt me bad."

"Here," Isback said, taking out a ten-dollar bill. "Maybe this will make the hurt go away."

Ida Rose's eyes grew wide as she clutched the bill. "You . . . you won't take it back, will you?"

"No. You earned it."

"Thank you! Oh, thank you!"

Isback started toward the door but before he reached it, he stopped and turned to look back at the bruised woman on the bed, still clutching the ten-dollar bill.

"Ida Rose, if I ever hear that you have told anyone what happened here tonight, I will be very displeased. And I don't think you want me to be displeased, do you?"

There was a smile on Isback's face, but there was absolutely no mirth in the smile.

Chapter Fourteen

Nuevo Pacifico

"Please, *Coronel*. I do not want my rooster to fight yours."

"Your rooster is named *Rey de Gallos* is he not? You think he is King of the Roosters?" Keno asked.

"The name means nothing, *Coronel*."

"Do not be such the coward, Lozano. Do you think your rooster is a coward? Or do you think he will fight?"

"He will fight, *Coronel*, but . . ."

"But what?"

"Coronel Keno, *Rey de Gallos* had been in ten fights and he has won every one. I fear that if my rooster defeats your rooster, you will be most angry. I am but a poor peasant, you are an important man. It is not good for me to have someone as important as you to be angry."

"You need not worry about that, Señor Lozano," Keno said. "Your rooster will not defeat my bird. Anastasio Bustamante cannot be beaten."

"Very well, *Coronel*," Lozano said. "I will allow my rooster to fight yours."

Word had spread that *Rey de Gallos*, a rooster that everyone knew, would be fighting, the cock of Coronel Keno. Many gathered for the fight, and those in the crowd were split as to their loyalties. The soldiers under Keno were making wagers on Keno's bird, Anastasio Bustamante. The people of the village were betting on *Rey de Gallos*, and even those who had placed no wager were secretly wanting Lozano's rooster to win, because his bird represented them. They believed that if *Rey de Gallos* could win, it would be a symbol of justice against this evil man.

"Lozano, you are our champion!" someone called out. "Your rooster fights for all of us."

"Have you bet money on him?" Lozano asked.

"*Sí.* I have bet twenty pesos."

"And I have bet one hundred pesos," another said.

There were more wagers placed, then Keno held his rooster up. "This is Anastasio Bustamante. He is named after one of Mexico's fiercest warriors, and he has the same fighting spirit as *El Presidente* Bustamante. Watch, as he will fight, and kill the puny bird that Lozano calls King of the Roosters!"

Keno and Lozano held the roosters out so that they were teasing each other, then they dropped them on the ground. The roosters immediately attacked with flapping wings, beak thrusts, and slashing talons. Feathers flew, then blood, until finally, Anastasio Bustamante lay dying on the ground.

"What was wrong with the *coronel*'s rooster?" one of the soldiers asked. "I've never seen him act like that. He had no fight in him."

"You did something to my rooster!" Keno charged, angrily.

"*Coronel*, how could I do something?" Lozano replied. "I have not been around your rooster."

Keno drew his pistol, and the villagers reacted in fear, thinking he was going to shoot Lozano. Instead, Keno walked over to Lozano's rooster, who had been slightly wounded, and was now sitting, exhausted, on the ground.

Keno aimed at the bird, and pulled the trigger. *Rey de Gallos* fell over, and flopped on the ground for a full minute before it grew still.

"All wagers made on this rooster are forfeited," he said.

The soldiers of Keno's army, all of whom had bet on his bird, now gave a cheer.

"Sontino!" Keno said.

"*Sí, Coronel?*"

Keno pointed to the bird he had just killed. "Take the bird to Manuel. Tell him I will have stewed chicken for my supper."

A wide smile spread across Sontino's face.

"*Sí, Coronel.*"

Keno and the soldiers walked away, leaving Lozano and the villagers standing behind, angry and shocked over what they had just witnessed. Most had won money in the wagers they had placed, and they weren't going to collect what was rightly owed to them, as they heard Keno say that their bets had been forfeited. They lost all the money they had wagered.

They knew, also, that there was nothing they could

do about it, and they all left the piazza in frustrated anger.

Only Lozano and Keno's dead bird remained behind. Lozano walked over to pick up Anastasio Bustamante, who was now lying still, in death.

"If the *coronel* can eat my rooster, I can eat his," Lozano said, quietly. The rooster would feed him tonight, but it was little compensation for the rooster he had lost.

The Wide Loop

By the end of the first week of breaking horses, Cal got the nerve to ask Katrina if she would like to go into town to have supper with him, and she accepted.

"Thing is, I don't know the town, so you're goin' to have to pick out the best place for us to go."

"I know just the place," Katrina said.

Tom Byrd made his surrey available that night, and Cal took Katrina to the War Drum.

"How did you meet Mr. Jensen?" Katrina asked as she and Cal sat across the table from each other, a candle lighting the distance between them.

"I never met Mr. Jensen," Cal replied. "He was dead before I ever run into Smoke."

"Dead?"

"Oh, wait, Smoke is who you meant, ain't it? Uh, I mean, isn't it? I was thinkin' maybe you meant Smoke's pa. The way I met Smoke was, I tried to rob Miz Sally."

"What?" Katrina asked, shocked by the response. "Are you serious?"

"I'm very serious. That's exactly what happened. I

wasn't nothin' more 'n a boy then, on my own, and it had been a while since I'd found any work, and two or three days since I had had anything to eat. I figured maybe I could hold somebody up, just for enough money to get somethin' to eat, and I picked Miz Sally 'cause she was a woman and I figured it would be easy and there wouldn't be as much a chance of anyone gettin' hurt. But when I tried to hold her up, why, she got the drop on me."

"That must have been very frightening for you."

"I guess it was at first, only, instead of takin' me down to the sheriff 'n' turnin' me in like she coulda done, she took me home with her, fed me, and give me some better clothes to wear. Then, when Smoke come home, she made him give me a job, and I've been workin' for 'em ever since."

Katrina reached across the table to put her hand on Cal's arm. "That is a wonderful story," she said. "Why, if you hadn't run into her, you could have wound up taking the outlaw trail and by now the chances are you would either be dead, or in prison somewhere."

"That's true," Cal agreed. "That's why I'll always be loyal to both of 'em, 'cause I figure they most likely saved my life."

"Cal, there's a dance tomorrow night," Katrina said with a seductive smile.

"A dance?" Smoke replied to Sally's announcement.

"Yes, it's to raise money for the school. Summer is almost over and school is about to start again. Don't you think that's a good cause?"

"Well, yes, sure I do. But we don't have to go to a dance. We can just donate some money."

"Smoke Jensen!" Sally said. "Are you saying you don't want to dance with me?"

"You know I'm teasing. Or at least, I hope you know. Of course I want to dance with you."

"All right then, I don't want to hear any more complaints about it. Tom has said he will make his country wagon available, and we'll ride in with Cal and Katrina."

"Cal and Katrina?"

Sally chuckled. "You don't pay attention to anything, do you?"

"I guess not."

"You want to wear my bolo tie, Cal? It's got a silver and turquoise slide," Pearlie asked.

"You don't mind my wearin' it?"

"No. It'll help you make an impression on Katrina. You know what I think you should name your first kid, if it's a boy?"

"Whoa, first kid? Aren't you gettin' a little ahead of the game?"

"Doesn't hurt to be prepared. You can call it Smoke."

"I was thinkin' about callin' it Pearlie."

"Really?"

"Yeah, really. If I can wear your silver belt buckle too."

Pearlie laughed. "Always playing the angles, aren't you? Well, I was goin' to let you wear it anyway."

* * *

"If you're really that anxious to meet Smoke Jensen," one of the cowboys in the Lone Star Saloon said to Isback, "you should go to the dance tomorrow night."

"What dance?" Isback asked.

"You ain't seen none of the signs, tellin' about it?"

"No, I haven't."

"There's one on the wall over there, just by the piano. Go take a look at it. Ever'body from ten miles around town will more 'n likely be comin' to the dance, 'n' that includes Smoke Jensen."

Ida Rose was standing at the table nearest the piano, and when she looked up and saw Isback coming, she moved away, quickly. Bridget was standing at the bar when Ida Rose approached.

"Ida Rose, I have noticed that every time Mr. Isback comes near you, you get out of his way. Has he done anything to you? Has he hurt you in any way?" she asked.

"What?" Ida Rose gasped. "No! Why do you ask? I haven't said anything about it."

"You haven't said anything about what?"

"About nothin'," Ida Rose said, the tone in her voice reflecting her fear. "Please, Bridget, don't ask me any more questions."

"He has done something, hasn't he?"

"Bridget, please, don't talk about it," Ida Rose said, a sense of desperation in her voice.

"All right, if you don't talk about it, we won't. But just know that if you ever do need to talk about it . . .

whatever it is, you can talk to me," Bridget said, putting her hand, reassuringly, on Ida Rose's arm.

"Thank you," Ida Rose said, looking over at Isback.

As the cowboy had told him, there was a poster on the wall next to the piano, advertising the dance for the following night.

DANCE – SEPTEMBER 5th
for the
Benefit of the San Vicente School

☞ Band from Brownsville to Play
Come One! Come All!

Isback smiled as he looked at the poster. The dance would be the perfect time for him to check out Mr. Smoke Jensen.

Turning away from the poster, he saw Ida Rose talking to Bridget, and both of them were looking in his direction. He smiled at them, and nodded his head. The smile offered no mirth, and the dip of his head contained no warmth.

He wondered what they were talking about. He was sure that Ida Rose had told Bridget about their little encounter of a few nights earlier. Before he left town, he would make certain that Ida Rose told nobody else. He would also take care of Bridget. It wouldn't do for things like his particular way of dealing with women to be spread around. He could kill a man in a gunfight, and if he killed enough men, he would earn the respect and fear from other men. But those same men would react differently, if they knew how he treated women.

Isback returned to the table he had been sharing with two locals.

"Did you check out the poster?"

"I did," Isback said.

"Will you be goin' to the dance? 'Cause, like I said, I expect Smoke Jensen will be there."

"What for, are you wantin' to meet Jensen anyway?" the other cowboy asked.

"He and I share a particular skill," Isback said. "I just want us to get together and compare those skills, to see which of us is the better."

"Sort of a friendly get-together, you might say?" the first cowboy asked.

"Exactly," Isback replied, again flashing a smile without mirth.

He glanced toward the bar and saw that Ida Rose and Bridget were still looking toward him. Yes, he would have to take care of them both.

The thought of it gave him pleasure.

Chapter Fifteen

Cal drove the country wagon, a four-passenger vehicle with leather-padded seats and a fringed top. He pulled up in front of the Big House where Smoke, Sally, and Katrina were waiting.

"My oh my, Cal, how handsome you look tonight," Sally said. "Don't you think so, Katrina?"

"Yes, ma'am, I sure do," Katrina said.

The blush on Cal's face was noticeable.

In a town that was no larger than San Vicente, all public events were big things and a dance was the biggest. All the local citizens, as well as the cowboys from the surrounding ranches, had made plans to attend. There wasn't a building big enough to accommodate the number of people anticipated, so carpenters had built a wooden floor in the middle of Front Street. Musicians, as advertised, arrived from Brownsville, and as they warmed up that afternoon, they drew a crowd of youngsters to watch.

Smoke, Sally, Cal, and Katrina arrived in town, by

design, before the dance was scheduled to begin. The four of them had dinner at the War Drum, Smoke's treat.

"Do you ever miss teaching?" Katrina asked Sally.

"I haven't stopped teaching," Sally said.

"Oh?"

Sally chuckled. "I don't teach school anymore, but when you are surrounded by men like Smoke, Pearlie, Cal, and all the other men who work at the ranch, you never quit teaching. At least, not as far as grammar is concerned."

"What about Old Mo?" Cal asked. "You don't ever teach him anything."

"Believe me, Cal, Mr. Morris is educated far beyond anything I could teach him. The fact that his education wasn't acquired in a schoolroom doesn't diminish it in any way. In fact, he taught me a lot of things during our drive down here."

"Mr. Morris is an interesting man," Katrina said.

"He sure is," Cal said. "And he's a good man too. Wouldn't you say so, Smoke?"

"Absolutely, I would say so," Smoke replied. "He is like Preacher, one of the men who opened up the West for the rest of us. Maybe Mr. Morris didn't study in school, but men like him will, one day, be studied in school."

"Speaking of school, are you enjoying teaching, Katrina?" Sally asked.

"Oh, yes, very much. School reopens in another week, and I'm looking forward to it. I intend to teach until . . ." She paused in mid-sentence.

"Until what?" Smoke asked.

Sally kicked Smoke under the table. "Just until she doesn't teach anymore," Sally said.

Sally and Katrina smiled at each other as they shared the silent communication, "until I am married," between them. Neither Cal nor Smoke had any idea what they were talking about, but Smoke had enough sense to know better than to ask. At least, he wouldn't ask now.

Lanterns were strung from overhead ropes and by nightfall men and women began moving from the outlying edges of town toward the bright bubble of golden light in the center of darkness. They were drawn to the light as moths are drawn to a flame, and they greeted one another happily. Many of the young men, most of them cowboys, teased one another about being all "gussied up."

There were youngsters there as well, most of them too young to dance, but there was an area set aside for them, and a few of the more matronly ladies of the town had volunteered to keep an eye on the children as they played.

"Ladies and gents!" the caller said. "We'll start this dance off with the grand march, so, choose up your partners!"

Smoke and Sally, Cal and Katrina stepped out onto the floor. Then the music started and the procession began as they marched, two by two and arm in arm, to the far end of the floor. Curving around, they came back to where they had started. Then, as the music continued, the marchers weaved back and forth until their numbers increased to four, this time including Smoke and Sally.

Between the sets of the spirited quadrilles, the band played some waltzes. This gave the more sedate attendees a chance to participate, and the more active dancers a chance to catch their breath.

There were many more men than women, so the women would be rationing their dances. Nevertheless, Cal was getting more than his share of dances with Katrina, and that was obviously with her approval. But about halfway through the dance, a cowboy from a neighboring ranch took issue with it.

"Tell, me, mister, how come it is that you're gettin' so many dances with that one, while the rest of us is left suckin' hind tit? 'Cause I'm tellin' you right now, I don't intend to let you get away with it."

There was anger in the cowboy's remark, and even an implied challenge.

"I don't know. Maybe it's just 'cause I'm better-lookin' than you are," Cal replied. He made the comment with a smile, clearly indicating that he meant it as a joke. He was hoping that by introducing humor into the moment he could defuse the situation. But it didn't work.

"Why you, low-assed, mealy-mouthed, tick-bit, mule-kicked, son of a bitch!" the cowboy shouted, and he swung wildly at Cal.

Cal leaned back just in time to miss the cowboy's swing. The cowboy tried a straight punch the second time and Cal leaned to one side to let it slip by.

"Oh, Smoke!" Sally said when she became aware of what was going on. "Do something!"

"No need to do anything," Smoke replied. "It looks to me like Cal has it fairly well in hand."

The cowboy tried several other punches and swings, none of which landed because Cal, dancing now, was adroitly avoiding every one. By now all other activity had stopped as everyone turned to watch the "fight" though there was no fight. The cowboy was growing increasingly agitated as he continued to swing wildly, while Cal managed to avoid his punches.

The musicians, seeing what was happening, began to play an Irish jig, as Cal danced, not only with his body movements, but with his boots which, by now, were beating a staccato rhythm on the board floor.

With a broad smile, Katrina put her hands on her hips and stepped out to join them, staying just far enough away to avoid both the swinging cowboy and Cal's gyrating dance.

The others began clapping their hands in rhythm and calling out to the three.

"Duke, I never knowed you could dance like that!" one of the cowboys shouted to the young man who continued his attack on Cal . . . but so far had been unable to make so much as one blow land. He was clearly getting more and more exhausted, and finally he stopped swinging and stood there, bent over, his hands on his knees, breathing hard.

"Duke, you want to dance with Katrina and me?" Cal said. "Put your hands on your hips like this, and join in."

The invitation was issued with a broad smile and after a second or two of hesitation, Duke put his hands on his hips, then joined in, leaping and cavorting about as best he could. The scowl on his face left, to be replaced by a smile as broad as Cal's. The three of them danced to the music and the rhythmic claps of the others until finally, the music ended.

There was a wide, appreciative applause from all the other dancers.

Cal extended his hand. "Duke, I'm Cal. I'm glad to meet you."

With a sheepish grin on his own face, Duke took Cal's hand. "It's good to meet you as well. I'm sorry about all this foolishness."

"Think nothing of it. And, if you want to, you can take my dance with Katrina."

"No, I can't," Duke said.

"Why not?"

"'Cause I'm all tuckered out. I'm too tard to dance."

The others laughed.

"That's all right," Katrina said. "When you get your wind, come see me. I'll be glad to dance with you. Even if you aren't as good-looking as Cal," she added with a tease.

There were no other altercations during the dance and shortly before it was over Cal and Katrina went outside, then walked down to the bank of the Rio Grande. The dark water, with moon-glow highlights, was a study in black and silver.

"I am very proud of you for not fighting back," Katrina said.

Cal chuckled. "Well, Duke and I wound up as friends. It's always better to make a new friend, than to make a new enemy, don't you think?"

"I absolutely think so."

"Like us, for example," Cal added. "We didn't even know each other last month, and now we are friends."

"Is that all we are?"

Cal didn't answer right away. Instead he leaned down, picked up a rock, and tossed it into the river, causing concentric circles of moonlight silver to spread from the point where the rock entered the water.

"I'm sorry," Katrina said, apologizing quickly. "I had no right to ask such a question."

"You have every right to ask it," Cal said. "But I don't have any right to answer it."

"What do you mean, you don't have any right? Why would you say such a thing?"

"Katrina, you are the daughter of a very wealthy man, and I'm nothin' but a cowboy. I may be a little better off than most of the cowboys you know, because my job is permanent and I work for a good man who pays me well. I also own my own horse and tack, and I've got a little money put away. But when you get right down to it, I'm still nothin' but a cowboy."

"Don't limit yourself by what you do, Cal, define yourself by who you are. And you are a fine, decent man with the courage and intelligence to avoid a stupid fight, and turn your adversary into a friend. And you must know that I have begun to feel something for you."

"It's only been a little over two weeks, Katrina. If there is going to be any more of this than friendship, I want us to be very sure."

"How can I be more sure than I am now?"

"Smoke will be wantin' to go back home when all the horses are broken."

"Will you be going as well?"

"Katrina, I . . ." Cal started, but he was unable to finish whatever he was going to say because Katrina moved to him and kissed him on the lips.

"Will you be going as well?" Katrina repeated, when, finally, she broke off the kiss.

"Do you want me to stay?"

"Yes, but only if you want to stay."

"Katrina, I want to stay here with you more than I have ever wanted anything in my life. But, I want you to be certain that this is also what you want."

"Yes, I very much want you to stay."

"Then, just so that we know this is real, let's do it like this. I'll go back with Smoke and the others. In three months, if you still feel this way, you send me a letter and I'll come back. I would need to go back up there anyway, to sort of get things settled. I couldn't just leave Smoke without so much as a fare-thee-well."

"I'll still feel this way in three months," Katrina said.

Cal smiled. "I'm very glad to hear that, because I will too."

They kissed again, then they walked back toward the bubble of light that marked the location of the dance floor.

"There you are," Pearlie said when they returned. "Are you going to let me dance with your girl or not?"

"Yes, so long as you realize that she is my girl," Cal said, squeezing Katrina's hand, intimately, before he let her go.

* * *

Rick Isback was one of the men at the dance. He stood out from the others, distinguishable by the clothes he was wearing: a forest green frock coat, and mustard-colored trousers. He was ever the gentleman: a smooth talker and a smooth dancer. He picked out Smoke early in the dance, and observed him from across the floor, always doing so in a way that didn't call Smoke's attention to him.

Isback made a study of the man, watching the way he moved and how he reacted to input from the people around him. He was particularly interested in seeing how Smoke handled the fight that broke out. He knew that one of the young men involved in the fight had arrived with Smoke, and he assumed that they were good friends

He watched to see if Smoke's wife, whose name he had learned was Sally, would dance with anyone else. When he saw that she had danced with someone other than Smoke, he approached the two of them.

"With your permission, sir," he said, recognizing Smoke with a slight nod of his head. Then he turned to Sally. "I wonder if I might have the pleasure of this dance?"

"I would be pleased," Sally said, smiling at him.

The dance was a waltz, but Isback was silent for the entire dance. Not until he returned her to her husband did he speak.

"Thank you very much, madam," he said. "Sir," he added toward Smoke, again with a nod of his head, before he turned to walk away.

"What a strange man," Sally said after her dance partner walked away.

"Strange in what way. Sally, he didn't . . ."

"No, no, nothing untoward," Sally said quickly. "It's just that he didn't say one word for the entire time. I would have thought that, perhaps he was a little unsure of himself, but he is very good dancer. Still . . ."

Sally let the word hang.

"Still what?"

"There is something a little frightening about him, like a hint of sulfur."

"That's not very specific."

"I'm sorry, but that is about as specific as I can get. Call it woman's intuition, but, for all his charm and polish, there is something frightening about him."

Smoke looked up, but the man Sally had danced with was nowhere to be seen. He didn't find that too strange; all a person would have to do to disappear is step out of the bubble of light. The surrounding darkness would envelop one very quickly.

Chapter Sixteen

As Isback walked away into the night, he could still hear the music behind him. He had been in town for almost three weeks now, just waiting until Smoke Jensen arrived. Isback liked to play the advantages. Tonight he had studied Smoke Jensen with the single intention of killing him. On the other hand, Smoke had seen Isback, only in the brief time it took him to dance with Sally Jensen. And of course, Smoke had no idea what Isback had in mind.

The advantage that gave Isback might have been slight, indeed, but when two men of comparative skill faced each other in deadly competition, a slight edge is all one of them would need, to best the other. Isback was convinced that he and Smoke Jensen were of comparative skill. And now he, Rick Isback, had that slight edge. He was now very much looking forward to the encounter that would elevate his name to one of instant recognition. He knew, also, that it would inscribe his name in history books, to be recognized for as long as there was history.

When he stepped into the Lone Star Saloon, it was

nearly empty, with but one man standing at the bar, and two others sharing a table.

"It's very quiet tonight," he said.

"Yes, sir, ever'one is at the dance."

"The women who work here? I was just there and I didn't see any of them."

"Oh, they was there all right," the bartender said. "It's just that most likely you coulda looked right at one of 'em 'n' not recognized her. There ain't none of 'em dressed tonight like what they wear when they're workin' in here. Out there, they look just like any other woman."

"Give me a bottle of whiskey," Isback said. "I know where Ida Rose's room is. I'll wait for her in there."

"I'd rather you not do that," the bartender said. "The thing is, the girls that work here, they don't get all that much privacy. It's the nature of their profession, you might say. So, whatever privacy they do get, why, they guard that pretty damn close. So if Ida Rose was to come back 'n' find someone waitin' in her room, she'd know I was the one that let you in, 'n' she'd be real upset with me.

"I don't like for any of the girls to get mad at me. It puts me off my feed."

"Would this help?" Isback asked, showing the bartender a twenty-dollar bill.

The bartender smiled, then pulled a box from under the bar. Opening it, he took out a key and handed it to Isback.

"She mighta left the door locked," he suggested, exchanging the key for the twenty-dollar bill.

* * *

Cal was the topic of conversation in the bunkhouse that night, not just because he had walked down to the river with the boss's daughter, but because of the way he had handled Duke Pearson, from the Bar W ranch.

"Pearson always has been a little quick to use his fists," Stan said.

"Ahh, me 'n' Duke wound up as good friends," Cal said.

"It takes a good man to turn someone who is fightin' him . . ." Stan paused in mid-sentence, then smiled before he continued, "that is, someone who is tryin' to fight him, into a friend. And tonight, you done that. You are a good man"

"Was there ever any doubt about it?" one of the other cowboys asked. "You know Miss Katrina, 'n' you know she ain't goin' to fall for just anybody who happens to come along. She's just real particular, 'n' she's done let it be known that you're the one for her."

"Oh, I wouldn't be so quick as to say that," Cal replied, pretending to be embarrassed by the conversation, but secretly, very much enjoying it.

"Well, if you won't say it, I will," Old Mo said. "I've seen the way she looks at you, Cal. That gal's got her cap set for you, sure as gun is iron."

One week after the dance, Smoke went into town to arrange for railroad tickets back to Big Rock, Colorado. He would need tickets for the five of them, plus five horses. He had only five horses to take back, because he had sold the remuda to Tom Byrd, along with the other horses he had brought down.

"When will you be departing?" the ticket agent asked.

"I'm not sure; we have a few more days before all the horses are broken. I'd like to just keep it open, if I can."

"Yes, sir, I see no reason why you couldn't do that."

The agent wrote out five tickets, with all the necessary transfers, then handed them to Smoke.

"As you can see, your departure date is left open. You can present them at any time over the next three months."

"Well, I certainly hope it doesn't take three more months to finish my business here. And I thank you."

"Isback, was you serious when you said you'd give a dollar to the first person to tell you when we seen Smoke Jensen come back into town?" someone asked, coming into the Lone Star.

"Have you seen 'im?"

"He's over to the railroad depot buyin' tickets. I think him, and the ones that stayed with him to break horses, is gettin' ready to leave pretty soon."

Isback pulled a silver dollar from his pocket. "Thank you," he said.

"If you're wantin' to talk to 'im, he'll more 'n likely take a meal over at the War Drum. I heard him say somethin' about it."

Isback nodded, then, finishing his drink, left the saloon and walked down to the War Drum.

The War Drum was run by a man named Dwight

Ring. He smiled at Isback when Isback came in.
Isback was not a cheap diner, and Ring appreciated
that.

"Mr. Isback, it's good to see you," Ring said.

"Mr. Ring, do you know Smoke Jensen?"

"Well, I can't say as I know him, actually. He's not
a citizen of our community."

"But you would recognize him, wouldn't you? I
mean if you saw him?"

"Oh, yes, yes, indeed. Mr. Jensen has come in here
quite a few times." Ring smiled, broadly. "I would say
that he is a gentleman of discriminating taste, so it
seems only normal that he would dine with us."

"Good. I have reason to believe that he will be
taking his lunch here today. When he arrives, I would
appreciate it if you would tell him that he can order
anything he wishes to eat, and that I will pay for it."

"You are going to pay for Mr. Jensen's meal? But
why would you do that? I understand that Smoke
Jensen is quite a wealthy man."

"I'm doing that because I would like to meet him.
So, after you tell him that I am paying for his meal,
please invite him to join me at my table."

"Yes, sir," Ring said. "I would be glad to."

After he left the depot Smoke went to the War
Drum Restaurant. He was met by the owner as soon
as he stepped inside the door.

"Hello, Mr. Ring," Smoke said, greeting him with a
smile. "What's good for lunch?"

"Anything that we have on the menu is good, you

know that," Ring said. "And for you, today, there will be no charge."

"No charge? Why would that be?"

"Mr. Jensen, would you happen to know that gentleman over there?" he asked, pointing.

The restaurant owner indicated a man who was sitting alone at a table in the far corner of the room. The man was wearing a low-crown hat with a silver hatband, a jacket, and a bolo tie. His boots were highly polished. It was the same man who had danced with Sally.

"I saw him at the dance. As a matter of fact, he danced with my wife. But I can't say as I know him."

"He has been waiting to see you. He asked that I seat you at his table. He also said I was to serve you anything you wished, because he would pay for it."

"Really?" Smoke smiled and put his hat on the hat rack. "Maybe he has heard about the horses I brought to Tom Byrd, and he wants to do business. All right, I'll have steak, a baked potato, some fried okra, and a couple of rolls."

"Very good, sir."

When Smoke reached the back table, the stranger stood and extended his hand. He was wearing an ivory-handled pistol tucked into a black, silver-studded holster. The holster was low, and well tied down. The skirt of the jacket was kicked back to allow a quick draw. Smoke wondered why a businessman would be wearing his gun in such a way.

"You are the man who danced with Sally," Smoke said.

"Yes, you were most gracious to allow me to do

so. And, she is a very skilled dancer. It was quite a pleasure."

"Well, I appreciate you buying my lunch, but you didn't have to do so, just because you danced with my wife."

The man laughed. "Oh, I assure you, Mr. Jensen, this meal has nothing to do with my having danced with your wife. At least, there is no direct correlation. My name is Rick Isback. Does that mean anything to you?"

The name was familiar, but Smoke couldn't place where he had heard it.

"I can't say that I recognize it," Smoke said. "I'm sorry, had we met before the other night?"

"No, we haven't met," Isback said. "But I must say that I'm a little disappointed you haven't heard of me. After all, I have heard of you."

"Yes, I often find myself at a disadvantage with people that I don't know, who know me," Smoke replied. "It can be a little frustrating at times."

"More and more, people are beginning to recognize my name, and, I've no doubt, the time will come when my name will roll as easily from the tongue as does your. Especially after today."

"Why, especially after today?"

Isback flashed a toothy smile. "Oh, we'll get to that after a while. Have you already ordered?"

"I have."

"Good. That is good. Tell me, Mr. Jensen, how many men have you killed?"

The question didn't come as a complete surprise to Smoke; he had been having suspicions almost from the moment he had approached Isback. Also, he remembered Sally's assessment of him.

"There is something a little frightening about him, like a hint of sulfur."

"Are you a newspaper man?"

Isback laughed. "Heavens, no. Why would you ask such a thing?"

"Because that seems like a rather unusual question to ask a person."

"I expected you to respond by asking me the same thing."

"All right, Mr. Isback, how many men have you killed?"

"I've killed seventeen men."

"That's quite a few."

"But not as many as you, I'd wager," Isback said.

Smoke didn't reply.

"Let me reword my question. How many men have you killed as an affair of honor?"

"What is an affair of honor?"

"Don't play coy with me, Mr. Jensen. You know perfectly well what an affair of honor is. It is when you met your adversary, face-to-face, with each of you having an equal opportunity to prevail."

"I see nothing honorable about killing," Smoke replied. "And I've never killed anyone unless I had to."

"If someone is trying to kill you, would that put you in a position where you had to kill them?"

"Well, yes, but, there has to be more to it than that. I mean, someone wouldn't be trying to kill you unless they had a reason."

"So, you've never fought a gunfight that had no reason for its being, other than honor."

"As I said, I can see no honor in killing."

"What a strange thing to say for a man who has killed as many as you have. You are aware, are you not, that your name is spoken of in awe from New York to San Francisco. Books have been written about your many brave encounters."

"I have nothing to do with that. Believe me, I don't seek such notoriety."

"That's very easy for you to say, Smoke Jensen, because you already enjoy such fame. And after today, it will be my name on everyone's lips."

"After today?"

"After I kill you in a fair fight." Isback smiled. "You see, Mr. Jensen, you and I are about to participate in an affair of honor."

"Suppose I tell you I don't want to fight?"

"Oh, you'll fight," Isback said. "Because I'm going to kill you today whether we fight or not."

"How would you explain that as honorable?"

Isback chuckled. "Really, Mr. Jensen, do you think I expect you to just sit there and let me kill you? No, I think not. As I said, I'm going to kill you, but not until after we have had our meal."

At a signal from Isback, the food was brought to the table.

"Since you are buying, I would like for you to pay the man now, if you don't mind," Smoke said.

Isback chuckled. "Do you think I'm going to change my mind?"

"No. It's just that after this affair of . . . *honor* . . . is over, I don't want to have to go through your pockets to get the money. I'm sure you agree, that would be very awkward."

Isback took a quick breath, then he forced a smile. "Oh, that's a good one," he said. "I'll try to remember that."

"Don't worry, you'll remember," Smoke said. "If you are serious about this foolishness, then you won't be alive long enough to forget it. Do pay the man, won't you?"

With the forced smile still on his face, Isback pulled out his billfold, then extracted enough money to pay for the meal and handed it to the waiter.

Over the next several minutes the two men enjoyed a leisurely meal. They exchanged stories and laughed so frequently that anyone who had not overheard the earlier conversation might think they were two very good friends.

Many knew better, however, because some of them had overheard the initial conversation between the two men, and had passed it on to others until soon, everyone in the restaurant knew. Word spread beyond the café as well, so that before Smoke and Isback were finished with their lunch, every table was filled and there were many more present who were standing along the walls, watching. As a result of the unfolding drama, all other conversation in the café had stopped as everyone waited, silently, to see what was going to happen.

As the last of the peach cobbler was eaten, Isback called for the waiter to pour them each another cup of coffee. The waiter did so, his hands shaking so badly that it was all he could do to get the coffee in the cup.

"Mr. Jensen, people will talk and write about this meal for years to come, especially as it was your last meal. I do hope you found the food to your taste," Isback said. He lifted the coffee cup. "I drink to our newfound but, of necessity, short-lived friendship, sir."

Smoke took a swallow of his coffee, then put the cup down. "This is your play, Isback, so I invite you to make the first move."

"Surely, sir, you wouldn't want the gunfight to take place here, in this crowded restaurant?"

"Why not?" Smoke asked. "Isn't that the whole purpose? Don't you need witnesses?"

"Yes, but they can watch us in the street. In here, there is too much of a danger of someone being hit by a wayward shot."

Smoke shook his head. "There won't be a wayward shot. You won't get a shot off, and I won't miss."

The easy smile left Isback's face and he reached for his pistol, drawing it very fast, considering that he was sitting down. The smile returned as he brought his pistol up and saw that Smoke had not yet even started his draw. He had won!

Then, faster than could be comprehended, Smoke's pistol appeared in his hand. Smoke fired and, as he had predicted, Isback didn't get his shot off, and Smoke didn't miss. A small black hole appeared in the middle of Isback's forehead and his chair pitched over.

With his gun still in his hand, Smoke stood up, then stepped around the table to look down at Isback's sprawled body.

Returning the pistol to his holster, Smoke turned and started toward the door.

"I've never seen anything like that before in my life!" someone said. "I thought for sure he had you. How can anyone be that fast?"

Smoke neither spoke, nor looked toward anyone. He had no reason to kill Isback, except for the fact that Isback had it in mind to kill him. If this was an affair of honor, he wanted nothing to do with it. He felt a little sick.

Chapter Seventeen

From the Brownsville *Cosmopolitan:*

GUNFIGHT IN SAN VICENTE

Strange Affair of Honor

Two of the best-known shootists in the American West, Smoke Jensen and Rick Isback, encountered each other recently in the border town of San Vicente. The two men, both known for the skill with which they could employ the pistol, settled for all time the question as to who was the better of the two of them.

The gunfight took place in the War Drum Restaurant, and according to witnesses, occurred at the conclusion of a meal which, to the casual observer, seemed full of congeniality and friendly discussion.

Witnesses, however, tell a different story. According to the reports of several who overheard the conversation, Mr. Jensen was forced into the fight by Isback, and had no recourse but to respond, or lose his own life.

Smoke Jensen prevailed in the contest thus precipitated, employing his pistol with a speed that amazed all who saw it. None, however, were more shocked than Rick Isback, who went to his grave knowing that there was someone faster.

On the same day the newspaper article appeared, Smoke, Sally, and Cal were invited to dinner with Tom Byrd and his family. Pearlie and Old Mo had also been invited but they had respectfully declined, knowing that the real reason for the invitation was to enable Katrina and Cal to spend a little time together.

"I'm sure you saw the newspaper today," Tom said.

"I saw it," Smoke said. "I wish the story had not been written, but there was no way something like that wasn't going to be reported."

"Does this happen often?" Tom Byrd asked. "I mean, are you often encountered by men whose sole purpose is to see who can kill the other?"

"Tom, please," Hazel said. "Do you really think something like this is appropriate conversation to be having at dinner?"

"I'm sorry, dear. Kirby, Hazel is right, forget about the question. I have no right in asking such a thing."

"That's all right, I don't mind answering it. And fortunately, the answer is no, I've not encountered a lot of men who are looking only to make a name for themself," Smoke replied. "And I am very sorry it happened here, to put a damper on what has otherwise been a most pleasant and productive visit."

Tom smiled. "It hasn't put a damper on anything,

young man. Your visit here has been most delightful and I have enjoyed it very much. The only one who might have enjoyed it more is Katrina." Tom looked pointedly toward Cal.

"Papa!" Katrina exclaimed. She looked down in obvious embarrassment, but she didn't dispute the comment.

"School will be starting for you on Monday," Sally said. "During the school year do you live here, or in town?"

"The school board furnishes a room at the back of the schoolhouse, and I'll stay there some of the time, but with Sundance, I can stay here and ride into school without any problem."

"Good, I'm glad Sundance has made that possible for you," Smoke said.

"Sundance is such a beautiful horse. I'm so glad Cal was able to break him for me."

Tom Byrd laughed. "Cal didn't break him for you, honey, he broke him for me. Isn't that right, Cal?"

"Well now, Mr. Byrd, I can't exactly agree with that, seein' as who wound up with the horse."

Tom laughed out loud. "Very good answer. You are a smart young man, Cal."

"He's a good man too," Smoke said.

Cal cleared his throat. "This is gettin' a little embarrassin'. Katrina, would you like to take a walk with me?"

"I would love to take a walk with you," Katrina replied.

The Big House of The Wide Loop ranch was shaded by cottonwood trees. To the west rose a line of sheer cliffs and grassy plateaus. The sun was just going down and it ignited a golden glow that stretched from end to end all along the rim of the cliffs, making them look as if they were on fire.

"Oh, look," Katrina said. "Isn't the sunset beautiful?"

"Not as beautiful as you are," Cal replied.

"Papa likes you," Katrina said.

"I like him."

"No, you don't understand. I mean Papa really likes you, the way a man is supposed to like his son-in-law."

Cal smiled at her. "I'm not even goin' to ask you to slow down, 'cause I can tell you right now, I will be comin' back."

"Do you promise?"

"Yeah, I promise. And it's not goin' to take me three months, either. Soon as we get back up there, I'm goin' to tell Smoke that he needs to hire someone else to take my place, 'cause I'm comin' back down here to get married."

"You are coming down here to get married?" Katrina questioned.

"Well, yeah, to get married. Look here, Katrina, ain't that what this here is all about?" The expression on Cal's face showed his confusion at her response.

"Well, I don't know, Mr. Calvin Woods. So far as I know, nobody has asked me to marry them."

"Oh," Cal said. "I guess I haven't asked you, have I?" Cal took both of Katrina's hands in his, and stared into her eyes.

"Katrina, will you marry me?"

"Yes, Cal! Oh, yes!" Katrina answered happily. She

threw her arms around his neck, plastered herself against him, and kissed him deeply.

The Mexican state of Tamaulipas

T. B. Keno rolled some spicy beef into a tortilla and took a bite, then addressed the *americano*, Johnny Lodge, who had come to see him with an offer to sell him a new kind of terrible weapon.

"With this weapon, one man can duplicate the efforts of twenty men. It would make your small army as powerful as one many times larger. And I have two of them."

"What kind of weapon can do such a thing?"

"I have brought two Gardner guns to you, Colonel," Lodge said. "They can fire very rapidly."

"No, *señor*, I am not interested. I know about the Gatling gun. They have to be pulled on wheels, behind a team of horses. My army must be very mobile. I cannot be bothered by such a thing."

Lodge shook his head. "This is not a Gatling gun, Colonel, it is a Gardner gun. The Gatling gun is very heavy, and, as you say, must be pulled on a gun carriage, such as artillery. The Gardner is much lighter, can easily be transported on horseback, and handled by one man. The Gatling gun has many barrels, the Gardner has but one barrel that is fed from a vertical magazine. When the crank is turned, a feed arm positions a .45 caliber cartridge in the breech, the bolt is closed, and the weapon fires. As you turn the crank, the bolt is opened, the spent case is ejected, a new bullet inserted, and fired again. If you would allow me, I shall set up a demonstration for you."

"Yes, I would like to see such a gun," Keno said.

Keno followed Lodge outside where, in addition to Lodge's horse, there were two mules tied to the hitching rack. On each of the mules, there was a cargo pack, each pack carrying a contraption of some sort.

"Here are the guns," Lodge said, pointing to the mules. "As you can see, a gun can be easily carried by one mule. And, when we get to a place where I can demonstrate the gun to you, I'll show you how easy it is for one man to take it from the mule, assemble it, and fire it."

"Do it here, *señor*," Keno said.

"Here, Colonel, in the middle of town?"

"*Sí.* I want to see you assemble the gun here."

Lodge nodded. "All right, if that's really what you want, I'll do it for you."

He took down the gun, which was in four parts. As he took down each part, he explained what it was.

"This is the tripod," he said. "As you said, the Gatling gun must rest on a caisson, but this gun rests on a tripod, which is so light it can easily be held by one hand."

Next came the base assembly, which not only connected the gun to the tripod, it was also the means by which the gun could be elevated or traversed.

"This is the barrel and breech assembly," he said, connecting the gun to the base.

"I have never seen a barrel so big around," Keno said. "Are the bullets so large?"

Lodge chuckled. "Look, this is the actual gun barrel," he said, pointing to a .45 caliber protrusion. "This is the water jacket," he added, laying his hand on the part. "The gun fires bullets so rapidly that the barrel becomes very hot, and it requires water to cool it. You should never fire the gun unless the jacket is filled with water."

"Is the jacket filled with water now?"

"Yes, it is. Now, the last part of the gun, is the ammunition magazine. Here, you see fifty bullets loaded. When you put the magazine here, and turn this crank, it will shoot all fifty rounds in just a few seconds."

"That is an amazing gun."

"Yes, sir, it sure as hell is. And you can have both of them for a thousand dollars apiece."

"A thousand dollars? I think that is much more than the guns cost."

"That may be," Lodge said easily. "But the ordinary person can't just go buy a gun like this. You have to get them from someone who has them, and who is willing to sell them." Lodge smiled. "I have them, Colonel, and I am willing to sell them, if the price is right. And my price is one thousand dollars for each gun."

"Before I agree to pay so much money, I would like to see the gun fired."

Lodge said, "I thought you might. Let me take the gun down, and we'll go somewhere, where it is safe to shoot it."

"Shoot it here, *señor*."

"Here?" Lodge said, a surprised look on his face. "Colonel, we are right in the middle of town. It wouldn't be a good idea to shoot the gun here."

"Shoot the gun here, *señor*. I want to see it."

Lodge shrugged. "All right, what the hell? I may as well, it's your town, not mine. If someone is hurt, it will not be my concern. What shall I shoot at?"

At the other end of the plaza, there was a kiosk, plastered with signs advertising goods that could be bought in town. Keno pointed to it.

"That," he said. "It is little larger than a man. I should like to see if you can hit that with this gun."

"Ha!" Lodge said. "That will be easy."

Lodge lay on his stomach behind the gun, then he fit the magazine into the slot on top of the gun. Lining it up with the sights, he started turning the crank.

The firing began then, a rapid-fire, staccato pop of bullets, the shots coming so close together the sound of shooting could not be separated. At the loud and unexpected sound of so many bullets being fired so rapidly, there were screams of fear, and shouts of surprise from the residents of the town.

As Lodge continued to fire, the effectiveness of the gun was immediately recognized. Bits and pieces of wood flew from the kiosk, each piece representing the impact of the bullets. Within a few seconds the part of the kiosk that had not been shredded by the bullets was filled with bullet holes.

Lodge rolled over onto his side and looked up at Keno.

"What did you think of that, Colonel?" he asked, a triumphant smile on his face. The smile left, when he saw that Keno was pointing a pistol at him.

"What the hell?" Lodge shouted in surprise, anger, and fear.

"How dare you shoot up this town, and endanger my people!" Keno shouted in a loud voice. Before Lodge could respond, Keno pulled the trigger, the bullet hitting Lodge in the middle of the forehead.

"Martinez," Keno said easily.

"*Sí, Coronel?*"

"Take that gun down and put it back on the mule."
Keno smiled. "We now have two marvelous guns."

"*Sí, Coronel.*"

Shortly after Martinez left, Vargas came back from
his scouting expedition down to the Byrd ranch, and
he went into the cantina where Keno had set up his
office, in order to render his report.

"There are two hundred of them, *Coronel*, fine,
strong horses already broken. It will not be hard to
steal them."

"The *rancho* is near the *pueblo* of San Vicente, is it
not?"

"*Sí, Coronel.* And there is but one sheriff and one
deputy in the village."

Chapter Eighteen

The Wide Loop

When the last horse was broken, and trained by Old Mo to be an effective cow pony, Tom Byrd decided to have a barbeque to tell Smoke and the others good-bye. To that end, half a steer was spitted and placed over a fire early in the morning, and the men took turns slowly rotating the meat throughout the entire day.

The ranch was permeated with the rich aroma of cooking meat, those smells augmented by the pies and pastries that were also being prepared.

Cal and Katrina found a place under a tree where they could be relatively alone.

As Katrina put the food out onto the two plates, Cal stretched out on his side, supporting his head on his hand, his body close to hers. His hat lay beside him, and his hair, dampened by the warmth of the summer day, was forming haphazard curls against his forehead. She reached out to brush the dark brown hair aside, and when she did he caught her hand.

Without a word being said, she leaned forward to kiss him. It was neither demanding nor hesitant, but the kiss of two people who had grown quite comfortable with each other.

"All of your friends will see us," Katrina said. "Does that bother you?"

"No. They'll all be jealous of me," Cal said. "Let 'em look all they want."

They kissed again.

"For cryin' out loud, Cal, let the girl eat, will you? She's goin' to starve to death, if you don't quit kissin' her," Pearlie called, and the other cowboys laughed.

Cal sat up quickly.

"Why, Cal, you're blushing!" Katrina said. "And here I thought you said you didn't care if your friends were watching."

"It's you I'm thinkin' about," Cal said. "I don't want you to be embarrassed."

"I'm not embarrassed at all," Katrina said, leaning forward to kiss him again.

After the meal the cowboys engaged in various activities, such as throwing horseshoes, lassoing, and shooting at targets. Then Old Mo surprised everyone when he produced a bow and a quiver of arrows.

"Where did that come from?" Pearlie asked.

"I found a good limb on that hickory tree by the barn," Old Mo said. "So I made myself a bow."

He showed the bow to the others, and several commented on how smooth the wood was, and the quality of the workmanship.

"Mo, can you actually shoot that thing?" Stan asked.

"I can shoot it."

"Shoot at something," Stan challenged.

Mo fitted an arrow into the string, then looked around. "What would you like me to shoot at?" he asked.

The name of the ranch, THE WIDE LOOP, was painted on the barn, just above the wide door opening. Stan pointed to the painted sign. "Can you hit one of the O's in that sign?"

"Which O?"

"The first one."

"Come on, Stan," Cal said. "That's more 'n a hundred yards away. Most folks would be doing well to hit that with a rifle. Find something else."

"No, it's all right," Old Mo said. "I'll do it for 'im."

Old Mo lifted the bow, pulled the string back, sighted along the arrow, then lifted his fingers.

The string sung as it whipped forward, and the arrow flashed away from the bow, made a long, swift, graceful arc, then stuck with a solid thock sound, almost exactly in the middle of the first letter O in the word "Loop."

Everyone who watched the demonstration applauded appreciatively.

"I'm very impressed, Mr. Morris," Tom said. "Where did you learn to shoot a bow so well?"

"I spent some time with the Injuns," Old Mo said without further explanation.

Both Thomas Byrd and his daughter, Katrina, went to the depot to see Smoke and the others off. Katrina and Cal wandered down to the far end of the platform to have a few private moments before the train would arrive.

"I don't want you to be late for school," Cal said.

"The train leaves at seven, school doesn't start until eight. I have plenty of time."

"Good. I wouldn't want you to get into trouble because of me."

Katrina chuckled. "Papa is the president of the school board. I wouldn't get into trouble even if I didn't show up."

"Good."

"Will you write to me?" Katrina asked.

"I will, but remember, I'm not educated like you are. I'm sure I won't spell all my words right. Oh, wait, I can get Miz Sally to . . ."

"No, don't do that."

"What?"

Katrina put her hand on Cal's cheek. "Don't you think you might want to say something that you want only me to see?"

Cal chuckled. "Yeah, I reckon you're right. All right, I'll write and you might just have to figure out what I'm saying."

"Cal, I read things written by first, second, and third graders. Trust me, I'll be able to read and understand anything you write."

"Here comes the train!" somebody shouted.

"Well, I guess we'd better get down there with the others," Cal said.

"Cal, I'll still feel this way, even after you have gone," Katrina said.

Cal smiled at her. "I'm glad that you do, because I'll be coming back as soon as I can. I'm not going to be waiting any three months like I said. It won't even be one month."

"Are you going to kiss me good-bye?" Katrina

asked. "Or, are you too embarrassed to do it in front of your friends?"

"If I wasn't too embarrassed to kiss you at the barbeque, I'm not too embarrassed to kiss you now. You sure you want me to kiss you in front of your pa?"

"Why not? Do you think Papa doesn't know how I feel about you?"

"All right," Cal said and, wrapping his arms around her, he pulled Katrina to him, and she raised her lips to his.

He had never kissed anyone in quite this way before, and he thought he actually felt the blood moving through his veins.

They held the kiss until the locomotive passed by them, clanking and puffing as it did so. Not until that moment were they aware that they weren't alone, but were in the wide open, being observed by her father and his friends.

They parted then walked slowly together down to where Pearlie, Old Mo, Smoke, Sally, and Tom Byrd were all standing.

The good-byes were said, and Smoke and the others boarded the train. Cal stayed on the step even as the train got under way, and Katrina walked along beside the slowly moving train. She and Cal held hands for as long as she could keep pace. Then as the train began to gather speed she stopped and held her hand up in a final wave. By now, tears were coming down her face.

Tom Byrd came up to put his arm around her. "Do you love him, darlin'?"

"Yes, Papa," Katrina replied. "I love him more than anything in the world."

"I just want you to be careful, is all. I don't him to break your heart."

"He won't hurt me, Papa. He said he is coming back as soon as he can, and I know that he will."

"Did he tell you that?"

"Yes, he told me that. Papa, you aren't against him just because he isn't rich, are you?"

"No, honey, that has nothing to do with it. I'm rich enough that I don't care whether the man you wind up marrying is rich or not. All I want for you is to have a man that you love, and one that loves you."

"I love him, and he loves me."

"I'm glad. I think Cal is a good man. He reminds me a great deal of another young man I used to know, a man who has made quite a success of his life."

"You're talking about Mr. Jensen, aren't you?"

"Kirby Jensen, yes."

The train whistle blew again, this time from far down the track and Katrina and her father stood there watching it until, finally, it went around a distant bend and passed out of view. All that remained to be seen of the train was a thin wisp of black smoke.

"I suppose I had better get to school," Katrina said. "I wouldn't want the children getting there ahead of me."

"Where are you going to leave Sundance?" Tom asked.

"I'll leave him in the stable; there's really no place for him at the school."

"I tell you what I'll do. I'll approach the school

board and ask them to build a stable behind the school."

"Oh, Papa, do you think they will?"

Tom chuckled. "I'll pay for it," he said.

Cal didn't sit with the others on the train. He sat alone at the front of the car, looking out the window, but not really seeing the passing scenery.

"I wonder if Cal is feeling all right," Smoke said.

"No, he's not feeling all right," Sally replied.

"Why not? What's wrong with him?"

Sally sighed. "Really, Smoke, haven't you paid any attention to anything but horses for the last month?"

"The girl?"

Sally smiled. "Maybe you aren't hopeless after all. Yes, of course the girl. I doubt Cal will be staying with us after we get back home."

"You mean you think he is going to want to come back down to Texas?"

"I know he is."

"I think I'll go up and talk to him."

"Smoke, don't say anything that will . . ."

Smoke put his hand out to touch Sally on the arm. "Don't worry," he said. "Cal is more than just a top hand. He's also a close friend. I'm not going to say or do anything that would change that."

Sally smiled up at him. "I know you won't."

Smoke walked up to the front of the car. Cal was looking out the window with such intensity that he didn't even notice the man who was standing in the aisle, looking down at him.

"Do you mind if I join you?"

Smoke's words startled Cal and he jerked around, quickly.

"Yes. Yes, of course you can."

"You're already missing her, aren't you?"

"You mean it shows?"

"Well, I suppose you could have painted the sign in larger letters, but I think most people can read it."

"What? What sign?" Cal asked, not understanding Smoke's joke.

Smoke laughed. "Never mind. How long do you plan to stay at Sugarloaf before you start back?"

"As soon as you can find a replacement for me, I plan to gather up all my things then head back down here. You don't mind, do you?"

"Cal, never let it be said that Smoke Jensen stood in the way of true love. I'm going to miss you. We all are. But there comes a time in a man's life when he has to go out on his own, and I'd say that time has just come for you. Go with my blessings. And you'll be getting a real fine woman. I know that, because I have known her since she was a baby."

"Thanks, Smoke," Cal said with an expression of relief on his face. "I knew you would understand."

"What about Pearlie? Have you told him yet?"

"I ain't told 'im, but I figure he's prob'ly already figured it out, anyhow."

"You mean you *haven't* told him," Smoke said. "If you think schoolteachers that you know are always correcting your grammar, wait until you marry one."

"You're right. I haven't even thought about that. But, bein' as you're married to a schoolteacher, I reckon you would know all about it, wouldn't you now?"

"I reckon so," Smoke replied with a smile. He

stood, then looked down at his young ranch hand. "Has she told you she'll marry you?"

"Yeah, she's told me that she will."

"Congratulations."

At that same moment, Katrina was sitting at her desk in the school building, back in San Vicente. The children had not yet arrived, and she was scribbling on a sheet of paper:

Katrina Woods.

Mrs. Calvin Woods.

Mrs. Katrina Woods.

She printed the name in block letters, then wrote it in cursive. No matter how she did it, the sight of it made her heart sing. This was the happiest she had ever been in her life.

"Hello, Miss Byrd," a young voice said.

Katrina looked up to see Lenny Potts, one of her first graders. She had a particularly warm spot for Lenny. She thought he was cute, and funny, and she couldn't help but think that if she ever got married and had children, she would want a boy just like Lenny.

"Hello, Lenny," she said. "You're the first one here today. You must really like school."

"That's because I like you, a whole lot."

"Well now, isn't it good that it works out that way? Because I like you too."

"Mama says I can give this to you." Lennie held out an apple. "Mama said I could give this to you."

"Isn't that sweet of your mama? Thank you, Lenny.

And when you get home this afternoon, you thank your mama for me as well."

"Can I ring the school bell, Miss Byrd?" one of the seventh graders asked, arriving at that moment.

"Yes, Mickey, I think it's about time for it. Go right ahead."

A moment later the bell began to toll, and young people streamed toward the school from all over town.

Chapter Nineteen

Keno held his hand up, halting the column. It was early afternoon, and just east, and down the Lodge from him, the town of San Vicente was undergoing a normal day of business. From here they could see a wagon rolling slowly down the street as well as men and women strolling along the boardwalk. School was out for recess, and the happy laughter of children at play could be heard.

Keno had only twenty men with him. It was his intention to strike against the town making as much noise and causing as much chaos as he could. Doing so would create a diversion that would draw defenders in from around the town. Keno had sent thirty men out to Tom Byrd's ranch with orders to wait there until Byrd's ranch hands rushed into town. That would leave the herd unprotected.

The school was located at the west end of town, and at the moment Katrina was out on the school ground, keeping an eye on the children at play. She was glad school had started, because when she was busy she didn't have time to dwell on Cal being gone.

She knew that Cal was a little intimidated, partly because of her education, and partly because her father was such a wealthy man. But Cal was a man of intelligence, confidence, and self-reliance. She had seen him demonstrate those very qualities, many times over the last month. And she knew that he would be able to overcome any misgivings he might have about marrying her.

"Miss Byrd, look," one of the boys said, pointing to the Lodge just to the south. "Who are all those men?"

Looking in the direction the boy had pointed, Katrina was confused by the sight of so many mounted men, just setting up on the ridgeline, looking down toward the town. She had no idea who they were, but she waved tentatively at them.

Her wave was not returned.

Up on the Lodgetop, Keno was sitting on his horse, looking down toward the town. Seeing all the children outside let Keno know that their approach had been unseen. He had the complete advantage of surprise.

"Chavez, Ortega, set up the Gardner guns here, and here," he said, pointing to positions on the Lodge. "When I give the word, start shooting."

"What shall we shoot at, *Coronel*?" Ortega asked.

"The town," Keno repeated.

"But, at what in town should we shoot?" Ortega asked, still not sure he understood what Keno was talking about.

"People," Keno said bluntly. "Shoot at the people. I will tell you when to start, and when to stop."

"*Sí, Coronel.*"

Keno peered at the town through a pair of field glasses, smiling when he saw how many people were out, just milling around. There would be plenty of targets for his rapid-firing guns to shoot at.

"Now!" he shouted, bringing his hand down sharply. "Begin shooting!"

Chavez and Ortega began turning the cranks, feeding ammunition into the breech of the guns. The two guns roared, spitting two streams of bullets toward the town at a combined rate of three hundred bullets per minute.

In the town the people out on the street heard the sound of gunfire coming from the Lodge to the west of town. In addition, they could hear the whizzing, whistling, and popping of bullets as they flew through the town, breaking out windows, punching holes in signs, kicking up dirt from the street, and splinters from the boardwalk.

"What is it? What is happening?"

"How can they be shooting so fast?"

The citizens of the town hurried to get off the street.

Although she had never heard gunfire so rapid and so close to together, Katrina recognized it immediately for what it was. It was gunfire! She had to get her children back into the schoolhouse!

"Boys and girls, back inside!" she shouted. "Hurry, please, back inside."

Lenny, her first grader, had never heard such a

sound before and, confused, he wandered off the school ground, out into the street. It was at that moment that the noise of the very rapid fire stopped, and mounted riders began galloping down the Lodge, shooting as they approached.

"Lenny! No! Get back here!" Katrina called.

Despite Katrina's warning, Lenny stood there, watching, as if mesmerized, the galloping horses. Whether he was too curious or too frightened to move, Katrina didn't know. She just knew that he was in great danger, and without giving it a second thought, she rushed out into the street.

"Lenny!" she shouted again. She managed to reach him, grabbing him, just as the riders reached the edge of town. The riders were shooting now, and though there weren't quite as many bullets flying around now as there had been a little earlier, they seemed to be closer, and she could hear them whizzing by, and see them kicking up dirt in the road. She picked Lenny up, then turning to put her body between him and the riders, started back toward the school.

Sanchez had not specifically aimed at the woman, but he saw his bullet hit her in the back, and he saw her go down. She was lying belly-down on the ground as the twenty men rode on past the school, shooting up the town.

"Shoot everyone who is on the street!" Keno shouted. "Burn the buildings!"

Out at The Wide Loop, Stan Hardegree heard the shooting. It wouldn't have caught his attention, except for the intensity of it. The sound of gunfire was loud and sustained. Then he saw smoke coming up from the direction of town.

"Somethin' goin' on in San Vicente!" he shouted, and as the others looked in that direction, Hardegree ran to the Big House.

"Mr. Byrd, there's shootin' comin' from town! Lots of it!"

Byrd stepped out onto the porch and he too could hear the many gunshots.

"Katrina is there!" he said. "Get the men mounted! We're going to town!"

Ramos watched until the *vaqueros* left the ranch, then he held up his hand, signaling the others.

"Come!" he said. "We will take the horses now!"

Ramos and thirty men swooped down onto the ranch with guns blazing. Only three of Byrd's hands had been left behind, and they went down under a hail of bullets. With all resistance gone, stealing the herd of horses was easy and within two minutes after riding onto the ranch, Ramos and his men were heading southwest toward the river, and Mexico.

"*Señor Coronel*, many men are coming!" Sanchez shouted.

"Come, we will leave now," Keno replied, and the twenty men rode off, leaving the dead and dying lying on the street behind them. Three of the buildings were ablaze.

By the time men from the surrounding ranches

arrived, the raiders were gone, and there was nothing they could do but help fight the fires that had been started.

Tom Byrd went straight to the school to check on his daughter. He saw a cluster of children, looking down at someone on the ground, and as he drew closer, he felt a grabbing constriction in his chest.

The person they were looking at was Katrina!

"Katrina!" he shouted in dismay. Dismounting, he moved toward her as quickly as he could.

"She saved Lenny," one of the older children said. "When the riders came they were shooting, and Lenny ran out into the street. Miss Byrd went to get him, and she was shot."

"Katrina, no, no!" Tom Byrd shouted in anguish. He knelt on the ground beside her.

"Papa?"

"Yes, honey, it's Papa."

"Are you and Mama all right?"

"We weren't hurt."

"That is good. That is very good. And Lenny?"

"Lenny is here, Miss Byrd," the same older boy who had spoken to Tom Byrd said. "He is crying, but he isn't hurt. You saved his life."

"Papa?"

"Yes, sweetheart, I'm here."

"Papa, tell Cal. Tell him it would have been so wonderful."

"You can tell him yourself, Katrina, I'll send a telegram and bring him back so you can . . ."

Katrina took a couple of short, audible, rattling breaths, then she stopped breathing, and her eyes, though still open, glazed over.

"Katrina!" Tom shouted. "Katrina!"

"She's dead, ain't she?" the boy asked.

Tom lowered his head and pinched the bridge of his nose.

"Is Miss Byrd dead?" one of the other students asked.

Soon, word spread among all the students that their teacher was dead. Many of the students began crying then, girls and boys alike.

Stan Hardegree rode up then, and seeing Tom Byrd squatting down by Katrina, knew without having to ask, that she was dead. Dismounting, he removed his hat and stood, respectfully, alongside his boss. He said nothing, thinking it would be better to give Tom Byrd a moment of privacy.

"I'm going to have to tell Hazel," Tom said. "I'd rather do anything in the world than that. But I'm going to have to tell her."

Before leaving town, Tom made arrangements with the mortician to take care his daughter. It wasn't that easy to do, as eleven more of the town's citizens had been killed in the raid.

"How will you handle that many?" Tom asked.

"I've sent word to Brownsville. There are two undertakers there. I'm sure one of them will be able to come over and help."

With Katrina in good hands, Tom started home to share the grim news with his wife of forty-eight years. Halfway home he was met by Hardegree, who had gone home earlier, taking the men with him.

"Stan?" Tom asked, puzzled as to why his foreman would have come to meet him.

"They was here too, Mr. Byrd," Hardegree said.

"What? Stan, my wife?" Tom gasped, in shock and fear.

"Miz Byrd is fine," Hardegree said.

"Thank God."

"But Lou, Jay, 'n' Booker ain't. They was kilt, Mr. Byrd. While we was in town, a bunch of men come here to the ranch. They kilt the three men that was keepin' watch o'er the horses, then they took the horses."

"Took the horses? How many did they take?"

"They took 'em all, the whole herd. Mr. Byrd, they took ever' horse they could find."

Tom rode on up to the house where he found Hazel sitting alone, on the sofa, in the living room, darkened because the shades and curtains were pulled shut.

"Hazel?" His voice was quiet and caressing.

"She's dead, isn't she? Our little girl is dead."

"Who told you?"

"Nobody told me. Nobody had to tell me. I just knew, that's all."

Tom hurried over to the sofa, and pulled Hazel into his arms.

"Did you get to see her, Tom? Was she, at least, able to say something before she died?"

"Yes, she spoke to me."

Tom wondered if he should tell Hazel that Katrina spoke of her, or if he should tell her the truth.

"She talked about Cal, didn't she?" Hazel asked.

"Darling, I'm sure . . ."

"Don't worry. I know she loves you and me. But I very much want to know that she had found love, before she died. What did she say about Cal?"

"She said that we should tell him that . . . 'it would have been wonderful.' I told her that she could tell him that, herself, but it was too late."

"I'm glad her last thoughts were of him. Now, we have to get him back for her funeral."

"They are on the train. How am I going to do that?"

"I don't know, but, please, do."

"We can do it," the Western Union operator said. "I have a schedule of where the train will be at any moment. All we have to do is send a telegram to a stop that is ahead of the train. They'll get word to any passenger."

"Are you sure they'll know how to do this?" Tom asked.

"Don't worry. It's been done many, many times." The telegrapher chuckled. "The telegram is a lot faster than a train. Now, what message do you want to send?"

Tom showed him the message, and the smile left the telegrapher's face.

"Oh, I'm very sorry, Mr. Byrd. Forgive me for laughing. I should have known."

"No need for forgiveness. Just see to it that this message reaches Cal Woods on the northbound train."

Chapter Twenty

"We're coming in to San Antonio," Smoke said. "From what I understand, we're supposed to be here for almost an hour. We may as well leave the train and get something to eat. I wonder if Cal wants to eat."

"Ha!" Pearlie said. "He may be pining over that girl, but have you ever seen a time when that boy wouldn't eat?"

Cal did join them and the five were sitting at a table in the dining room of the depot.

"Smoke, Miz Sally," Cal started. "I hope you two know that you're both the most important people in my entire life, up to now. But there's someone else important too. Maybe you don't know it, 'cause I haven't said anything, but me 'n' Katrina, uh," he cleared his throat and looked at Sally. "Excuse me, I mean Katrina and I, well, we saw quite a bit of each other during this past month. And the truth is . . ."

"For cryin' out loud, Cal," Pearlie said, interrupting him. "Next, you'll be tellin' us that you got blue eyes. Do you think there was even one of us who didn't know that you 'n' Katrina had gone nuts over each other?"

"Yeah. You mean you already knew that?"

"You might say we figured it out," Old Mo said.

"Oh. I thought we was keepin' it pretty much to our ownselves."

"Cal, are you trying to tell us that you'll be leaving Sugarloaf?" Sally asked.

"Yes, ma'am, I reckon that is what I'm sayin'. I hope you don't mind."

"Of course we don't mind," Sally said with a broad smile, reaching her hand across the table to lay it on Cal's hand. "We are both very happy for you."

Now the troubled expression on Cal's face was replaced with a smile as large Sally's.

"It won't be for at least another month, though. It's prob'ly goin' to take me that long to get everythin' all took care of so's I can leave."

"If it means you'll get out of my hair any faster, I'll be glad to help you get ready to go," Pearlie teased.

"Ha! You're goin' to miss me somethin' fierce. You know you are," Cal said.

As Smoke and the others continued with their good-natured banter over lunch, a boy of about fourteen approached their table. He was wearing a hat with the words "Western Union" written on the front.

"Excuse me, sir, I'm looking for Mr. Calvin Woods," the boy said.

"I'm Woods," Cal said.

"This telegram is for you, sir." The boy handed a folded piece of paper to Smoke.

"For me? Who would be sending a telegram to

me?" Cal asked, the expression on his face showing his curiosity.

Smoke gave the boy a dime.

"Thank you, sir," the boy said with a big smile.

"Please come back! I can't live without you!" Pearlie teased.

Cal was smiling at Pearlie's antics as he unfolded the paper. Almost instantly, the smile left his face to be replaced by an expression of horror.

"Cal, what is it?" Sally asked.

Cal looked up from the message, but he said nothing.

"Smoke, what is it?" Sally asked. "Cal is frightening me."

Smoke reached across the table and, gingerly, removed the paper from Cal's hand. Smoke was already wearing a look of concern, but as he read the message, the concern changed to sorrow.

"Smoke?" Sally's voice was choked with emotion, and the expression on the faces of both Pearlie and Old Mo mirrored hers. They didn't yet know what had happened, but they prepared themselves for the worst.

"There was an attack at San Vicente, shortly after we left this morning. Many were killed, and several buildings were burned."

"Oh, no! How terrible!" Sally said.

"One of those killed was Katrina."

Sally gasped, and she looked across the table at Cal. Tears were now streaming down Cal's face, and though he wasn't crying aloud, it was obvious he was weeping, because his shoulders were shaking.

Sally got up to move around to Cal's side of the

table. Old Mo got up so she could sit beside Cal, and she put her arms around him, cushioning her head on his shoulder.

The telegram had not only told of Katrina being killed, it also relayed the information that the entire herd of horses Smoke had brought down from Sugarloaf had been stolen.

"I'm going back!" Cal said.

"We all are," Smoke said. "That is, Sally and I are. Pearlie, you and Mr. Morris can come with us, or go back home. It's up to you."

"I'll go back with you," Old Mo said.

"Cal is my best friend," Pearlie said. "If he goes back, I'm damn sure going back too. Pardon my language, Miz Sally."

Sally, whose eyes were now filled with tears, just nodded at him.

"No need to pardon your language, Pearlie," she said. "It is obvious that those words were spoken for the love of a friend."

"I'll get the tickets," Smoke said. "Pearlie, you get our luggage taken off the train. Mo, you take care of the horses."

"I'll help," Cal said. Those were the first two words he had spoken since receiving the telegram, and they were quiet, and choked. He started to get up, but Sally held him down.

"No," Sally said. "Please, sit here with me."

"All right," Cal said.

Smoke, Pearlie, and Old Mo left to attend to their tasks.

"Why, Miz Sally?" Cal asked. "Why did it have to happen?"

Sally shook her head. "I don't know, Cal. Nobody

knows why such terrible things come into our lives. Preachers will tell you that it is to strengthen your faith, philosophers will say it is to strengthen you. But when you get right down to it, it's all the same. It's a pain that is so hard, that it takes everything you have to be able to endure it."

"I don't know that I can endure it," Cal said.

Sally put her arms around him, pulled him to her, and patted him on the back.

"Cal, you are one of the finest and the strongest people I know. Just take joy in the time that you did have with her, keep close to those of us who love you, and you will get through this. I promise you, you will get through it."

A half hour later they were all on the southbound train, heading back to San Vicente.

"What time will we get there?" Sally asked.

"It's an all-night train ride," Smoke said. "We should get there around ten o'clock tomorrow morning."

And talk among the five, when it did occur, was generally quiet and specific. There was no general conversation and when night fell, everyone tended to look out into a black void, interrupted only occasionally by the dim lights of an isolated house alongside the tracks.

There were no Pullman or Wagner Palace cars on this train, so everyone tried to get as comfortable as they could, right where they sat.

Katrina was beautiful in her wedding gown . . . but then, why wouldn't she be? Cal thought she was beautiful, no matter what she wore.

Once she got married, she had to quit teaching, but that was all right. Cal had over five thousand dollars saved,

Smoke gave him twenty-five hundred as a wedding present, and Tom Byrd gave him five hundred acres that not only had a year-round source of water, but was also directly adjacent to fifteen thousand acres of free range land. It didn't take him long to get a very good ranch going.

He and Katrina named their son Kirby, and their daughter, Hazel. Kirby was a really big help, learning to ride and rope when he was still just a boy. But it was Kirby's ambition to go to college, so Cal and Katrina took him to the railroad station to see him off.

Hazel was married soon after that, and Cal and Katrina became grandparents. Kirby graduated from college, then medical school, married, and also had children.

The whole family was there for Cal and Katrina's fiftieth wedding anniversary.

"We have grown old together," Katrina said.

"And you are as beautiful today as you were the day I first saw you," Cal replied.

Katrina took Cal by his hand and looked into his eyes.

"It has been a wonderful life," she said.

The train whistle nearly drowned out the words.

The train whistle awakened Cal with a hypnagogic jerk.

He had been dreaming! The whole thing had been a dream, the wedding, the ranch, the children, the grandchildren, the fiftieth wedding anniversary; it had all been a dream.

At first, Cal was upset, and he wished he had not had the dream. But, the more he thought about the dream, the more peace it provided him. It was as if, through the dream, he had been able to live an entire lifetime with Katrina. When he closed his eyes to go back to sleep this time, it was with a peace that surpassed all understanding.

Sally was right. He would take joy in the time that he did have with her, and keep a part of her locked away in his heart, forever.

As the train rolled into the town of San Vicente, Smoke looked through the window at the damage done by the raid. The leather goods store had been completely destroyed by fire. The apothecary, and a ladies' shop, showed a charred exterior, but the damage wasn't so severe that the buildings couldn't be repaired.

There was a funeral procession going down the main street, a black hearse pulled by a team of matching black horses, followed by mourners in surreys, buckboards, wagons, and on foot.

"San Vicente! This is San Vicente!" the conductor called, coming through the car.

They got off the train in San Vicente, and as Smoke and the others took care of the luggage and the horses, Sally waited in the depot for them. She saw a copy of the Brownsville *Cosmopolitan* for sale, bought it, and began to read.

TERRIBLE RAID !

Fifteen Slain

But one day previous, a man so foul as to defy description, Taurino Bustamante Keno, came across the Mexican border with as many as fifty men to strike against the Texas village of San Vicente. T. B. Keno portrays himself as a revolutionary and has assumed the title of colonel, but he is neither revolutionary nor colonel. He is, however, known throughout northern Mexico and southwestern Texas as a bandit and a murderer.

On his most recent adventure twelve innocents were killed in the town of San Vicente, including the schoolteacher, who is said to have surrendered her life that she might save that of one of the young students in her charge. During Keno's invasion of our country, he committed widespread larceny to include rustling. As many as two hundred head of fine, broken horses were taken from The Wide Loop, the ranch of Tom Byrd.

In addition to having his horses stolen, Mr. Byrd suffered the terrible, personal loss of his daughter, for the abovementioned heroic teacher was Miss Katrina Byrd. Three of Mr. Byrd's cowboys were also killed in the raid.

Because there will be so many funerals conducted in such a short time, morticians have been brought in, not only from Brownsville, but also from San Antonio. Additional ministers have also come to San Vicente that they might assist the lone pastor in residence. Already the bell has commenced rendering its mournful toll so that those unable to attend the funeral will be given the opportunity to stop what they are doing, in order that they may pay a moment of respect to the dead.

"I was coming back, Mr. Byrd," Cal said. "I told Katrina before we left that, as soon as I could, I would be coming back. I . . . thought I would be coming back so we could be married. I had no idea I would be coming back to . . . to bury her."

Cal choked on the word "bury."

"I loved her," he said.

"I know you did, son," Tom said. "And she loved you as well. Her last thoughts were of you."

"It would have been a wonderful life," Cal said.

Tom gasped. "What did you say?"

"I said it would have been a wonderful life."

"How did you know that?"

Cal was confused by Tom's reaction to his comment.

"I just know that it would have been. We loved each other, how could it be anything but a wonderful life?"

"No, I mean, how did you know that those were the last words Katrina spoke, before she died?"

Cal shook his head. "I didn't know that," he said.

Tom put his arms around Cal and drew him to him in an embrace.

"You and she are both right. It would have been."

Chapter Twenty-one

Katrina's funeral was held out at the ranch, and because it was the very last funeral to be conducted, it was attended by nearly everyone from town. But that was only part of the reason her funeral was so well attended. She had been a very popular school-teacher, so the parents of all the children who were in school attended. In addition, news of her saving the life of young Lenny Potts had spread throughout the town and even many of those who had lost their own loved ones had come to pay their final respects.

The service was to be held in the great room of the Big House, and every ranch hand was there, dressed in his finest and cleanest jeans and work shirt. A very beautiful coffin sat on sawhorses in the parlor, the sawhorses themselves hidden by purple drapery.

The mourners filed by for one last look at the beautiful young woman who, but a short time earlier, had been a vibrant part of their community. After they viewed the body, they greeted Tom and Hazel Byrd. At Tom and Hazel's invitation, Cal was standing right beside them. One of the young men who came through the viewing line, then stopped to offer his condolences, was Duke Pearson, the cowboy with whom Cal had had an altercation during the recent dance. He reached out to take Cal's hand.

"Pardner, I'm just real sorry about this," he said. "Miss Katrina was one of the purtiest women I ever seen, and I think you two was just meant for each other."

"Thank you, Duke. I very much appreciate that."

There weren't chairs for everyone, but Smoke, Sally, Pearlie, and Old Mo were given reserved seats in the second row. Cal sat on the front row alongside Katrina's parents.

Tom Byrd had asked Cal if he would say a few words at the funeral.

"I couldn't do that," Cal said. "I've never gotten up in front of people to speak before."

"You can do it, Cal," Sally told him, taking both his hands in hers. "I know you can. And you know that Katrina will be listening."

Cal nodded.

"Would you like me to write a few words for you?"

Cal shook his head. "No, ma'am. I reckon if I'm goin' to do this, I'll just sort of say the words I'm thinkin'."

"I was hoping you would say that," Sally said.

The church organist played, and Marylou Parker, a good friend of Katrina's, sang "There's a Wideness in God's Mercy."

When the song was over, Reverend T. Barnabas Bixby nodded toward Cal.

Cal stepped up to an ambo that had been placed at the foot of the coffin, cleared his throat, looked out at the many people who had gathered there, then began to speak.

"Most of you good people don't know who I am, and you wonder how it is that someone like me, a perfect stranger, would be talkin' to you at Katrina's funeral.

"I may be a stranger to you, but I'm not a stranger to Mr. and Mrs. Byrd, nor am I a stranger to any of the good men who work here on this ranch.

"I arrived here a little over a month ago with my boss and friends, to bring a herd of horses. I stayed here to help break those horses, and while I was here, I met the most wonderful woman I had ever met in my life.

"Katrina Byrd was everything a woman should be. I would tell you that she was beautiful, but I don't have to tell you that. Anyone who had ever seen her knew how beautiful she was. I could also tell you that she was a woman with a heart as big as all outdoors, but all of the children she taught, as well as mothers and daddies of those children could tell you that.

"She was courageous, she willingly climbed onto a horse that had just been broken. But I don't have to tell you about her courage. We all know how she gave up her life to save young Lenny Potts.

"She was also a loving woman. I know that because she loved me, as much as I loved her. And the reason I am here talking to you about her, is because, had this tragic thing not happened, Katrina and I would have been married.

"I know that the preacher is going to talk all about Heaven, and maybe streets that are lined with gold, or diamonds and rubies and emeralds everywhere. But I don't believe that."

There were a few gasps of shock and surprise scattered through the room.

"No, sir, I don't believe that at all," Cal continued. "If Heaven is supposed to make us joyful, then Katrina isn't walking around on golden streets. I believe she is with her ma and pa; she is with her brother, and her niece, she is with all of her schoolchildren, and she is with you, Miss Parker. And she is with me. Anytime I want her to be, all I have to do is think about her, and she is with me.

"Now, I don't know about you folks, but I plan to hold on to that for the rest of my life, until we can be together, forever."

Cal nodded one more time, then he walked back to his chair and sat there quietly throughout the rest of the funeral.

When the last song was sung, and the last words spoken, everyone left the house and went out to a small, fenced-in, and beautifully landscaped area where Katrina would be buried, right here on the ranch.

Sally stepped up to Cal and put her arms around him.

"Cal, I have never heard more beautiful words spoken, anywhere. I know that Katrina is with you right now, holding on to your arm, and smiling lovingly up at you."

"Yes, ma'am," Cal said, managing a smile. "Yes, ma'am, she is at that."

After Katrina was buried, Cal, Pearlie, and Old Mo

were invited up to the Big House to take part in the repast, the meal provided by the people of the town.

After the meal, Cal, Pearlie, and Old Mo returned to the bunkhouse. Cal lay on his bunk, his hands laced behind his head, staring up at the ceiling. Old Mo came over to sit on the bunk next to his.

"There can't nobody fault you for mournin'," Old Mo said. "'Cause the truth is, we know exactly what you're a-feelin'. There didn't none of us know Smoke then, but we do know how it was that his first wife, Nicole, and his baby, was kilt by outlaws. And you might remember that Pearlie once lost someone he loved."

"Yes, but at least he got to marry her, just before she died."

"The marryin' wasn't the important part, the lovin' was the important part. And you knowed Miss Katrina long enough to love her."

"That's true."

Old Mo stood, then reached down to put his hand on Cal's shoulder.

"Smoke has it in mind to go after the people that done this. You'll get some satisfaction out of that . . . and I will too. We all will. Satisfaction is a good thing, it helps with the healin'."

Old Mo was quiet for a moment, and he got a far-away look in his eyes. "Only thing is, it ain't possible to get satisfaction from snow and starvation."

Cal knew that Old Mo was referring to the tragedy at Donner Pass.

"So, if you don't mind, I'll just kinda share in the satisfaction you'll be gettin' when we catch up with the sons of bitches that done this."

"It will please me to have you along," Cal said.

* * *

"I believe Keno hit San Vicente as a diversion," Smoke told Tom over breakfast the next morning. "Their target, all along, was your horses. But he isn't going to keep them. I didn't bring them all the way down here, and break them, just to see someone like Keno wind up with them."

"That's what they wanted, all right," Cal said. He had been invited to breakfast as well.

"Oh," Tom Byrd said, lowering his head and pinching the bridge of his nose. "Compared to losing my daughter, and the others who were killed, the horses mean nothing to me. If I had known something like this was going to happen I would have given him the horses."

"They may mean nothing to you, but they are very important to Keno, and I don't intend to let him get away with it. I'm going to get them back," Smoke said.

"Kirby, I've known you for a long time," Tom said. "As a boy, you were resourceful enough to make a success of the farm, even when Emmett and Luke were gone. And your reputation has grown considerably since then. But there is no way you are going to be able to recover those horses, short of taking the army into Mexico. And our government isn't going to do that."

"I'll be taking *an* army, I just won't be taking *the* army," Smoke replied.

"What army would that be?"

"I'll be part of that army," Cal said.

"As will Pearlie and Mr. Morris," Smoke said. He

paused for a moment, then added, "We'll also be taking Sally."

"Kirby, don't do it. Keno has an entire army. I don't want to see anyone else killed because of those horses."

"It isn't just the horses, Mr. Byrd," Cal said. "I tell you the truth, I would be going to Mexico after that son of a bitch, whether Smoke goes or not. He not only took Katrina's life, he same as took the rest of my life from me. We would have married, we would have given you grandkids, and they would have given us grandkids." Again, tears welled in Cal's eyes. "He the same as killed a hundred years of what would have been."

No one spoke for a long moment, but Tom looked at the young cowboy who was sitting across the table from him.

"If you put it that way, son, then by all means go. And go with my blessing."

"How soon will we be going?" Cal asked Smoke later that same morning.

"Anxious to go, are you?"

"I'm so ready to go that I would strike out on foot if I had to."

"I know, but you need to wait just a while longer. One of the things I learned from riding with Asa Briggs during the war was that any action you took would have a much greater chance of success if you planned them out in advance."

"We ain't a-goin' to have to wait too long, are we?"

"Not too long. We'll get these bastards, Cal. I promise you, we'll get them."

"All right," Cal said. "You've always been right before, so I got no reason to think you ain't right this time."

The first thing Smoke did in preparing for his campaign against Keno, was visit the newspaper office in Brownsville, the *Cosmopolitan*. A bell attached to the front door signaled his arrival.

Greg Goldstein, the newspaper editor, was standing by his Washington Hand Press. Goldstein wiped his hands on the ink-stained apron he was wearing and, with a smile, approached Smoke.

"Yes, sir, would you like to buy an advertisement in the paper? We have over one thousand readers, you know."

"How much does an ad cost?"

"It depends on the size, of course. A classified ad is only one penny per word."

"What about half a page?"

Goldstein's smile grew broader. "Yes, sir! Half a page would be twenty-five dollars."

"I'll take half a page, provided you give me some information."

"What information would that be?"

"I need as much information as I can get about the Mexican bandit that raided San Vicente a few days ago."

"Yes," the editor said. "We are well aware of Keno's raid against San Vicente. You may have read the article we published about the raid."

"I did, and I thought it was an excellent article," Smoke said. "That's why I came to you."

"You came to me to buy an ad? Or to get information about Keno?"

"Both."

"If you don't mind, can we get the ad taken care of first?" Goldstein asked.

Smoke smiled. "Always the businessman, are you?"

"It puts food on the table," Goldstein replied.

Smoke gave Goldstein twenty-five dollars. "Here is for the ad."

"And what is the ad to say?"

"It should say: 'The *Cosmopolitan* is a fine newspaper,'" Smoke said.

"That's it? You're buying an ad, and the only thing you want to say, is that the *Cosmopolitan* is a good newspaper?"

"Yes."

"All right, Mr. . . ." Goldstein paused, waiting for the name to be supplied.

"Jensen. Smoke Jensen."

The newspaper editor's eyes grew large in recognition.

"*The* Smoke Jensen?"

"I don't know if I'm—the—Smoke Jensen, but I am the only Smoke Jensen that I know."

"Mr. Jensen, it will be a pleasure for me to do business with you. Now, how else can I help you?"

"I would like to find out as much as I can about this man Keno as I possibly can."

Chapter Twenty-two

"Well, sir, you have come to the right place," Goldstein said. "You have indeed. What specific information are you looking for?"

"I want to know who he is, and what is his background? And I especially want to know where his headquarters is now. How can I find him?"

"May I ask why you want this information, Mr. Jensen?"

"I want the information because I am going after him."

"Mr. Jensen, I am well aware of the reputation you have garnered by your many exploits, and even if only half of them are true, you are a remarkable man. But surely you understand that you won't be going after Keno alone. As far as I've been able to determine, Keno is never alone, he practically has an entire army with him. In fact, he calls himself Colonel Keno, for that very reason."

"Yes, I am aware."

"But you are still going after him?"

"Yes, I am going after him."

Goldstein drummed his fingers on the counter for a moment before he spoke again.

"You must have some personal reason for such a thing, because as I'm sure you know, there is no reward being offered for this man. Not by the American government, and certainly not by the Mexican government. In fact, Keno is regarded as somewhat of a hero in Mexico."

"You're right," Smoke said. "The reason I am going after him is personal."

"I almost hate to provide you with the information that could lead to you being killed."

"You let me worry about that," Smoke said.

"All right. Come back here tomorrow. By that time I will have gathered as much information on him as I can."

When Smoke returned to the office of the Brownsville *Cosmopolitan* the next day, Sally went with him. They were leading a packhorse and though Sally wondered what the packhorse was for, she didn't ask, because she knew that Smoke would tell her in due time.

They tied their mounts to the hitching rail in front of the newspaper office, then stepped inside. Perhaps, because of her education background, Sally had always believed there was something almost sacrosanct about a newspaper office, whether it be the *New York Times*, the *Big Rock Journal*, or the Brownsville *Cosmopolitan*. There was the editorial bay, where the publisher had his desk, the composing room with its tables and drawers of type, and the press room, where reposed, in this case, the Washington Hand Press.

Goldstein looked up at the jingling bell.

"Mr. Jensen," he said. "You're back, I see."

"Yes. Mr. Goldstein, this is my wife, Sally."

"It is nice to meet you, Mrs. Jensen. I do hope you are able to talk some sense into your husband."

Sally chuckled. "Mr. Goldstein, we have been married for a number of years, and I've never been able to talk any sense into him. What makes you think I could do so now?"

"A forlorn hope, I suppose," Goldstein said. He picked up a paper from among many on his desk. "Here you go, Mr. Jensen. I'm sure this is what you were looking for."

The editor handed the report to Smoke. Smoke held the paper so that Sally could read it as well, and she couldn't help but notice that it was written in a very neat hand.

> Colonel Taurino Bustamante Keno was born to a sharecropper in the Mexican state of Tamaulipas. He grew up a peasant, and when his father died, he murdered the owner of the farm where he lived, stole all the money the owner had in his hacienda, then took off to live in the mountains. He has subsequently made the statement that he shot the landowner when he discovered him raping his 12-year-old sister. However, that story cannot be verified, as his sister died soon thereafter.
>
> Keno lived in the mountains for several years,

running from the law. While on the run he joined a bandit band, becoming the leader of that band when he killed Xavier Acosta, the original leader.

Once Keno took over the Acosta band he began to expand by incorporating other bandit groups into his own, intimidating some of the leaders into following him, and killing the others, who would not submit to his command. Eventually he had enough men to create his Ejército Mexicano de la Liberación, *or Mexican Army of Liberation. Estimates of the size of Keno's private army run as high as sixty men.*

Keno and his group of bandits have stolen cattle, robbed shipments of money, and committed crimes against the wealthy. Occasionally Keno will distribute money and food to the poor, and it is this latter activity that has caused some to regard Keno as a Mexican Robin Hood. That commendation is falsely applied, however, for he preys upon the poor far more often than he helps them. Some also admire his ability to escape capture, and a few even believe that he is, ultimately, a revolutionary who will one day be president, and end the suffering of the poor.

Today it is believed that Keno makes his headquarters in the small village of Nuevo Pacifico, which is suffering under his presence.

Smoke read the document, then nodded. "You have done an excellent job, Mr. Goldstein. And to show you my appreciation for your research and cooperation, I intend to buy three more half-page advertisements."

Goldstein held up his hand. "I appreciate that, Mr. Jensen. But I fear that four newspapers with consecutive half-page ads would be counterproductive. Not only would I be tooting my own horn, so to speak, the readers might think that I am unable to sell legitimate ads."

Smoke chuckled. "Use the half pages as you wish, Mr. Goldstein. You can put stories there, or even sell it a second time to another advertiser."

"Thank you, Mr. Jensen. That is most generous of you."

"I consider it fair pay for the information you have provided."

"Mr. Jensen, now that you have the information, and a clear assessment of the strength of Keno's bandit army, do you still intend to go after him?"

"Yes."

"Mrs. Jensen, surely you can disabuse him of such a notion."

"On the contrary, Mr. Goldstein, I intend to go with him."

The newspaper editor shook his head. "I had hoped that the information would make you aware of the folly of such a notion. I wish now that I had not helped you, for I've no desire to be a party to your demise."

"You're a good man, sir," Smoke said as he gave the newspaper editor the additional seventy-five dollars. "Please don't fret so."

Goldstein shook his head sadly as Smoke and Sally left his establishment.

"What now?" Sally asked as they left the newspaper office.

"Now? We're going to do something that you always enjoy doing. We're going shopping."

Sally laughed. "Why do I think we won't be buying clothes, or something pretty for the house?"

Sally and the packhorse followed Smoke down the street to a gun shop, its function advertised by the oversized cutout of a rifle, hanging in front of the store. A sign on the store bragged that it was THE BEST-STOCKED GUN SHOP IN THE ENTIRE STATE OF TEXAS.

Smoke wasn't quite ready to acquiesce to that claim, but he had looked through it when he was there yesterday, and he had to admit that it did offer an exceptionally large array of weapons, both in quantity and quality.

"Yes, sir, you're back, I see," the shop owner said, greeting Smoke and Sally.

"I am. And I have come today, ready to do some business with you. I noticed, yesterday, that you had the latest model Sharps rifles."

"I do indeed, sir. Breechloaders they are, single-shot .44-90 caliber, brass-jacketed shells."

The gun shop owner took one of the rifles down from its display case and handed it to Smoke. "Feel the balance of that piece," he said. "Look down the sight. In the hands of an expert marksman, this rifle is accurate for up to one thousand yards."

"Do you have scopes?" Smoke asked.

"Yes, sir, we do. We have the William Malcolm scope, and they are the finest telescopic sighting devices in the entire world."

"I'll take them," Smoke said.

"Yes, sir, you are making an excellent choice," the gun shop owner said. "One Sharps .44-90 and one William Malcolm scope."

"Five," Smoke said, holding up five fingers.

"I beg your pardon, sir?"

"I want five Sharps rifles, and five scopes," Smoke said.

"You . . . you want five?" the gunsmith asked in a disbelieving voice.

"I do," Smoke said. "I also want one thousand rounds of .44-90 cartridges.

"One thousand rounds?"

"Can you fill my order?"

"Yes, that will take every rifle and nearly every .44-90 bullet that I have, but I can do that. May I ask you, sir, and I don't mean this facetiously, but are you going to war?"

"Yes," Smoke replied. "And I don't mean that facetiously."

With the rifles and ammunition wrapped in a canvas bundle, and attached securely to the pack-horse, they proceeded to the Matthews Mercantile store. This time Smoke let Sally do the ordering.

"I'm looking for a small hand mirror," Sally told the clerk.

"Oh, we have just the thing for you," the clerk, a rather small man with a narrow moustache, replied. He picked up a mirror in a gilt frame, with a pearl handle. "Isn't this just the most elegant thing you have ever seen?" he asked.

"I'm afraid that won't do," Sally said.

"Oh, dear, but that is the best we have to offer. I can't go up from that one."

"I don't want you to go up. I want you to go down."

"Is it the price? Because I think you will find that this is very reasonably priced."

"This is what I want," Sally said, picking up a small, square, frameless mirror.

"That one? But, for a beautiful lady such as yourself, surely you don't want such a pedestrian mirror."

"I want five of them," Sally said.

"Five?"

"Yes."

After paying the bewildered clerk, Smoke and Sally went to the hardware store, where they bought fifty sticks of dynamite and a keg of nails.

Then, with the packhorse carrying their purchases, they went back to The Wide Loop to make plans for the upcoming expedition into Mexico.

Chapter Twenty-three

Nuevo Pacifico

Thirteen-year-old Rosita Salinas looked into the mirror and preened, her long black hair glistening in the single candle that barely managed to illuminate the *cabaña*. She thrust her chest forward in such a way as to make her just-emerging breasts more prominent, proud of what she could see.

"Papa, do you think boys will think I am pretty?" she asked.

Miguel, who had spent an entire day working in the field, looked over at his daughter. She was the oldest of four children, all of whom lived, slept, and ate in the same room. "You are not yet old enough to think about boys," he said. "Better you should think of more ways to help your mama with your brothers and sisters."

"But I have helped, Papa. Today I ground the corn, and I washed the dishes. Didn't I, Mama?"

"*Sí*, Rosita, you are *una gran ayuda*."

"Do you see, Papa? Even mama says I am a great help."

Miguel spoke more softly. "I know you have done much, my daughter. I don't know what we would do without you." He smiled. "And if the boys don't think you are pretty, they are *muy loco*, because I think you are *muy hermosa*."

One mile from the small, crowded house of Miguel Salinas, T. B. Keno sat at a table in a cantina, listening to a report from Ramos, one of his men.

"We have the horses in a dead-end canyon in the Sierra Veinte Casas mountains," he said. "We can make our camp there. There is a cabin near to the place that you can use for your headquarters."

"Is the cabin empty?"

"No, *Coronel*, it is occupied by a *gringo* prospector."

"One man?"

"*Sí.*"

"He will be no problem. Have you found a buyer for the horses?

"*Sí*. I have found someone who will give us fifty pesos for each horse. He will sell them to the army."

"*Sí*, and he will get one hundred pesos for each horse," Keno said with irritation in his voice.

"But we cannot sell them to the army," Ramos said. "Already newspapers have carried stories of our raid into Texas."

"I know. When will he take the horses?"

"He will take them anytime we deliver them."

"We will leave here and go to the place you have found in the mountains," Keno said.

"*Sí*, but before we can do that, we must gather food," Ramos said.

"I am sure the people of Nuevo Pacifico will be more than generous," Keno suggested. "Send a messenger to every *hacienda*, every *casa*, and every *cabaña*. Tell the people that they must bring food to town within two days. Corn, flour, beans, sugar, coffee, beef, bacon, and chickens."

"How much shall each give, *Coronel*?"

"Each citizen shall bring five pounds of corn, flour, beans, sugar, and coffee. But they shall only be taxed for one of the meat, either five pounds of beef, or five pounds of bacon, or five chickens."

"I think they will be happy to do this," Ramos said.

Miguel was feeding the chickens when two riders came onto his small farm. Both men were wearing bullet-filled bandoliers and carrying rifles. They weren't in any kind of uniform, because, except for Keno himself, his "army" didn't wear uniforms.

The men didn't have to be wearing uniforms. Miguel recognized them at once for who they were, and he felt a lightness in his head, and a constriction in his stomach. He had no idea what they wanted, but it couldn't be good. It was never good to be visited by Keno's "soldiers."

"You are Miguel Salinas?" one of the men asked.

"*Sí, señor.*"

"I see that you have many chickens. Have you pigs as well?"

"*No, señor.* I have only chickens."

"But I see that you have a garden. What is in your garden?"

"It is the end of summer, *señor*, there is nothing left in my garden."

"You have saved nothing from your garden? Do you not have a family?"

"*Sí*. I have a wife and four children."

"What kind of father would not save vegetables from his garden for his family?"

"I have saved some vegetables," Miguel said. He didn't like where this conversation was going.

"Bring five live chickens to the cantina."

"What? But that is one-third of all the chickens I have. Why should I do that?"

"It is a tax, *señor*."

"But I cannot afford that. I have a family to feed."

"You have one week, *señor*."

The two soldiers turned, and rode away.

The Wide Loop

"I stopped by the telegraph office when I was in town, and had him write down the Morse code for me. I had Sally make a copy for each one of us. I think if we practice on this for a few days, we can learn it well enough to use it . . . at least for our purposes. And that's what we're going to do," Smoke said, as he handed out the mirrors.

"Smoke, before we start learnin' any kind of a code, maybe we ought to learn how to use these things," Pearlie said. "I mean, if the sun is behind you, why, you can't use it at all, can you?"

"From midmorning till midafternoon, the sun will

be high enough that it won't matter where it is," Smoke said. "Here's how you catch it."

Smoke picked up the mirror to demonstrate, as he explained the use to them.

"The first thing you do is grip the mirror edges with your fingertips. Don't let any of your hand get out over the front of the mirror, 'cause if you do, it could partially block the surface. Now, let me see all of you hold it."

The other four gripped the mirrors with varying degrees of correctness. Sally was the most accurate.

"Sally, help them out there," Smoke said.

Once he was satisfied that everyone was holding the mirror properly, Smoke proceeded to the second step.

"Hold out your other hand in front of you, then pick up the sun's reflection and put the spot on that hand. Once you've got the spot on that hand, sort of lift the hand, keeping the sun spot on it, until that hand is lined up with your target. One you've got that hand lined up with your target, drop it, and the sun spot will go exactly where you want it. Do that, and we'll be able to keep in touch with each other from a mile away."

The others began experimenting with finding the sun, and the spot.

"Look over there," Smoke said. "The side of that barn is dark. You should be able to see the spot once you put it there. One at a time now, let me see you put the spot just below the window.

"All right, now once you have your target picked out, all you have to do is send dashes and dots, just like with a telegraph. And you can do that by holding your hand over the mirror like this"—Smoke demonstrated—"and this lets you control the length of your signal. Do it quickly and it is a dot. Let the light linger, and it is a dash. Cal, this is your name. Watch as I do it, and I will say it to you. C is dash dot dash dot. A is dot dash. And L is dot dash dot dot. See if you can do it."

Cal sent his name, making the spots appear on the dark barn.

"Ha!" he said. "If anybody happened to see that, and could read Morse code, they would know it's me."

"Easy for you," Pearlie said. "You just have three letters in your name."

"All of us are going to have just three letters, except Mo. He'll have only two. You'll be PEA, which is dot dash dash dot, which is P, a dot by itself is E, and dot dash for A. Now, you send your name."

With the charts before them the first thing they learned was how to do their own names, then they learned a few simple phrases such as: all clear which they sent as AL CLR; many men, as MNY MN; come in, CM IN; I'm coming, IM CMG; and WT, which meant wait. They also learned how to send look north, look south, look east, look west, in abbreviated terms. They also learned how to say "understood," which they sent as UD. That was quick and simple to learn as the letters U and D were just the opposite of each other, dot dot dash for U and dash dot dot for D.

All the abbreviated phrases were written out on a tablet which each of them had, and they practiced for the next two days until they were beginning to get quite proficient at it.

"What if we have to send something we haven't learned?" Sally asked.

"Good question. Do you have a suggestion?"

"I do. We'll send the word "new." That will mean that whoever is sending the message is going to have to use the guide to send it, and whoever is receiving it will just mark it down on the paper as dots and dashes, then, we can used the guide to decipher it."

Smoke laughed. "Good idea," he said. "It wouldn't exactly work for a telegrapher to warn a train that the bridge is out in front of them, but it'll do for our purposes. Suppose you send a message like that, and let us decipher it."

Sally smiled, and taking the code sheet and the mirror with her, walked all the way back to the porch of the Big House. Once there she started sending the message, while Smoke and the others recorded it, only by the dots and dashes.

Pearlie was the first to decipher the series of flashes emanating from Sally's mirror.

"Ha!" Pearlie said. "She is saying 'Come for lunch.'"

"Easy enough for you to decipher," Old Mo teased. "You've been ready for lunch ever since I've known you."

"Do you think she really means that?" Cal asked.

"Why not?" Smoke replied. "It's time for lunch."

"Smoke, are you sure you want to go after Keno?" Hardegree asked later that afternoon.

"Yes, I'm sure. Why do you ask?"

"I just found out that he has Gatling guns. That's how he was able to shoot up the town the way he did."

"Does he have artillery?" Smoke asked.

"Artillery? No, I don't think so."

"We do."

"You have a cannon?" Hardegree asked, surprised by the response.

"Not exactly. But we do have Mo."

"What do you mean?"

"Mo," Smoke called. "Show Hardegree one of the arrows you've been working on."

With a smile, Old Mo held up an arrow. Tied to the arrow was a stick of dynamite, and glued to the dynamite were several nails.

"Whoa!" Hardegree said with a laugh. "I reckon you do have artillery at that."

The next day, as the others were practicing signaling with their mirrors, Smoke happened to see a brown lizard crawling through the dirt. When the lizard crawled into a clump of grass, it turned green.

Smoke smiled.

"Folks, I'm going to buy all of you a new pair of jeans and a new shirt," he said.

"What? Why?" Pearlie asked.

"Because we're all about to become lizards."

"Smoke, what are you talking about?" Sally asked, as confused as the others by his strange comments.

"You ever notice how a lizard looks just like the land where he is? That's what we're going to do. We're going to be going through mostly brown and tan dirt, and the reason I'll be buying you some new clothes is because we're going to dye one our outfits the color of sand."

"How?" Cal asked.

"With butternut dye." Smoke smiled. "Everyone

likes to think that the Confederate army wore gray, and I guess the officers, and some of the sponsored regiments did. But a lot of the Confederate soldiers, if not most of them, wore butternut tan. And butternut dye is easy to make. All we need are about fifty walnuts, in their shells."

Smoke supervised the making of the dye, first by cracking open the walnuts, removing the nut meat, then crushing the shells.

"What do we do with the walnuts?" Cal asked.

Smoke popped a walnut into his mouth, and grinned. "I don't know about you, but I'm going to eat them."

When all the walnuts were cracked, and all the shells crushed down, they were put into a pot and boiled.

Before nightfall of the second evening, Sally made one more check of the five sand-colored pants, and five similarly colored shirts she had hung out after removing them from the dye pot. They were all dry, and ready to be worn the next day.

"Sally, I've been having second thoughts about this," Smoke said as they lay in bed that night.

"You mean about us going?"

"No, I mean about you going."

"If you're going, I'm going," Sally said, resolutely.

"I'd rather you not."

"Kirby Jensen, you're not going to keep me out of this," Sally said.

"Kirby, is it? You call me Kirby instead of Smoke?" Smoke teased.

"Yes, if you're going to be like this. Please, Smoke, don't leave me behind. We've been in some tight spots before, you know that."

"Never like this. Sally, we are going up against an army. An entire army. And there are only five of us."

"Yes, five, and you want to cut it down to four, to decrease your strength by twenty percent before we even start. Why would you want to do such a foolish thing?"

"Sally, if something happened to you, I'd be . . ."

"No more than I would be if something happened to you," Sally said, interrupting him in mid-sentence. "Smoke, wouldn't we both be better off knowing what was going on? At least if we are together, there's none of the anxiousness."

Smoke chuckled. "Sally, if we're married for seventy-five years, I might win an argument with you someday. You win."

"Oh, but, darling, I don't like to think of it as I won. I prefer to think that you simply see that I'm right."

Chapter Twenty-four

Nuevo Pacifico

For the entire week, the villagers had been bringing in food to supply Keno and his men. They stood in lines, holding live chickens, rabbits, some even had pigs. All had fruit and vegetables, as well as flour and cornmeal.

Miguel Salinas was one of the peasant farmers standing in line. He was holding two live chickens by their legs, the chickens long ago having grown too tired to continue to resist. Miguel had been told that he must give five chickens, and his wife, Eva, was frightened that he would be punished for not bringing his quota.

"I will have my whole family with me," Miguel said. "When Coronel Keno sees how many I must feed, he will have compassion, and he will accept the two chickens. You will see."

As he had said he would, Miguel Salinas took his entire family with him, including his thirteen-year-old daughter, Rosita.

"You! Come!" one of the guards shouted to Miguel and his family who, after a long and tiring wait, were finally next in line to approach the table where sat T. B. Keno.

"Two chickens?" Keno said when Miguel made his offering. "Two chickens is all you bring to feed the army of revolution, the army that is fighting for your rights. That is not enough. You must give us at least three more chickens."

"Please, *señor Coronel*," Miguel said. "You can see that my family is here. I have four children. I cannot feed them all if I give you what you ask for."

Keno lifted his pistol and cocked it. "That is not a problem, *señor*," he said easily. "I will kill one of your children, then you won't have so many to feed." He smiled, a twisted, evil smile. "And I will let you choose which of your children you want me to kill. I am sure that there is at least one who is a troublemaker."

"Papa!" the children called as one.

"No! No!" Miguel shouted, holding out his hand. "Wait, please wait! I will give you three more chickens. I beg of you, do not hurt any of my children."

"You," Keno said, pointing to Rosita. "You must stay with me until your papa returns with the other three chickens."

"Papa, no!" the young girl cried out in terror.

"Do not worry, Rosita. I will be back with the other chickens, and soon," Miguel promised.

As he had promised, Miguel returned within the hour with three more chickens. He handed them to one of Keno's men.

"Here are the three chickens you asked for, *Coronel.* Now, please, may I have my daughter back?"

"It is too late," Keno said. "You should have brought the five chickens when you were told to do so. Now, you must be punished. And to punish you, I will keep your daughter with me."

"If you must punish me, then do so," Miguel said in an anguished voice. "But, *Coronel,* please, punish me, not my daughter. I am the one who offended you. Please let my daughter go, so that she can return to her mother."

Keno smiled, an evil smile, and shook his head. "No. I think if I keep the girl, it will be more punishment for you than anything else I might do. Besides, do you not have three other children? I am a compassionate man, *señor.* I will not take you from your children, I will take only your daughter from you."

"Please, *Coronel,* I beg of you. Let my daughter go!" Miguel got down on his knees, and put his hands together as if praying.

"Get him out of here," Keno said, gruffly. "What kind of man would grovel so?"

Rosita had watched the whole thing, and when she saw her father sink to his knees to beg, she wanted to cry out, but there was such a restriction in her throat that she could make no sound. She was both hurt and embarrassed for her father, and she felt a sense of shame, as if by being Keno's prisoner, she was the cause of all this.

After her father was taken to the front door and brutally thrown out into the street, Rosita turned to her captor.

"What is to become of me now?" she asked. The

tone of her voice was exceptionally calm, so calm that it surprised Keno.

"Are you frightened, little one?"

"Yes."

"And yet, your words do not betray your fear. Why is that?"

"If I cried, would you let me go?" Rosita asked.

"No. Even if you cried, I would not let you go."

"Then why should I cry?"

"Listen to the girl," he said to the others. "She is much braver than her father."

"What is to become of me now?" Rosita repeated.

Keno stepped over to her, and ran his finger over the smooth skin of her cheek. The feel of his finger on her skin was repugnant to her, but she showed no reaction.

"Do not worry, my pretty little one. I will find some way for you to be useful to me."

"*Coronel*, we have gathered all our supplies," Vargas said.

"Very well. Call in all the men and we will leave," Keno replied.

Keno and the others left the village a short while later, but before they did so, Rosita's hands were tied and she was put up on a horse. Although she had ridden on the back of a donkey before, this was the first time in her life she had ever been on a horse, and as they rode out of town, one of the soldiers held on to a rope that was tied to the harness of her horse.

They rode for several hours until they reached the mountains, then they started through a canyon which was narrow enough that the clatter of the horses' hooves on the rocky floor echoed loudly back from the bracketing walls. Just before nightfall they reached a cabin, and here, they stopped. As they approached the cabin, Rosita thought that it must belong to Keno, but when they stopped, an old man, with white hair and beard, came out.

"So, you have come back," the old man said. "Have you decided to pay what I have asked, for allowing you to keep your horses in my canyon?"

"You are a *gringo*?" Keno replied.

"*Sí*, I'm an American. What of it?" the old man asked.

"You are an American, this is a Mexican canyon. How can it be your canyon?"

The old man laughed, though it sounded more like a cackle than a laugh.

"It's my canyon because I was here first. You have two hundred horses, that will cost you ten pesos per horse. That will be two thousand pesos."

Because of the challenging way he spoke, Rosita thought he must either be very brave or very foolish.

"I will pay you nothing, and I will take your house, *gringo*," Keno said.

"Like hell you will. This is my place. Get out of here, now! And if you aren't going to pay to keep your horses here, take them with you!" The man pointed.

"You will not be needing money or the house anymore," Keno said, and at a nod, at least three of his soldiers shot the man.

Rosita had never seen anyone killed before, and watching the man shot down in front of her, knowing that one moment he was alive, and the next moment he was dead, had shocked her into horrified silence.

Her eyes reflected the terror she felt, but was too frightened to express.

Rosita was lifted down from the horse, and as the man did so, his hands managed to squeeze her breasts. She gasped in pain and surprise, and the smile on the man's face told her that it wasn't an accident.

"Take her inside," Keno ordered. "And do not put your hands on her that way again."

"Sí, Coronel."

Rosita's cheeks burned with embarrassment. Her shame of being handled so had been seen by the others.

"Did you see what happened to the *gringo*, when he did not listen to me?" Keno asked Rosita when he came into the cabin with her.

She nodded.

"That is exactly what will happen to you, if you do not do everything I tell you to do," Keno warned. "Do you understand me?"

Rosita nodded but, again, made no audible response.

"Is the girl *loco*?" Vargas asked. "Why does she not speak?"

"What does she have to talk about?" Keno asked, then he laughed out loud at his own joke.

"Why does she not scream in fear?" Vargas asked.

"Who, besides us, would hear her scream? Would it do her any good to scream?" Keno asked.

"No," Vargas agreed. "It would do her no good to scream. Still, I do not know why she does not cry."

Rosita wanted to cry. She wanted very much to cry,

but for some reason that she couldn't understand, the tears wouldn't come.

"Sit in that chair," Keno ordered.

Rosita did as he directed, sitting in a straight-back, wooden chair.

"Vargas, tie her hands behind the chair."

"Please do not tie me, *señor*," Rosita said. "My wrists hurt." These were the first words Rosita had spoken since they had left the village.

Keno tossed a short piece of rope to Vargas.

"Do as I said."

Vargas pulled Rosita's arms around behind the chair, then tied her hands. As he did so, it became obvious that, though she was only thirteen, she was developing into a woman.

"How old are you, girl?" Keno asked.

"I am thirteen."

"Are you sure you aren't just telling me that? You know what I will do to you if you lie to me."

"I am thirteen!" Rosita repeated, desperately wanting him to know that she wasn't lying.

Keno pulled a knife from his belt and approached her.

"You aren't going to cut her up, are you, *Coronel*?" Vargas asked, surprised to see his leader approach the young girl with a knife in his hand.

"I am not lying!" Rosita said. She closed her eyes and took a deep breath. She felt the point of the knife sticking her through the top of her dress just between the breasts. She felt his hand move quickly and she gasped in fear, then relief as she felt, not the sting of the blade, but the coolness of the night air. Keno had just cut her dress.

"Let's get a better look," Keno said, and he took the two halves of the dress then split it all the way down. He pulled it down across her shoulders so that her frontal nudity was completely exposed to the lustful staring of Keno, Vargas, and at least two more of the soldiers. Someone said something, speaking in a voice that was too quiet for her to understand. Whatever he said elicited laughter from the others. The just-burgeoning young breasts she had been so proud of, the same breasts the man had grabbed as he lifted her down from the horse, were now a source of shame for her. And not only shame, they were also reason for her to be frightened.

"You are going to be a beautiful woman someday," Keno said, speaking in a voice that was almost respectful. "You could become a *puta* and make a lot of money."

"Please, *señor*, cover me," Rosita begged.

"Vargas, find a needle and thread. Then sew the dress back so that the girl is covered."

"*Sí!*" Vargas replied with a broad smile.

Because her hands were tied behind the chair, there was no way Rosita could close the gap in her dress that left her exposed. She kept her eyes tightly shut as Vargas began sewing the dress back together. She felt her flesh crawl as his hands found every opportunity to grope and fondle her.

"*Pequeñas y agradables tetas,*" he said in a lecherous voice.

"*Por favor, señor.*"

"Please? You mean you want me to make a woman of you?"

"*No, señor!*" Rosita gasped.

"Vargas!" Keno said. "Leave the girl alone."

"*Sí, señor.*"

"*Gracias, señor Coronel,*" Rosita said with a sense of relief. That relief was short-lived, however, when Keno spoke again.

"If anyone is going to make a woman of you, I'll be the one."

Rosita wasn't exactly sure what "making a woman of her" meant, but the lewd smile that followed Keno's comment suggested that it wasn't something that she wanted to experience.

"Vargas, when you are finished, take the rope from her wrists. I think there is no need to keep a young girl tied up to the chair. Surely an army can keep track of one young girl."

Rosita breathed a prayer of thanks. The ropes were beginning to hurt her wrists, and having them free would be some improvement in her situation.

Once the ropes were removed, she began rubbing her wrists in an effort to restore circulation.

"Can you cook?" Keno asked.

"*Sí.*"

"Good. Find whatever food the *gringo* had and cook something."

"For everyone, *señor*? I do not think there is enough food for everyone."

"No, not for everyone. For me," Keno said. "You do not belong to everyone, *niña.* You belong only to me."

Chapter Twenty-five

Having become sufficiently proficient in the use of the Morse code to warrant Smoke's confidence in their use of the mirrors, and with their weapons and ammunition packed, the group made final preparations to leave. Smoke and the others were wearing their butternut uniforms as they stood by their horses, just after dawn on the day Smoke had chosen for them to get under way.

Tom and Hazel Byrd, as well as Stan Hardegree and the other cowboys of The Wide Loop, turned out to see them off.

"Prepare to mount. Mount!" Smoke called.

"Don't you go ordering me around, Smoke Jensen. This is no army," Sally said, and the others laughed.

"Uh, would you folks kindly get mounted, please?" Smoke asked, and again the cowboys laughed.

"If you put it that way, yes, we would be glad to get mounted," Sally replied, a triumphant smile spreading across her face.

"Well, I guess we can see who is foreman of this outfit," Hardegree said.

Hazel waited until everyone was mounted, then she stepped down from the porch. It wasn't until then that everyone noticed she was holding a couple of cloth bags.

"I know you've got jerky, bacon, and beans," Hazel said. "But I hope you don't mind that I've fried up a few chickens and made some biscuits. I've got 'em in these bags here."

"Oh, Mrs. Byrd, you didn't have to do all of that," Sally said.

"I know, but I wanted to. I'm sure Katrina would have wanted to do something like this for you if she was still alive. I do hope you will take it." She held the two cloth bags up toward Sally.

"Of course we will take it, and we thank you for it." Sally tied the two bags to her saddle horn.

"Miss Sally, if them bags is goin' to be in your way, I'll take care of 'em for you," Pearlie offered.

"Lord no, Miss Sally, don't do that," Cal said. "Pearlie would have everything ate up before we stopped for our first lunch."

"That's the truth," Hardegree said, and all the cowboys who had gathered to watch them leave, laughed.

"Thank you, Pearlie, but I'm sure they won't be a problem for me to handle," Sally said. "But it was a nice try," she added with a smile.

"We'd better get going," Smoke said, and clucking at his horse Seven, he turned and started away. The others followed him.

"I'll be praying for you!" Hazel called as she and the others waved good-bye.

* * *

As they rode away from the Big House their route took them past a little mound of earth, still covered with flowers, and marked by a shining new headstone. All removed their hats as they rode by Katrina's grave.

"I'll always love you," Cal said, though he spoke the words so quietly that none of the others heard him. Neither did anyone see the tears that had sprung to his eyes.

Fifteen minutes later the hooves of their horses were churning up the water of the Rio Grande as they rode across a shallow ford. Emerging from the river into Mexico, they continued on down to Nuevo Pacifico, which was where Smoke believed they would either find Keno, or at least find some information that would lead them to the bandit colonel.

Nuevo Pacifico was a small town consisting of a group of low-lying, flat-roofed, adobe buildings. Smoke and Cal rode into town together, leaving the other three behind, where they had set up camp in an arroyo. Just ahead of them, on the right-hand side of the street, they saw a cantina.

"If you want to find out what's going on in the States, you go to a saloon," Smoke said. "My guess would be that it is pretty much the same here. What do you say we get us beer?"

"Can we get beer here?" Cal asked. "Or just tequila?"

"That looks like a beer to me," Smoke said, pointing to a painted mug of beer.

"A beer would taste good about now," Cal agreed.

The cost of the beer was fifty centavos, but using

Mexican money wasn't a problem. Before leaving Brownsville, Smoke had converted five hundred dollars to just over five thousand pesos.

They tied their horses off out front, but before they could go inside, they were met by three men, all of whom were wearing bullet-filled bandoliers angled across their chest. They were also holding pistols in their hands.

"*Gringos*, welcome to Nuevo Pacifico," one of the men said.

"Not a very pleasant welcome when you are holding guns in your hands," Smoke said.

"Oh, this?" When he spoke the word, it sounded like "theese." "We carry guns because we must collect a tax from all *gringos*, and sometimes a *gringo* doesn't want to pay."

"What is the tax for?"

"It is for the people's *revolución*."

"I wasn't aware there was a revolution."

"*Sí*. Coronel Keno is leading a revolution of the people against the government in Mexico City." The armed Mexican smiled.

"I thought the people of Mexico were pretty well satisfied with their government. What do they think about this Keno person attempting to make a revolution?" Smoke asked.

"Coronel Keno is much loved by the people of Tamaulipas. They do not mind paying a tax. And *gringos* who come into our land should not mind either."

"All right, how much is the tax?" Smoke asked.

"It is fifty pesos."

"Fifty pesos? That is a lot of money, just to be here."

"It is fifty pesos for each of you. That will be one hundred pesos."

Smoke whistled. "Oh, that really is a lot of money."

"*Sí*. It cost much money to fight a *revolución*."

"But we are *americanos*. Why should we have to pay the tax?"

"It is so you will do what is right for the people."

"All right," Smoke said. "I do want to do what is right for the people, so I'll pay the tax."

Smoke took out a bound packet of money, making certain that the three men saw it. He counted off one hundred pesos, which did little to decrease the size of the stack, then passed the bills over to the man who had been the spokesman for the three.

"You have a great deal of money, *señor*," the spokesman said.

"Yes, we have come to Mexico to buy horses. Do you know where we might find some?"

"*Sí*," one of the other three said. "Coronel Keno has . . ."

"We do not know where any horses are, *señor*," the spokesman said, interrupting the other in mid-sentence.

"You say no, he said yes," Smoke said. He addressed the man who had responded in the affirmative.

"Do you know where we can buy horses?"

"No, *señor*."

"That's too bad. Well, now that we have transacted our business, my friend and I would like to go into the cantina to enjoy a drink. May we do that?"

"*Sí*," the spokesman of the three said. "You may go into the cantina." He waved Smoke and Cal in, and as they stepped up onto the porch of the cantina, the three Mexicans who had stopped them holstered their pistols.

Instead of the swinging batwing doors Smoke was used to, the entrance to the cantina was guarded by hanging strings of multicolored glass beads. The beads clacked audibly as Smoke and Cal pushed their way through them.

There were only six small windows to the building, and the light the windows let in was filtered through the dirt on the panes. As a result, the cantina was in so much shadow that it required several candles to push away the darkness.

Smoke ordered two beers, and as they were waiting for them, he noticed there were two men gathered around a third man at the far end of the bar. The third man appeared to be very distressed.

"Your beers, *señores,*" the bartender said, setting two golden mugs before them.

"What is wrong with the man at the other end of the bar?" Smoke asked.

The bartender shook his head, but said nothing.

"What is wrong?" Smoke repeated. "Why is he upset?"

"I cannot say, *señor.*"

"You can't say, or you won't say?"

"It is . . . dangerous . . . to say."

Smoke put fifty pesos on the bar, covering it with his hand so that only the bartender could see it.

"It is his daughter, *señor.* She has been taken by Coronel Keno. He demanded more payment, and Miguel gave him more, but Keno did not give the girl back. Now Keno has gone, and he took the girl with him."

"What is the girl's name, and how old is she?" Smoke asked.

"Her name is Rosita, and she is but thirteen years old."

"Do you know where Keno has gone?"

"I do not know, *señor.*" As the bartender answered the question, he looked around, in obvious fear.

"That's all right," Smoke said. "I don't want to cause you any trouble, or get you in danger. But I am looking for him, because I have my own score to settle. If I find him, and I see the girl, I will do what I can to get her back safely to her family."

"Gracias, señor." Without any further conversation, the bartender walked away.

"Smoke," Cal said after the bartender left. "Can I ask you a question?"

"Sure."

"Why did you pay those men out front? You know they are just going to use the money for something evil. And why did you show them that we had so much money?"

"Why do you ask? Do you think they might try and hold us up as we're leaving town?"

"I think they just might."

Smoke chuckled. "Yeah, that's what I think too."

For just a second Cal stared at Smoke, then a big grin spread across his face. "I'll be damn, that's what you want them to do, isn't it?"

"Let's face it, Cal, we are so badly outnumbered, that the only way we are going to come out on top of this is by fighting a war of attrition."

"A war of what?"

"We're going to have to cut their numbers down,

wherever and whenever we can, and we may as well start with these three. I just thought it best not to do it in the middle of town. We won't have to go to them, they'll come to us."

"Yes," Cal said.

Just as they got up to leave, Miguel came over to them.

"*Señores,* I am grateful that you have shown concern for my daughter. *Que Dios esté con ustedes.* May God be with you," he repeated in English.

Miguel reached out to shake Smoke's hand, and as he did so, Smoke felt him pass a piece of paper.

Nobody else in the cantina, not even Cal, realized that Miguel had passed anything to Smoke.

Chapter Twenty-six

Not until they were outside and mounted, did Smoke look at the piece of paper Miguel had given him. It was written in Spanish, but Smoke was able to make it out.

"I think Keno may be in the Sierra Veinte Casas mountains."

"What? How do you know?"

"Miguel told me."

"Miguel told you?"

"Don't you think that's what this means?"

Smoke passed the paper over to Cal.

Keno es en la Sierra Veinte Casas montañas.

Cal nodded. "I don't speak the lingo, but yeah, I'm pretty sure that's what that says. Do you know where those mountains are?"

"We brought a map. We'll find them," Smoke said.

As Smoke and Cal rode out of town, both men kept their eyes open for the ambush they were sure was to come.

"Do you think they'll shoot at us from behind cover, or will they come out?" Cal asked.

"We have to be ready for anything," Smoke said. "But the way we gave in so easily back at the cantina, I believe they'll be somewhat bold about it. They will enjoy facing down the *gringos.*"

"If they are going to shoot us from behind cover, that's the best place for it up there," Cal said, pointing to an outcropping of rocks just to the right of the trail.

"You're right. What do you say we force their hand?"

"How will we do that?"

"We'll make them think that we're going to camp here for the night." Smoke chuckled. "If they aren't behind those rocks, we're going to look pretty damn foolish."

Stopping, the two men dismounted, then took the saddles from their horses and set them aside. Smoke unrolled the blankets, and made a big show of getting out a coffeepot, while Cal started gathering wood for a fire.

Smoke saw something over by the rocks, a movement, or perhaps just a shadow. Whatever it was, it caught his attention.

"Cal, get ready," he said. "I think we are about to have company."

Cal came back to the site and dropped the wood on the ground. He no more than did so, than three men appeared from behind the rocks. With guns in their hands, they started walking toward Smoke and Cal.

"*Buenas noches, señores,*" the one in the middle said. This was the same one who had done all the speaking when they were braced by the three men in front of the cantina.

"Good evening," Smoke said. He glanced around furtively, purposely making it look as if he were frightened. "We're about to make some coffee. Perhaps you gentlemen would like to have some."

"We will have some coffee later," the spokesman said. "But first, I am sorry to tell you that we made a mistake at the cantina, and the time has come to correct that mistake."

"Oh? What kind of mistake?"

"We didn't charge you enough taxes. I think, maybe, you owe more."

"I don't know, I thought we paid quite a lot in taxes, considering that we don't even live here. How much more do you want?"

The Mexican smiled. "All of it, *señor*. We want all of it."

"I see. Well, I don't think I want to do that. I think I'll just keep my money, and ask, politely, that you return the money that you took from us."

The timidity had left Smoke's countenance, and the expression on his face now was chiseled and hard.

"You want us to give the tax money back to you?" the Mexican asked, obviously surprised by Smoke's comment. He smiled, arrogantly.

"And if we do not give the money back to you, *señor*, what will happen?"

"We'll kill all three of you, and take the money," Smoke said, speaking the words as calmly as if he had just asked the time of day.

Now the Mexican's smile turned into laughter. "*Gringo*, there are three of us, and we are holding guns in our hands. I think you have gone *loco*."

"This is your last chance. Give the money back to us."

"Manuel, I do not like this. Let us kill them now and take the money," one of the others called out in alarm.

"*Sí,*" Manuel replied, and he started to thumb back the hammer, but even as his thumb twitched, Smoke had his gun in his hand. He killed the one named Manuel, as well as the man who had called out in alarm.

Cal got the third one, who was so shocked at the sudden turn of events that he, like the other two, did not get off one shot. The three shots that were fired by Smoke and Cal now came rolling back from the nearby elevations as if there was a life-and-death gun battle going on over in the Lodges as well.

The three Mexican *bandidos* lay dead on the ground. Smoke walked over to his saddlebags, took out a tablet and a pencil, then began to write.

KENO
   I AM COMING AFTER YOU. YOU WILL NOT ESCAPE. WE WILL KILL YOU TO AVENGE THE PEOPLE YOU KILLED IN TEXAS. I AM SMOKE JENSEN, AND I AM AN AMERICAN AVENGER.

"That is in English. Do you think he can read English?" Cal asked.

"If he can't read it he'll find someone to read it to him," Smoke said. "I want it written in English, because I want him to know that it is Americans who are coming after him, and killing his men."

"What are we going to do with the note?"

"We're going to mail it to him," Smoke said.

"Mail it to him?"

Smoke saw that the man who had been doing all

the talking was wearing a knife. Smoke pulled the knife from the man's belt.

"Yes, by special delivery," he added. Then using the knife, he pinned the note he had just written to the man's chest.

Because the man was already dead, there was very little blood, even though Smoke had plunged the knife in to the hilt.

After that, he found six rocks, just the right size to put on the eyes of each of the dead men.

Before returning to the arroyo where Sally and the others had made camp, Smoke took out the small signaling mirror, and catching the last rays of sunlight, flashed two dots, two dashes, and a pause, then dash dot dash dot, two dashes, and dash dash dot. IM CMG, or I'm coming.

The response came back, dot dash, dot dash dot dot, a pause, then dash dot dash dot, dot dash dot dot, dot dash dot. AL CLR, or all clear.

"What if it isn't clear?" Pearlie had asked when Smoke was explaining the signaling procedure to the others. "What if we are prisoners? If we are, they aren't likely to let us send any signaling back."

"If we don't get a return signal, we'll just assume that the bad guys are here, and we'll start shooting," Smoke teased. "So I suggest that you return the signal quickly."

"No, no, you don't need to do that. We'll signal back," Pearlie insisted.

Old Mo had built a fire and the smell of wood smoke and coffee permeated the area as Smoke and Cal rode in. Sally had spread a piece of canvas on the ground and was now laying out the chicken and biscuits Hazel Byrd had prepared for them.

"Did you get a lead?" Sally asked.

"Yes," Smoke replied. "They've taken a thirteen-year-old girl as a hostage. The girl's father told us where to find them."

"They've got a thirteen-year-old girl with them? Just how cruel are these people?" Sally asked.

"They killed Katrina, didn't they? We've already seen how cruel they are," Cal said, quietly.

"Of course we have," Sally said quickly. She put her hand, comfortingly, on Cal's shoulder. "I'm sorry, Cal. That was insensitive of me."

"No, ma'am, I know you didn't mean nothin' by it," Cal said.

Normally, Sally would have corrected his grammar, but she realized this wasn't the time for it.

"You said the girl's pa told you where to find them," Pearlie said. "Where are they?"

"They are in the Sierra Veinte Casas mountains," Smoke said.

"That's a strange name for a mountain range," Sally said. "Twenty House Mountains."

"I didn't know you could speak Spanish," Pearlie said.

"I can't, I just know a few words, and I recognize the word for twenty, *veinte*, and house, which is *casa*."

"If they are hiding out in a mountain range, isn't that a little like saying someone is in the Rockies?" Pearlie asked.

"Not quite. This range isn't all that large. Besides, we may not have to look for them."

"What do you mean, we won't have to look for

them? Why do you say that. Do you know exactly where they are?"

"No, but we've started the ball rolling, and I'd say that it is more than likely that they will come looking for us."

"What happened?" Sally asked.

"We ran into three of Keno's men. A little disagreement over money led to shooting."

"And Smoke left a message pinned to one of 'em, tellin' Keno who he was, and that we were comin' after 'im," Cal said, completing the tale.

"So much for surprise," Sally said with a little chuckle.

"Surprise takes too long and I don't know how much time we have," Smoke said. "Don't forget, they've got a young girl they are holding captive."

Keno had just rolled some spicy beans into a tortilla when two of his men, Lopez and Salazar, came toward him. Keno had sent them out earlier to find the three men he had sent out to forage supplies for them.

"Did you find them? What is keeping them so long?" Keno asked.

"They are dead," Lopez said.

"Dead? How do you know?"

"I saw all three of them. I took this note from the body of Zamora." Lopez showed Keno the note Smoke had written. "It is written in English, so I don't know what the words say."

"I can read English," Keno said, reaching for the note. As he read it the expression on his face turned from curiosity to anger. He wadded the note up in his hand.

"Who is this man, Smoke Jensen?" he asked, angrily. "Has anyone ever heard of him?"

"I have heard of him."

"You have heard of him, Mendez?"

"*Sí*."

"What have you heard?"

"He is a hero to the *gringos*," Mendez said. "They have written books about him because he is so brave. He has killed many murderers and thieves in America, and it is said that no outlaw gang is safe from him. They say that Smoke Jensen cannot be killed."

"Of course he can be killed. Anyone can be killed."

"Many have tried to kill the man Smoke Jensen, but have been unable to do so. Why do you ask about him?"

Keno showed Mendez the wadded-up note. "He has killed three of my men. He says he is coming for me."

"What will you do, *Coronel*?" Lopez asked.

Keno smiled. "He does not understand. I am not a bandit; I am a commander of soldiers. We will see how he does against one who employs military strategy against him."

"Do you have a plan, *Coronel*?" Chavez asked.

"*Sí*, I have a plan. Chavez, bring twenty men here. Choose the men wisely. I will speak of my plan then."

As Chavez went out among the encampment to gather the men Keno had asked for, Keno continued to eat his bean burrito.

"Mendez, tell me more about this man Jensen," he said.

"It is said that he can draw his gun so quickly that

it seems to appear in his hand, as if by magic. And it is said that he can shoot a fly from a stick at a distance of one hundred meters, without breaking the stick."

"That's impossible. Have you ever seen him do such a thing?"

"No, *señor.* I have never seen Jensen. I tell you only things that I have heard."

"Talk, it is all talk," Keno said with a dismissive wave of his hand. "We will see what the talk is once he has been killed."

Chavez arrived with his twenty handpicked men then, and Keno, having finished eating, wiped his mouth with the back of his hand. "You, stand over here," he said, pointing to one man. "You stand over there," he said to another, and a moment later he had two groups of ten men each.

"You are the First Platoon," he said to one group. "You are the Second Platoon," he said to the other.

"Chavez, I am appointing you to the rank of lieutenant. You will be in command of the First Platoon."

"Gracias, Coronel Keno," Chavez replied, smiling broadly over the promotion.

"Vargas, you will command the Second Platoon."

"Gracias," Vargas replied, his smile as broad as the smile of Chavez.

"You will lead your commands as if you are fighting on the battlefield. It is said that ten men, wisely led, are worth one hundred, without a head.

"In this case you will be ten men wisely led, not against a hundred, but against one man." Keno interrupted his instructions to flash a big smile. "And the head I want is his. I will pay twelve thousand pesos to the platoon who brings me the head of the *gringo*. Two thousand I will pay to the lieutenant, and one thousand pesos to each soldier."

The two lieutenants smiled.

"When this is over, if you need to borrow money, I will lend it to you," Vargas said.

"That is very good of you, but I won't need money," Chavez said. "I intend to win."

"Find this man," Keno ordered. "Search every mountain, search every canyon, search the streams and forests. Search the villages, and if you find that a village is hiding him, raze the village."

Both lieutenants saluted smartly, then left to get their platoons organized for the search.

Rosita was sitting on the chair, her hands no longer tied behind her. She heard Keno and his soldiers talking, and though she didn't know who the man Smoke Jensen was, she did hear one of the men refer to him as a "hero."

She had read about heroes. In school she had read about knights in shining armor, riding upon a white horse, dispatched by their king to save the princess who was being held captive by someone evil.

Keno had said that he was only one man, and he would be confronting Keno and his entire army. But, isn't that what heroes did? And, didn't Mendez say this hero couldn't be killed?

Had her father found a knight in shining armor to come to her rescue? Obviously, it wouldn't be a real knight in armor, but she had heard one of the men refer to him as a hero. And, perhaps her father had not sent this hero to rescue her. But, whoever he was, he was coming after Keno. And if he succeeded, she knew that he would free her.

It pleased her to keep this in mind, and she said a prayer for the hero, Smoke Jensen

Chapter Twenty-seven

As Smoke and the others rode into the Sierra Veinte Casas mountains, they approached a draw that split, one side going north of the mountain, and the other to the south.

"Which way?" Cal asked.

"Cal, climb up to the top and take a look to the north. Let us know if you see anything," Smoke directed. "Pearlie, you do the same thing, but look up the southern side of the draw."

The two men nodded, then set forth on the task given them. Smoke, Sally, and Old Mo waited down in the valley.

Cal and Pearlie climbed to the top of the mountain, taking their signal mirrors with them, and Smoke was waiting for their report.

"There's a flash from Cal," Sally said. She read the message. "He says it is all clear."

"Nobody there," Smoke said. "Tell him to come back down."

Sally flashed the signal for Cal to come in and Cal

responded with dot dot dash, and dash dot dot, for understood.

Almost immediately thereafter, Pearlie sent the same signal Cal had earlier. There was no one on his side of the draw, so Sally called him in as well.

For the next several days, Smoke looked for Keno and his men, while Keno's men looked for Smoke. Neither found the other, and the frustration was growing on both sides.

"Smoke, we're going to get some more vittles here soon," Old Mo pointed out. "We're runnin' mighty low, and I don't intend to ever be caught out without food again."

"At least there's no snow this time," Smoke said.

"No, there ain't," Old Mo replied, grimly.

Smoke had passed the comment off lightly, but he realized quickly that Old Mo didn't find it humorous.

"I'm sorry, Mo, I meant nothing by that remark. I should've known better."

"That's all right," Old Mo said. "But the fact remains, we're runnin' low on provisions 'n' we're goin' to have to come up with food from somewhere pretty soon."

"We'll start looking," Smoke promised.

They discovered the farm midway through the day after the conversation between Smoke and Old Mo. A man, whom Smoke took to be in his late thirties or early forties, and a boy about fifteen were out in a cornfield, hoeing the weeds. As Smoke and the others rode up, the man greeted them cautiously.

Smoke couldn't help but recall his own time on

the farm where he too had grown corn, and the boy reminded him of himself, then.

"Do you speak English?" Smoke asked.

The man looked at the boy.

"*Americano?*" the boy asked.

"Yes. *Sí.*"

"*Mi padre* does not speak the language of the *americano,* but I do."

"Tell your papa that we are friends," Smoke said.

The boy translated, and his father smiled.

"*Mi nombre es* Smoke."

"*Humo?*" the boy replied, confused by the name.

"No, Smoke is my name."

"That is a funny name, *señor.*"

"I suppose it is," Smoke said with a smile. Smoke pointed to the others, identifying them in turn. "This is Sally, Pearlie, Cal, and Mo."

"Juan Alvarez," the boy said, pointing to his father. "Pablo," he said, pointing to himself.

"Pablo, tell your papa that if you have any food to spare, we would like to buy it. I will pay you in pesos."

After a series of exchanges, Juan Alvarez agreed to sell them three dozen eggs, some cornmeal and flour, a sack of beans, and a side of bacon.

Smoke paid the amount Juan had asked for without haggling. Juan smiled broadly at his luck, then he said something to Pablo, and the boy translated.

"Papa says that you are a good man and you didn't try to cheat us. He thought you would"—he paused, looking for the word—"*negociar,*" he said.

"Negotiate?"

"*Sí,* negotiate. He thought you would negotiate, so he asked for more money than he should. Now he feels bad because he overcharged you." The boy tried to give some of the money back.

Smoke shook his head, and held out his hand, not to take the money, but to tell the boy he didn't want it

"Tell your papa that he is a very good man, for only a good man would make such an offer. Tell him also, that we have no other place where we can get supplies, so I am pleased to do business with him."

The boy smiled broadly, then translated Smoke's response to his father. Alvarez smiled as well, then he spoke to the boy again.

"You are looking for Keno and his soldiers?" Pablo asked.

"Yes."

"Is it because you wish to join him?"

Smoke hesitated a moment before he responded. He had read in the report given him by Goldstein, the editor of the *Cosmopolitan,* that many poor Mexicans regarded Keno as a heroic character. Is that how Alvarez saw him? He decided to take a chance and tell the truth.

"No, not to join him. He crossed into America and killed many, including our friends, and the *esposa* of this young man." Smoke said that Katrina was Cal's wife, because he knew that it would have more impact with the boy and his father. And had Katrina lived, she and Cal would have been married.

"We are looking to bring Keno and his men to justice."

"*Justicia?*" Pablo replied, saying the word in Spanish.

Smoke looked at Sally who, though she didn't speak Spanish, did know a few words, and was aware of the Spanish method of giving the H sound to the letter J.

"*Sí,*" she said. "*Justicia.*"

Pablo translated the conversation to his father, and Juan's reaction told Smoke that he had made the right choice in telling the real reason they were looking for Keno.

Juan looked at Cal with great sadness, then spoke to the boy.

"Papa says that he is saddened for you. His *esposa,* my mama, died when I was very young, but he still misses her."

"Tell him I thank him for his kindness," Cal said.

Juan spoke again, and again Pablo translated. He pointed to the northwest. "Go five, maybe six kilometers in that direction. You will see a canyon that goes into the mountains. Papa saw some men there three days before. He thinks they are Keno's soldiers, maybe."

"Thank you for that information," Smoke said.

Smoke gave Pablo anther fifty pesos, and Pablo said something to his father. His father shook his head, held out his hand, and responded.

"*Sí,*" Pablo said, then he turned back to Smoke. "Papa says the information isn't for sale. He says that Keno is a very evil man, and should be stopped from hurting all the people."

"Your father is a good man, Pablo. And you are a good man as well."

Pablo smiled at being called a man.

"Would your father sell us some more eggs?" Sally asked. "We will give you fifty pesos for more eggs."

"Oh, *señora*, we do not have enough eggs for fifty pesos."

"Sure you do," Sally said. "They are very good eggs, don't you say so, gentlemen?" she asked the others.

"Best eggs I ever seen," Old Mo said.

They reached the place Alvarez told them about by midafternoon. A hot dry wind was blowing through the canyon, pushing before it a billowing puff of red dust. The cloud of dust lifted high and spread out wide, making it look as if there were blood on the sun. Just as they got to the mouth of the canyon, something caught Smoke's attention and he twisted in his saddle to look up toward the high denuded wall of the red mesa which boxed in the canyon. That was when he saw the sun's reflection off polished metal.

"I think I know where they are," Smoke said, pointing.

"Vargas, someone is coming into the canyon."

"Franco, Barrera, go there with Guzman," Vargas said. "Keep an eye on our visitors."

Franco and Barrera joined Guzman.

"Are we looking for only one man?" Guzman called back.

"*Sí*, one man, named Smoke Jensen."

"Then I think maybe we have made a mistake. There are five of them. They are looking up this way. They may have seen us."

"Perhaps the man Jensen has gathered some to come with him," Vargas said.

"What shall we do?"

"Kill them," Vargas ordered.

Smoke was still studying the top of the rock wall where a second earlier he had seen a flash of light. Now he saw a little puff of smoke just an instant before a bullet hit a rock nearby and whined as it ricocheted away. That was followed a second later by the low thump of gunfire. A little cloud of smoke drifted over the edge of the cliff.

"That's them all right! They're shooting at us! Get over there, behind that pinnacle!" Smoke shouted, and all five of them urged their horses into a gallop, covering the fifty yards to a pinnacle that stuck out into the canyon, running parallel with it. The iron-shod hooves clacked loudly on the hard rock floor of the canyon, the sound echoing back from the canyon walls.

There were at least three more shots fired at them as they were hurrying for cover and, fortunately, all three missed.

There was an offshoot from the canyon, going behind an upthrust slab of rock, the pinnacle providing them with cover from anyone who might be shooting at them from the opposite wall. Here, they dismounted.

"Sally, you and Mo hold the horses," Smoke ordered. "Pearlie, Cal, grab your Sharps, and come with me to the top of this pinnacle to see if we can get a shot at them."

The three men, with scoped rifles, climbed up to the top of the rock. Reaching the top, they stopped

just below the crest so that they couldn't be seen.
Smoke stuck his rifle over the top and looked through
the scope. On the other side of the draw, he saw five
men lying on their stomachs. All five had crept up to
the edge of the wall, thinking that because they were
prone, they were out of danger.

They were mistaken.

"Do you see them?" Smoke asked.

"Yeah, I do," Cal said.

"Me too," Pearlie added.

"Cal, you take the one in the middle. Pearlie, you've
got the one on the extreme left, I'll take the one on
the extreme right. The two men that will remain will
have had a man hit on each side of them. I expect
that will shake them up a bit."

"We need to all three pull the trigger at the same
time," Pearlie said.

"Yes. We'll shoot on three."

Smoke counted, and as he said the word "three,"
all three rifles boomed, the concentrated sound very
loud and echoing back and forth from wall to wall
across the canyon floor.

Chapter Twenty-eight

Santos was lying on the rim of the wall between Pacheco and Cabara, when all of a sudden he saw blood and brain detritus literally explode from the back of their heads. Some of it got on him.

"Ayiee!" he shouted in shock and fear. He got up and ran back from the rim.

Garza was lying between Pacheco and Nunez, and he too got up to run away from the rim.

The others shouted in alarm as well.

"They are devils, those men," Santos said. "No one can shoot that well."

"You're our leader, Vargas. What do we do now?" Montoya asked.

"Take a look. See if you can see what they're doing."

"I'm not going to stick my head over the edge. Their bullets are coming too close."

"Take a look," Vargas ordered. "Unless you are a woman, and too frightened to do it."

Montoya glared at him, then, staying on his stomach, scooted out to the edge of the mesa. He raised his head up just enough to look over to the other side.

"See anything?" Vargas asked.

"No," Montoya replied. He inched a little farther forward on his stomach, then he saw a flash from the top of the rock on the other side of the draw. In almost the same instant he heard a loud pop, and felt a sharp, stabbing pain in his right ear.

"Ow!" he called out in pain and, putting his hand on his ear, he backed cautiously away from the edge of the mesa. When he pulled his hand away, a little piece of the flesh of his ear came with it.

"My ear! My ear has been shot off!" he said, his voice strained with pain.

"Quit crying like a *niño*. You still have your ear," Vargas said. "The bullet hit only a piece of your earlobe."

"What are we going to do now?" Santos asked. "Our horses are down there, we can't get to them without being shot."

"We will go down on the other side of the mountain to return to our camp," Vargas said.

"Do you intend to leave our horses behind?" Santos asked.

Vargas laughed. "Santos, we have two hundred horses."

Smoke kept someone on top of the pinnacle for the rest of the day, keeping watch. He knew there was no way he could get to the men on the other side of the canyon, but there was no way they could get to him either.

As darkness fell, Smoke called up to Old Mo.

"Mo, come on down. Even if they started across now, you wouldn't be able to see them in the dark from up there."

Old Mo came down, and saw that Pearlie and Cal were laying a fire. "You're buildin' a fire?"

"You want to eat your bacon raw?"

"No. I was just wonderin' about buildin' a fire. Seems like it might draw 'em to us."

"Yeah, doesn't it?" Smoke said.

Old Mo chuckled. "I shoulda knowed that's what you had in mind."

After they cooked their bacon and beans, they threw enough wood onto the fire to keep it going, then laid out their bedrolls around the fire. They didn't bed down by the fire though. Instead they pulled away then, back into the darkness, hoping by that ruse to draw Keno's men in, if they decided to try it again.

Keno's cabin

So far Rosita had not been harmed, but she didn't know how long it would be before Keno, or one of the other men, did something to her. She had never been with a man, or a boy for that matter, but she did know what men and women did with each other. There had even been times when she thought of it, and wondered what it would be like when she was married, and with her husband.

But the thought of Keno, or any of his men, coming to her now, filled her with revulsion and fear. And though nobody had done anything to her, she was sure that it would only be a matter of time until someone did. After all, Keno had said that he would "make a woman of her," and she was pretty sure she knew what that meant. She knew, also, that if anyone did decide to force themselves on her, there would be nothing she could do to prevent it.

It was those thoughts, and that fear, that caused her to sleep fitfully, when she was able to sleep at all.

As she lay on the floor in the corner, thinking about this, she heard several loud voices coming from just outside and she stayed very quiet, there in the darkness of the cabin, listening to the spirited conversation.

At first she feared it might have something to do with her, but she learned quickly that it was about something altogether different. They were talking about the man called Smoke Jensen, the knight in shining armor that Rosita was certain was coming to rescue her.

"He isn't alone," one of the men was saying, clearly agitated. "You said we would be an army against Jensen, but he isn't alone, he has people with him."

By now Rosita had heard enough of the men speak that she could recognize some of them by their voice alone. Vargas was one that she could recognize, and he was the one who was speaking now.

"How many are there?" Keno asked.

"There's five of them," Vargas said.

"Five? And you ran from five men? You have ten men with you."

"I had ten," Vargas said. "Now I have only seven. They killed Pacheco, Nunez, and Cabara."

"And how many of them did you kill?"

"None, *Coronel.*"

"You were in a gun battle, ten of you to five *gringos*, and in this gun battle you had three men killed, but killed none of them?"

"It was not a gun battle, *Coronel.*"

"If it was not a gun battle, what was it?"

"It was a killing, *Coronel*, as if hunting and killing an animal. Pacheco, Nunez, and Cabara were all shot at the same time. Smoke Jensen and the *gringos* with him, have rifles that can shoot from very far off. They can shoot us, but we can't shoot back because our bullets cannot reach them. They are devils, these men are, with the skill to use such a rifle."

"Where are Pacheco, Nunez, and Cabara now?"

"We had to leave them, and our horses."

"So, like a coward, you ran from the *gringos*, left your *amigos* and your horses behind."

"If we had gone to recover the horses, we would have all been killed. It was not cowardice, *Coronel*. It was good sense."

"What kind of man is this Smoke Jensen?" Keno asked, though he had no expectation of the question being answered.

As Rosita lay in the dark, listening to the fear in their voices, she smiled. It was her first smile since being captured.

Smoke and the others spent the entire night away from the fire, which hadn't been needed for warmth, and had been built only for a ruse. Apparently, Keno's men had had enough because no one showed up. By the next morning, Smoke was convinced that the men they had exchanged fire with the previous day were gone.

"I'll find out," Cal said.

"Cal, no, it's too dangerous," Sally said.

Cal chuckled. "Would you rather your own husband take the risk?"

"Well, no, not that. It's just that . . ."

"Cal is right, Sally," Smoke said. "We need to find out if anyone is there, and Cal is the best choice. He is the youngest, and the most agile. If he goes by himself, I think he will have the best chance of getting over there without being discovered."

"If I see that anyone is still there, I'll flash you a signal," Cal said. "What shall the signal be?"

"Just flash your mirror until you get a response from us," Smoke said. "Once you get a response, and we are in communication, don't try to use a code. Two flashes will mean they are still there. Three will mean they have gone."

"Cal," Sally said. She put her arms around him and hugged him. "Please be very careful."

"Miz Sally, you ain't never saw no one who is goin' to be as careful as me."

Sally shuddered at the grammar. "I'm not even going to correct you," she said with a smile.

Cal returned the smile. "I was just funnin' you. What I meant to say was, you've never seen anyone who is going to be as careful as I will be."

"Very good," Sally said.

"Smoke, I'm not takin' a gun with me. It'll just get in the way of my climbin', and if they're still there, and they see me, one gun isn't going to do me much good anyway."

"I think you might be right," Smoke said.

"Good luck, and be careful," Pearlie said. Old Mo just nodded toward him, and Cal started out on his mission.

At first the route Cal selected had looked passable from the ground, but once he started climbing it proved to be much more difficult than he had thought. After more than half an hour of climbing he wasn't sure that he had gained so much as an inch. But when he looked back toward the ground, he could see that he was making progress, for by now he was dangerously high.

Cal clung to the side of the mountain and moved only when he had a secure handhold or foothold . . . tiny though they might be. Sweat poured into his eyes and he grew thirsty with his effort, but still he climbed.

He found an indentation in the side of the cliff, almost like a chimney, and climbing into it he realized that it was providing him not only with cover, but concealment. At about the same time it became easier to climb, and easier still, until he reached an incline that was no steeper than about sixty degrees. This allowed him to crawl up, rather than climb, and as he got even closer to the top, it eased down to between thirty and forty-five degrees, so that he was able to walk up.

Then, just before he reached the top, he got down onto his stomach and slithered up to where he could see over the edge. He saw three men lying there and as he studied them more closely, he realized that they were dead. He was certain that these were the men they had killed yesterday afternoon. There were also a few burned-out campfires, but there was no sign of anyone else there.

Cal made a careful, but very thorough examination of the rest of the area, and he saw footprints leading south, along the top of the ridge. He was certain, then, that everyone had left.

Cal walked over to the edge of the mesa where, standing up in plain sight, he began to flash his mirror. When he got a return flash, telling him that he had established contact, he sent the signal that everyone was gone. Three flashes.

The return signal was one they had worked on before leaving The Wide Loop. It was dot dash dash, a pause, then dash. WT, which meant for him to wait right where he was.

Cal flashed back UD, which meant that he had received and understood the message Then he sat down on the edge of the rim, with his legs dangling over the edge and watched as Smoke and the others reappeared from behind the pinnacle where they had taken cover the day before. When they reached the canyon floor, Smoke called up to him.

"What did you find?" The last word came echoing back, "*find, find, find?*"

Cal cupped his hands around his mouth. "There is nothing up here but three dead bodies!" he shouted.

"Send them down!"

"What? How 'm I going to do that?"

"Easy. Just push them over the edge and let 'em fall!" Smoke called back.

Cal wondered why Smoke would make such a strange request, but he had learned long ago not to question him. He didn't like the idea of pushing someone off a high cliff, but in this case, what did it matter? They were dead, so the fall sure wasn't going to hurt them.

He pulled them to the edge, one at a time, until all three were there. Then he pushed them over, and started back down.

Going back down required a lot less effort than going up had, not only because he could let himself down some of the ledges easier than it had been to climb up them, but also because he was no longer worried about maintaining cover and concealment.

When he reached the canyon floor, he was surprised to see several horses in addition to their own, gathered by Pearlie and Old Mo.

"Looks like them boys walked back home," Old Mo said. "There was at least ten horses tied up there. We let six of 'em go, and brung these four back."

"What are we goin' to do with 'em?" Cal asked.

"We're goin' to send Keno another message," Smoke said.

Fifteen minutes later the three bodies were draped, belly-down, across the saddles of three of the horses. One of the bodies had a note attached to it in the same way Smoke had sent the earlier note, by using a knife to hold the note in place. This note read exactly as the first one had.

> *KENO*
> *I AM COMING AFTER YOU. YOU WILL NOT ESCAPE. WE WILL KILL YOU TO AVENGE THE PEOPLE YOU KILLED IN TEXAS. I AM SMOKE JENSEN, AND I AM AN AMERICAN AVENGER.*

"All right, boys, give 'em a lick, and send 'em on their way," Smoke said.

"Shouldn't we follow them? They'll probably lead us right to Keno, don't you think?" Pearlie asked.

"Not yet. There are still too many of them for a direct confrontation," Smoke said. He smiled. "We've killed six of his men now. I'd say we just let all of this start working on him for a while."

"I see what you're getting at," Pearlie said. "You're going to make it so he starts jumpin' at shadows."

"That's the plan," Smoke said, returning Pearlie's smile.

Chapter Twenty-nine

Keno's cabin

"*Coronel!*" Santino called, pointing to the horses that came trotting into the camp. "Look!"

"Stop the horses!" Keno shouted. "Stop them!"

Several of Keno's soldiers ran out in front of the trotting horses, and holding up their arms, managed to corral the horses.

"There are bodies on the horses!" Santino said. "It's Pacheco, Nunez, and Cabara. How did they get there?"

"Vargas?" Keno asked.

"I don't know, *Coronel.* We left them back on top of the mountain," Vargas replied.

"Get them down."

"*Coronel,* look," Santino said. He pointed to Cabara's body, which had a knife sticking from his back. The knife was holding a note pinned to Cabara's body.

Keno walked over to the body, pulled the knife free, then read the note. He let out a loud curse.

"It is Smoke Jensen again! Who is this man Smoke Jensen?"

"I told you who he is, *Coronel*," Mendez said. "He is a *pistolero americano*. He is a very famous man in *Estados Unidos*."

"Why is he doing this? Why has he come to Mexico?"

"It is as the note says, *Coronel*," Mendez said. "When we went to Texas, some of the *gringos* we killed were his friends. I have heard that he is a man who will avenge the death of his friends."

"And so, to avenge the death of his friends, he has come after me? With only four men beside himself, he has come to attack an army? How can anyone be so foolish?"

"I have heard that he is a man without fear."

"You have heard, you have heard, you have heard!" Keno said, his voice raspy with exasperation. "I am tired of what you have heard!" He literally shouted the last eight words.

"I am sorry, *Coronel*," Mendez said.

"Chavez!" Keno shouted, calling the lieutenant he had appointed to take command of the First Platoon.

"*Sí, Coronel?*"

"Take ten men. No, take twenty men. Find that *gringo* hero, and kill him!" Keno was so angry, and shouting so loudly, that spittle was coming from his mouth.

"*Coronel*, may I take one of the rapid-shooting guns with me?"

The angry expression left Keno's face as he contemplated the question. "*Sí!*" he said with a broad smile. "*Sí, sí*. The *gringos* do not know we have such a weapon. We will have the advantage of numbers, and surprise. Perhaps you will be able to do what Vargas could not do."

"*Coronel,* that is not fair," Vargas said. "We did not have the weapon with us."

"What if you had had the weapon? Would the outcome have been any different?"

"I believe it would have been different, *Coronel.* If we had had the weapon, I believe Smoke Jensen would be dead by now."

"Good, I am pleased to hear that. That means that, with the gun that fires very rapidly, Chavez will be able to kill Jensen. Is this what you believe?"

"*Sí,* it is what I believe."

"Then, do not be jealous, for it will be better for us all, if he is dead."

When Keno went back inside the cabin, Rosita was sitting on the chair.

"You will not be able kill Señor Jensen," Rosita said.

Keno looked at her with a flash of irritated surprise at hearing her say Jensen's name.

"What do you know about this man, Smoke Jensen?"

"I know that he is a knight in shining armor," Rosita said. "And I believe my papa has asked him to come rescue me."

Keno laughed, though his laugh was without mirth. "There is no such thing as a knight in shining armor, and nobody is coming to rescue you. Soon, the man Smoke Jensen will be dead."

* * *

Smoke decided that it might be better if they didn't ride down the middle of the canyon. If they encountered more of Keno's men in the middle of the canyon, there would be no opportunity for maneuver. They left the canyon, deciding instead to ride parallel with the mountain range, and shortly after they did so, they happened onto another little town. The village was very small, with probably no more than three hundred to three hundred fifty residents. It had a grocery store, a cantina, and a café.

The sight of five Americans riding into the town was most unusual, and the villagers who were out and about stopped to stare at them.

"I wonder why everyone is looking at us?" Cal asked.

Old Mo chuckled. "How many times do you think this many Americans have ridden into town at the same time?"

"Probably not that many times."

"Then don't you think our ridin' in like this might be a bit unusual to 'em?"

"Yeah, I guess that's right."

"Do you think we could get any information if we ate a meal in that café?" Pearlie asked.

"I don't know if we will get any usable information," Smoke said. He smiled. "But I think we might be able to get a meal there. That is, if anyone is hungry."

"I'm hungry," Cal said quickly.

"You're hungry? Well, I never would have thought that," Smoke teased.

The five tied their horses off in front of an adobe building. The sign in front of the building read: RESTAURANTE MAMA MARIA, which was easy enough for them to understand, but even if they hadn't been able to understand the words, they would have been able to tell what it was by the delicious-smelling aromas that wafted into the street.

"I'm pretty sure that in a place like this, there isn't going to be a menu," Smoke said. "Whatever they have cooked is what we will be served."

"*Norteamericano?*" a man asked, as the five sat at the only empty table in the place.

"*Sí,*" Smoke said. "*Hablas inglés?*"

"*No, señor. Quieres comer?*" As he spoke the words, he made a motion as if eating, and Smoke understood that he was asking if they wanted to eat.

"*Sí,*" Smoke said. He repeated the same motion the proprietor had made. "We want to eat."

The man smiled and nodded. "*Sí,* eat," he said, repeating the motion to make certain he understood. When Smoke returned the nod, the man went out back.

"You think that's Mama Maria?" Cal asked with a chuckle.

"More than likely it's Papa Maria," Smoke said. "I expect his wife does the cooking, and he does all the greeting and serving."

A few minutes later the man who had greeted them returned, carrying a tray with food. On this day the fare was baked goat, corn on the cob, liberally sprinkled with chili powder, refried beans, and tortillas. It looked, smelled, and tasted very good.

About halfway through their meal, the proprietor came over to their table, accompanied by a young woman. He spoke to her and she nodded, then she spoke to Smoke and the others in English.

"I am Leticia Delgado. I can speak English."

Smoke stood, and as he did, so did Old Mo, Pearlie, and Cal.

"It is very nice to meet someone who can speak our language so far from home."

"You are Smoke Jensen?" the woman asked.

"Yes!" Smoke said, surprised to hear her speak his name. He looked at the others, and the expressions on their faces mirrored the surprise on his own.

"How is it that you know my name?"

"All of Tamaulipas know of the *americano* hero who has come to help us."

"But how do they know this?"

"Three of Keno's bandits tried to rob you at Nuevo Pacifico, is this right?

"Yes, this is right."

"They were very evil men, and they have killed many people." Señorita Delgado smiled. "But now it is said that after trying to rob you, that they will never kill again. Is this true?"

"Yes, that is true," Smoke said. "You don't have to worry about them anymore. They will never kill any more of your people."

"That is why the people of Cruillas and all the people of Tamaulipas believe that you are a hero from America come to help us."

Smoke decided not to say anything about the real reason they had come. If the Mexican people wanted to think he had come to help them, then it might mean that the Mexicans would be more likely to help Smoke and his group.

"Yes, Smoke said. "We have heard of the evil things

Keno has been doing to the Mexican people, and we have come to help."

Leticia Delgado turned to speak to the other diners in the café, all of whom had stopped eating in order to see what was going on. She spoke in Spanish so that neither Smoke nor the others with him could understand what she was saying. They had a pretty good idea of what it was, though, when everyone else in the café began applauding.

Smoke and the others acknowledged the applause with a little wave.

"Señorita Delgado, what is the name of the man who served us?" Sally asked.

"His name is Trinidad Castineda," Leticia said. "He is the owner of this place."

"Not Mama Maria?" Pearlie asked.

"Señora Maria Castineda is his *esposa*. It is she who cooks the food."

"You got that right, Smoke," Cal said, referring to Smoke's earlier pronouncement that the wife of the man who had greeted them was probably the Mama Maria of the restaurant's name.

"Well, you tell Señor and Señora Castineda for us, that the meal is excellent, and we are very much enjoying it."

"*Sí*, I will tell them."

Because the little town of Cruillas was close to their search area, Smoke decided it would be good if they could stay here for a while, using the town as their base. Using Señorita Delgado as his "voice" he rented two very small one-room adobe structures that sat side by side just on the outside of town. Over the next few days he and the others were frequently in the café or the cantina, letting it be known that they were searching for Taurino Bustamante Keno.

"I know that he has been terrorizing small villages," Smoke said. "He has also taken a young girl from her parents, and he is holding her against her will. I would appreciate any information anyone can provide me to help me find and stop this evil man."

Smoke wasn't surprised that nobody responded right away. Even though they had applauded his presence on the first night they were here, it would take a great deal of courage for anyone to actually take the risk of giving them any information. T. B. Keno had held sway over the entire state of Tamaulipas for some time now, and nearly everyone was very frightened of him.

There was one person, however, who saw an opportunity in the situation. Smoke's presence in the community, and his openness as to why he was here, gave Ygnacio Pena an idea as to how he may turn some information into money. He shared his idea with Gabriela Castillo.

"I am going to go to *Coronel* Keno and tell him about Señor Jensen and the *gringos* who are looking for him," Pena said.

"But why would you do that?" Gabriela asked. "Keno is a very evil man. You have heard what people have said about Keno. He extracts money from the citizens, and he kills those who will not pay what he demands. And he has captured a young girl. Do you not think it would be good if Señor Jensen stopped such evil?"

"Jensen has but three men and one woman with him," Pena said. "Keno has many men, maybe even one hundred. It is not possible for Jensen to stop him with so few people. And if anyone helps Jensen, after Keno has killed Jensen and his friends, he will kill those who have betrayed him.

"But I will remain loyal to Keno, and by so doing, I am sure that I can make a profit."

"How will you make a profit?"

"I think that when I tell Keno where Jensen is, he will pay a lot of money. I think he will pay me so much money that we can leave here and go to another place, perhaps to a place where Keno does not bother the people."

"No, Ygnacio, do not do this. I do not think you can trust Keno. He is a very evil man."

Pena smiled, and held up his finger. "I have something he wants. He will not harm me."

"How will you find him?" Gabriela asked.

"I will find him," Pena said, without being more specific.

What neither Gabriela nor anyone else in the village knew, was that this wouldn't be the first time Pena had sold information to Keno. And because he had dealt with Keno before, he knew exactly where to find him. It had been he who told Ramos where he could keep the horses, even telling him about the cabin that was occupied by the *gringo* prospector.

Chapter Thirty

Ciudad Victoria

Captain Juan Cortina of the Mexican *Federales* read the report from the *alguacil* of Nuevo Pacifico, then looked across his desk to Lieutenant Gomez.

"Have you seen this letter from Sheriff Gomez of Nuevo Pacifico?"

"No, *Capitán.*"

"It says that an American named Jensen has come into our country to find Keno. Jensen intends to kill him."

"One man?"

Cortina shook his head. "When he was in Nuevo Pacifico, another man was with him."

Gomez laughed. "He must be very foolish to think that, with but one other man, he can find and kill Keno."

"He has already killed three," Cortina said. "He killed them just outside of the town, and he left a note pinned to a body. That is how Rivas knows the intentions of Jensen."

Cortina read the note. "'Keno. I am coming after you. You will not escape. We will kill you to avenge the people you killed in Texas. I am Smoke Jensen, and I am an American avenger.'"

"Rivas has such a note?"

"No. He says, in the letter, that he let the note remain so that it would be taken to Keno."

"This man, Jensen, has killed three of Keno's men?"

"*Sí.*"

Gomez smiled. "Good. Maybe he will kill all of them."

Cortina shook his head. "No, this is not good, Gomez. We cannot allow someone from America to come to Mexico to start killing our citizens."

"Keno's men are evil, *Capitán*, you have said so yourself, many times."

"*Sí*, but, still, Keno and his men are Mexican citizens. If they are to be dealt with, they must be dealt with by Mexican authorities, not by some *vengador* from *los Estados Unidos*. How do you think such a thing would make us look?"

Keno's encampment

Because Pena had been there before, he knew the proper signal to give to gain entrance. He stopped at the junction of Rapido and Blanco Creeks, then he tied a blindfold across his eyes. That done he removed his sombrero, then resting his rifle, barrel-down on the pommel, put his hat on the rifle butt. He sat there without making a move or a sound for almost fifteen minutes, then he heard the rattle of horse hooves on rocky ground as a rider approached.

"Lower your rifle, but keep the blindfold on," he was told.

"*Sí, señor.*"

The rider who came for Pena took the reins of Pena's horse, then led him through the canyon and up a path for about fifteen minutes, then they stopped.

"You can take off your blindfold and get down from your horse," his guide said.

Pena complied, and as he dismounted, he saw Keno coming from the small cabin, walking toward him.

"Why have you come?" Keno asked. "Have you news for me?"

"*Sí,*" Pena said. "I have news that you will find very valuable. I know where Jensen and his men are."

"Where are they?"

"How much will you give me for this information, *Coronel?*" Pena asked, knowing that his bargaining position was very strong.

"I will give you thirty pesos."

Pena was stunned by the paucity of the offer. He had expected ten times as much money.

"Thirty pesos?" Pena asked. "I come to give you news of Jensen and the other *gringos,* and you say it is worth but thirty pesos? Surely it is worth more than that."

"Why should it be more? Do you not know your Bible, Señor Pena?"

"The Bible?" Pena shook his head in confusion, puzzled as to why Keno, of all people, would ask such a question.

"*Sí,* the Bible. If you have read the Bible, you know

that Judas was paid but thirty pesos to betray Jesus," Keno said. "So, tell me, Pena, do you think the *gringo* Jensen is worth more than Jesus?"

Pena's face registered shock as the biblical comparison was made between what he was doing and what Judas had done. Quickly, he crossed himself. How could he have blasphemed so? He wished he had listened to Gabriela when she cautioned him against coming.

"Now, you will take thirty pesos, or you will get nothing."

"I . . . I have changed my mind," Pena said. "I will get nothing." He turned to leave, but at a nod from Keno, a couple of his men reached out to grab him.

"You don't understand, *señor*," Keno said with an evil smile. "You will get thirty pesos, or you will get nothing. But either way, you will give me the information."

"I have made a mistake," Pena said. "I thought I had some information but now I know that I was wrong. I will leave now."

The two men who had reached out to grab Pena were still holding him, and Keno pulled his pistol.

"I think you will give us the information, Pena," Keno said as he began pushing all the shells from the cylinder of his revolver. When every shell was out, he put one back in, spun the cylinder, then pointed it at Pena.

"Where are the *americanos* who are looking for me?"

"I don't know," Pena answered. "I told you, I have made a mistake."

Keno pulled the trigger, and the hammer fell on an empty chamber. Pena shook in convulsive fear.

"Well, it would appear that Jesus is with you," Keno said in a mocking voice. "Perhaps Jesus does not mind if you betray Jensen for thirty pesos."

"Please, *señor*, I made a mistake. I know nothing."

Keno pulled the trigger, and again the hammer fell on an empty chamber. Again, Pena jerked spasmodically.

"Where are the *gringos*?"

"Please, *señor*, I have made a mistake."

Keno pulled the trigger two more times, and at the second pull, Pena wet himself.

"Now there is one bullet and two chambers," Keno said. "Shall I pull the trigger again?"

"Cruillas! They are in Cruillas!" Pena shouted.

"Thank you," Keno said. "You may go now."

"The thirty pesos?"

Keno chuckled a low, throaty, and contemptuous laugh.

"But, *señor*, when I offered the thirty pesos, you did not sell the information to me. I had to find another way to get the information, and that way cost me nothing."

"Please, *Coronel*."

"Carlos, blindfold him, and take him back to where you found him."

"*Sí, Coronel.*"

"Chavez. Get your men together. Tomorrow, you will go to Cruillas, and you will kill Jensen."

"*Sí, señor.*"

Pena heard the orders being given as the blindfold

was put back on. Then he mounted and, as before, his horse was led while he sat in the saddle, holding on to the saddle horn.

Pena felt angry and betrayed. He had provided Keno with information before, and Keno had paid for it. He had never paid very much money, but Pena had never given him information as valuable as that which he had provided today.

Pena had not been providing the information just for the money. He truly believed that someday, soon, Keno would actually mount a revolution against the Mexican government, and appoint himself as the new president. When that happened, Keno would need many officials, men that he could trust.

It had been Pena's intention to be one of those trusted officials, perhaps even governor of Tamaulipas. That all seemed very unlikely now. He was lucky to have gotten away from that encounter without being killed.

As he rode back to town, Pena got another thought.

If he couldn't sell information to Keno, perhaps he could sell information to Jensen.

A broad smile spread across his face. Yes, that is exactly what he would do. He would not only make some money, it would also provide him with the satisfaction of getting back at Keno for the way Keno had treated him.

It was early evening when Pena rode back into town, and the rich and spicy aromas of many dinners being prepared greeted him. He had not eaten since this morning and his stomach rumbled with hunger. He knew that Jensen and the men, and the one woman who was with him, often took their meals at the café of Mama Maria, so he decided to go there. Perhaps, as he ate his supper, he would see Jensen, then negotiate with him.

He was sure that he would get more than thirty pesos.

Pena had been correct in thinking that Smoke Jensen would be taking his supper at Mama Maria's. Smoke and the others were gathered around one of the four tables when Pena stepped into the restaurant.

"Señor Pena," Mama Maria said, greeting him. "Will Señorita Gabriela be with you tonight?"

"No." He pointed to the table of Americans. "Do any of the Americanos speak Spanish?"

"No."

"I must talk to them. I have something important to tell Señor Jensen."

"Leticia Delgado speaks English. She is next door."

Pena nodded his thanks, then stepped next door to a shop that sold notions to women. Leticia looked up when he came in, and smiled.

"You have come to buy something for Gabriela?"

"No, I have come to borrow your power of speech. I have some information for the Americanos. I wish you to speak for me."

Smoke saw Leticia Delgado coming toward their table, accompanied by a man. He stood.

"No, *señor,* remain seated," Leticia said with a wave of her hand. "This is Señor Pena. He has something to tell you, but he does not speak English, so I must speak for him."

"*Gracias, señorita.* Señor Pena, you have information?"

The word "information" was close enough to the Spanish *información,* that Pena understood the question.

"*Sí.* I have come to warn you that, tomorrow, Coronel Keno will come to town with many men to kill you."

Pena spoke the words in Spanish, and they were immediately translated by Leticia.

"How many men?"

"*Veinte años, tal vez más.*"

"Twenty, maybe more," Leticia said.

Pena spoke again, and it was clear that Leticia didn't quite understand what he was saying, so she had him repeat it. Then she turned to Smoke.

"Señor Pena says they will have a gun that is special because it can shoot many bullets, very fast."

"He must be talkin' about a Gatling gun," Pearlie said. He shook his head. "It was said that they had one when they shot up San Vicente. I wouldn't be worrying about that. They have to pull those things around on caissons, like a canon."

Old Mo laughed. "Do you know what Crazy Horse said when he was shown a cannon? He asked, 'How do you get someone to stand in front of the gun?'"

Pearlie laughed as well. "Yeah, that's my point. Any gun mounted on wheels isn't going to be worth much if they are trying to shoot people who are moving around. And I expect we'll be moving around."

"Ask Pena this," Smoke said. "Does Keno actually plan to come into town with that gun and all those men?"

Leticia asked the question, but that question was followed by an exchange between the two of them. Smoke didn't know what they were taking about, but whatever it was, Leticia had become, visibly, irritated with him.

"Señorita Delgado, what is it? What is wrong?"

"He says that he will not give you any more information unless you pay him."

"I see," Smoke said. He stared harshly at Pena. "So, the safety of your friends and neighbors means nothing to you? If I don't pay you, you are perfectly all right with them shooting up the town? You don't care if the villagers get killed or wounded?"

Leticia translated Smoke's question to Pena. The expression on Pena's face didn't change.

"*Cuánto va a pagar?*" he asked.

"How much will you pay?" Leticia translated.

"Fifty pesos, if he answers my question. Is he actually planning to come into town with that gun and that many people?"

Leticia translated the offer, and the question.

"*Sí,*" Pena replied, then he held out his hand for the money.

"Señor Jensen," Leticia said, speaking quietly, and in English. "You must be careful with this one. It is said that he sometimes gives information to Keno."

"I don't doubt it," Smoke replied. "I'm sure that's

how Keno learned that we are here in the first place. Don't tell him that we suspect him."

"No, *señor*, I will not tell him."

"Gracias," Smoke said as he put fifty pesos in Pena's outstretched hand. He was actually thanking Leticia, but Pena accepted it, as if it had been for him.

Chapter Thirty-one

"What are we going to do, Smoke?" Sally asked after Pena left with the fifty pesos. "We can't let Keno and that many men in town. If we do, I'm afraid many innocent people will be hurt."

"You're right. That's why we aren't going to fight them here. We're going to bushwhack them as they are coming in."

"Bushwhack?" Old Mo asked.

Smoke smiled. "That is what they called Missourians, like me, who fought with irregular forces. We were effective against greatly superior forces, because we learned the art of bushwhacking. We are going to set up an ambuscade."

Cal laughed. "Yeah!" he said. "I always regretted that I was too young to be a bushwhacker."

The next morning Smoke lay on the top of a flat rock, looking west toward the Sierra Veinte Casas mountains. They were at Snake Head Canyon, which was a place where the trail narrowed down to no more than one hundred fifty feet from side to side. This caused a choke point and there was no way Keno and his men could avoid it, if they intended to come to Cruillas.

Smoke had chosen this point as the best place to establish his ambush, and now he had everyone in place. Sally was fifty feet to his right. Pearlie and Cal were on the other side of the canyon, and all four had their signaling mirror with them.

Old Mo was with Smoke.

Pearlie was the first to see Keno's men approaching, and he flashed the notice. The other three flashed that they had received his signal, then Pearlie began telling the others how many were coming. Morse code for numbers was much easier than the code for letters, as it was a simple matter of regression, and progression. The number one was one dot and four dashes, number two was two dots and three dashes, increasing the number of dots and reducing the number of dashes until the number five with was five dots. Then the procedure started in reverse, reducing the number of dots and increasing the number of dashes. He signaled that twenty-one men were coming.

Shortly after Pearlie's signal, Sally flashed that she had seen them as well.

Smoke signaled that everyone should wait until he gave the signal to fire. They had already discussed that when Smoke fired the first shot, that would be the signal for everyone else to shoot as well. The only problem was that, from this distance, it wasn't possible to pick out a specific target. There was a chance that they might all choose the same target. It wouldn't really make that much difference, once the shooting began.

Behind Smoke, Old Mo was chewing on the root of a grass stem. He had the bow lying across his lap, and there were at least ten arrows, to which were attached sticks of dynamite. Each stick of dynamite had several nails glued to it.

"You see 'em, yet?" Old Mo asked.

"No, I haven't seen them yet, but both Pearlie and Sally have. I expect they're about a mile the other side of the bend in the canyon now. Once they come around the bend, we'll be able to see them as well."

Smoke could hear them before he could see them. It was impossible for that many horses to move over such ground without making a great deal of noise. And, soon after he heard the sound of eighty-four footfalls, he began hearing conversation, sometimes followed by laughter but often issued in a way that was harsh and guttural, as if they were cursing.

Smoke smiled. This was, in no way, a disciplined army.

The "army," such as it was, appeared around the bend, and Smoke waited until all twenty-one of the men were committed.

"Mo," he said. "Get an arrow in your bow. As soon as I light the fuse, I want you to put it behind the last men in the column. That should cause them to run forward, and that's what we want. We don't want them disappearing back around the bend where we can't get to them."

"All right," Old Mo said. He picked up an arrow, notched it, then held it for Smoke. Smoke struck a match and held the flame under the fuse. The fuse began sputtering, and spewing out sparks.

"Now!" Smoke said.

Old Mo lifted the bow so that it was at about a forty-five-degree angle, pulled the string back, and let it go. Smoke followed the smoking arrow as it made a huge arc from the top of the cliff, then starting down behind the last two horsemen in the column.

Just before the arrow struck the ground, Smoke saw a flash of light, then a billowing cloud of black smoke. There was a mighty blast that filled the canyon with a thunderous roar.

Smoke had picked out a target with his Sharps, and he pulled the trigger almost concurrent with the dynamite blast. His man went down and, almost immediately, he heard the shots of Sally, Pearlie, and Cal. Two more men went down, and Smoke was certain it was because two of the shooters had chosen the same target.

The riders started forward at a gallop, but Old Mo, without having to be told, put another explosive arrow in front of them. Now the riders didn't know what to do, and they began milling around. Smoke was looking for the Gatling gun but didn't see a caisson.

At an order from their leader, the men below dismounted, and they hurried to one side of the canyon, then found rocks to shield them. The position they had taken had gotten them out of the line of fire for Pearlie and Cal, because they were right at the base of the wall where the two men were.

They were still in the line of fire for Sally and Smoke, so they continued to shoot, firing as rapidly as they could eject one cartridge and load another. Now, though, the targets weren't as readily available to them, so while the shooting was effectively keeping Keno's men down, the number of hits they were scoring was reduced.

Suddenly, from one of the positions behind the rock, there was a stream of rapid fire, as if from a Gatling gun. Smoke was surprised; he hadn't seen the gun being transported, and he realized that they must be using some other kind of gun.

Whatever they were using, it was effective, because bullets were buzzing like bees as they whipped by overhead. The rapid-firing gun had also emboldened the others so that they too were firing.

Although none of the bullets being fired toward them found their mark, the shooting was effective enough to keep Smoke and Sally from being able to improve their position. Also their shooting, limited to a single round which had to be reloaded after each time the rifle was fired, meant that they were getting no more than four shots per minute, compared to more than a hundred rounds being directed toward them.

Old Mo fired two more dynamite arrows toward them, but one of the charges detonated on the ground in front of the rocks, and the other against the cliff wall behind the men. Neither effort was effective, and rather than waste more arrows or sticks of dynamite, Smoke told him to stop.

"Sally?" Smoke called. "Get back to that rise behind us, and signal for Pearlie and Cal to withdraw. Tell them to meet us at the point."

"All right," Sally said.

"Give Mo your rifle. Mo, get where you can take a few shots. We may as well keep up as much pressure on them as we can."

Sally, who was now far enough back from the edge of the wall to be out of danger, gave her rifle to Old Mo, who, on his belly, moved up to the edge of the wall.

As Smoke and Old Mo continued to keep up the shooting, Sally flashed a signal to Pearlie and Cal. She sent the word NEW, which meant that Pearlie and Cal would have to take down the dots and dashes, then refer to their chart to decipher the message. That was exactly what she had to do to send the message.

WITHDRAW FROM YOUR POSITION. MEET US AT THE POINT.

She waited for a minute after sending the last word, then she got the signal back, UNDERSTOOD.

Coming down from the rise, she moved back to where Smoke and Old Mo were keeping up the shooting.

Smoke saw one of the men raise up from behind the line of rocks to see if he could pick out a target. That was a fatal mistake, because Smoke dropped him with a head shot.

"Damn, that's three you got, and I only got one!" Old Mo complained.

"Smoke, I sent the message and they signaled back that the got it," Sally said.

"All right. I say that we get out of here now," Smoke replied.

Their horses were tied just below the crest on the other side, well out of danger, and Smoke, Sally, and Old Mo backed away from the edge of the wall, then, when they were out of sight from anyone on the canyon floor, they were able to walk upright, and quickly, back to their horses.

Behind them, Keno's men continued to keep up a steady volume of fire. But now the shooting was in frustration as much as it was anything else, for there were no longer any targets available to them.

Fifteen minutes later they were at the point, which was the east end of Snake Head Canyon. Pearlie and Cal had gotten there ahead of them, and were waiting for them.

"What do we do now?" Pearlie asked.

"Let's go back to Cruillas and wait for a while. We'll give Keno a little more time to think about what is happening."

Keno's encampment

"Nine men?" Keno said, shouting the words in anger. "You took a platoon of twenty men to do battle with only five men, and you lose half of your force? No, I am mistaken. It isn't five men, it is four men and one woman. How many of them did you kill?"

"I do not think we killed any, *Coronel*," Chavez said.

"Fifteen men the *gringo* has killed. Fifteen!" he shouted. "We have not killed Jensen, and we have not killed anyone who is with him."

"I had only nine killed, not fifteen," Chavez said.

"I am talking about every man Jensen has killed.

First the three men we sent for supplies, then the three men who were killed with Vargas, and the nine men who you let be killed. I made you and Vargas lieutenants, because I thought I could depend on you. But Vargas failed me, and so have you! You are no longer a lieutenant, and neither is Vargas."

"*Coronel*, you do not understand," Chavez said. "This man Jensen is a devil."

"*Diablo*, is he?"

"*Sí*. He is a devil, and those with him are angels from hell."

"*El diablo y sus ángeles*. That is how we will speak of him now. The devil and his angels," Keno said.

Cruillas

Three days after the confrontation between *El diablo y sus ángeles* and the *Ejército Mexicano de la Liberación*, Ygnacio Pena was having a drink in the cantina when he saw Uvo Ramos coming through the front door. Ramos was Keno's second-in-command, and Pena was surprised to see him here.

What was Ramos doing here? Recalling his last meeting with Keno, Pena felt a sense of fear. Had Ramos come to kill him?

"Tequila, *señor*," Ramos said to the bartender.

After getting his drink, Ramos brought it over to Pena's table, where he sat without being invited.

"Why are you here, Ramos?" Pena said. "You have taken a big chance by coming to Cruillas."

"I think not much of a chance, Pena," Ramos replied. He took a drink of his tequila before speaking again. "You are the only person in this village who can recognize me. You are not going to give me away, are you?"

The comment was more of a veiled warning than a question.

"No! No, *señor*, I will say nothing."

Ramos reached into his pocket, then pulled out some money.

"Here is three hundred pesos," he said. He put it on the table, then pushed it across to Pena. "It is for you."

Pena's face lit up in a broad smile. "For me? But why? I do not understand."

"*Coronel* regrets the unpleasant thing that happened when last you visited us. He wants to make amends, and wishes to buy our help in our war with *El diablo y sus ángeles*."

"The devil and his angels?"

"Jensen."

"But, how can I help?"

"We have heard that they are staying here, in this village. Is that true?"

"*Sí*, it is true."

"Where does he stay?"

"He has a house on Calle San Gabriel."

"Is it a big house?"

"No, *señor*, it is a very small house."

Ramos smiled. "That is good. It will make it very easy to kill him."

Pena shook his head. "I think Jensen will not be a man who can be killed, easily."

"Tonight at midnight, be in the plaza. I will have three men with me. You can lead us to the house where Jensen is sleeping. I think five men can kill one man, even if that man is the devil, if we shoot him while he is sleeping."

"You said you will have three men with you. That makes four men, not five. I will lead you to the house where Jensen is, but I will not help you try to kill him."

"Are you afraid of Jensen?"

"*Sí.*"

"Do not be afraid. I won't need you. It will be easy for four men to kill one man, as he is sleeping."

Chapter Thirty-two

Pena stood in the dark shadows, next to the well in the town plaza. The town clock had struck twelve a few minutes earlier, but as yet, neither Ramos, nor any other of Keno's men, had shown themselves. He was about to leave when he heard the sound of approaching horses. Pena stared toward the sound until four men materialized from the darkness.

"Ramos, I am here," Pena called out, quietly.

The four riders came toward him, then they dismounted.

"Are you ready to help us?" Ramos asked.

"*Sí.*"

"We will leave the horses here," Ramos said to the others, and as he tied his horse to a hitching rail in the plaza, the others followed suit.

"Now," Ramos said, his pistol in his hand. "Take us to the house of Jensen."

"It is this way," Pena said. "I have a key," he added, holding up a small piece of brass that gleamed softly in the moonlight.

"How did you get a key?" Ramos asked.

"It is a *llave maestra*," Pena said proudly. "It will open any door."

"Good. Let us go."

Pena led them down Absolo Street to San Gabriel Street. He pointed to two small houses that sat side by side. "That one," he said, pointing to the house in the right, "that is the house of Smoke Jensen."

As he took a step to improve his position, he stepped on a stick, which cracked loudly.

"Be silent!" Ramos ordered.

"*Sí,*" Pena whispered in reply.

Pena handed the skeleton key to Ramos, then, as Ramos and the others started toward the house, Pena began backing away in the opposite direction.

Something awakened Smoke. He didn't know if it was a dream or a sound he heard. He just knew that he was lying in bed, feeling a strange sense of disquiet. His gun belt was hanging from the headboard of the bed, and he reached up to pull the pistol from its holster.

He still didn't know what had awakened him, nor could he point to the source of his apprehension. Nevertheless, he had learned over the years to trust these intuitions. His life had been saved almost as many times by this sixth sense he had developed, as it had been by his skill with guns. At this moment he and Sally were in danger. From what or whom, he didn't know, but he knew that the danger was real.

"Sally," he said, speaking quietly, but just loud enough to penetrate Sally's sleep.

"What?" she asked, groggily.

"Get out of bed, now. Move to that corner."

Smoke's voice was quiet, but emphatic, and Sally

had learned, long ago, not to question him when he spoke in such a way.

"Take your gun."

As Smoke had done a moment earlier, Sally extracted her pistol, then she and Smoke stepped into the shadows of the front corner of the little house.

The door opened quietly, and only the spill of moonlight into the room gave away the fact that it had opened at all.

Sally reached out to put her hand on Smoke's arm.

Four men came in through the door and stepped toward the foot of the bed. It was then, in the dim silver glow, that they could see the bed was empty.

"*Qué?*" one of the men asked in surprise.

"Are you men looking for us?" Smoke asked. As he asked the question he pushed Sally gently, but forcefully enough for her to move out of the corner. He stepped in the other direction, just as the four men started shooting toward where Smoke and Sally had been but an instant earlier.

The room exploded in noise, and was lit by a series of bright gun flashes, not only from the guns of the four would-be assassins, but from Smoke's and Sally's as well. Then the shooting stopped.

"Sally?" Smoke asked anxiously.

"I'm all right," Sally replied. "You?"

"I wasn't hit."

By now noises were coming from outside, dogs barking, men shouting, and babies crying.

"Stay where you are," Smoke said, and he moved across the dark room until he encountered the first body on the floor. He nudged the body with his foot, but got no reaction. Then he stepped over to the bedside table, lit the kerosene lamp, and turned it

up. In the light that filled the room, he could see all
four intruders lying on the floor.

"Smoke! Smoke! Miss Sally! Are you all right?"

The anxious call came from Pearlie as he, Cal, and
Old Mo, with guns drawn, came into the room from
their house next door.

"You boys are a little late for the party," Smoke
said.

Captain Juan Cortina of the Mexican *Federales*
arrived in Cruillas two days after the shoot-out in
Smoke's house. The four men Smoke and Sally had
shot were laid out in one of the cells in the jail. Sheriff Rivas had held them there until Cortina arrived,
and now Cortina stood there looking down at them.

"I know two of them," he said. "This is Uvo Ramos,
and this is Urbano Jimenez."

"The other two are Tobais Luna, and Stefan
Dominguez," Sheriff Rivas said.

"They are all Keno's men, aren't they?" Cortina
asked.

"*Sí.*" He pointed to Ramos. "I think Ramos was
Keno's deputy."

"And Jensen killed all four of them?"

"*Sí.*"

"Murder?"

"No, *Capitán.* The four men went into his house in
the middle of the night and tried to kill Jensen, but
he killed them instead."

"How do you know this?"

"It is what I was told by Señor Jensen."

"Do you believe him?"

"*Sí.* I went to the house, and I saw all four of them.

They all had guns in their hands, and the guns had been fired. You could still smell the gunpowder."

"I think maybe the time has come for me to speak with Señor Jensen."

"I will bring him to you," Rivas offered.

The involvement of the law in the shooting that took place in the middle of the night neither surprised nor bothered Smoke. He wasn't surprised, because he had personally gone to fetch the sheriff immediately after the shooting happened. And he wasn't bothered by it because he knew that the shooting had been a case of self-defense, and he was in the right.

It was with that same frame of mind that he met Juan Cortina.

Cortina's first question did catch him by surprise, though.

"How many of Keno's men have you killed, Señor Jensen?"

"Are these four men Keno's men?"

"Of course they are. Señor Jensen, you are not going to try and tell me you didn't know they were Keno's men, are you?"

"The truth is, Captain, the subject never came up. One minute my wife and I were sleeping, and the next minute these four men were in our house, shooting at us."

"How is it that you were in your bed, and yet neither you nor Señora Jensen were struck by bullets?"

"Because we weren't in our bed when the shooting started." Smoke described the incident in detail to the *Federale* officer, including in the telling that something, perhaps a sound, had awakened him.

"Why do you think they came to kill you?" Cortina asked.

"If these four men were Keno's men, and I've no reason to doubt it, I suppose Keno sent them to kill me."

"Does Keno have reason to kill you?"

Smoke nodded. "You might say so."

"Señor Jensen, have you come to Mexico to hunt down Keno?"

"Yes," Smoke answered bluntly.

"You do understand, do you not, *señor*, that American authorities have no jurisdiction in our country?"

"I do not represent American authority."

"Oh? I have been told, *señor*, that you are a deputy U.S. marshal. Is this not true?"

"I am a deputy U.S. marshal, but I am not here in that capacity. I am here on my own. Keno came into Texas and killed many men and women. He also stole two hundred of my horses. I am here to recover my horses."

"And to kill Keno?" Cortina held up a copy of the note Smoke had sent to Keno, then he began to read.

"'Keno. I am coming after you. You will not escape. We will kill you to avenge the people you killed in Texas. I am Smoke Jensen, and I am an American avenger.'"

Cortina looked up at Smoke. "Did you write that note, *señor*?"

"I did."

"And so I ask you again. How many of Keno's men have you killed, since you came into our country?"

"I don't know," Smoke said, truthfully. He had no

idea how many they had killed at the encounter in the canyon.

"I know that you have killed at least seven. The four men who came into your house, and the three men who tried to rob you. I don't know if you have killed any more than that or not. But, *señor*, this killing has to stop."

"Captain Cortina, the seven men you mentioned tried to kill me. I was acting in self-defense and, even here, in this country, a person has the right to defend his own life if it is threatened. Isn't that true?"

"*Sí.*"

"Like I said, Captain, I'm here to recover my horses. I'm sure that after Keno went to all that trouble to steal them . . . he's not going to want to give them back. And I'm equally sure that he will try and kill me to keep me from getting them. If I kill him while he is trying to kill me, that too will be self-defense, will it not?"

"Regardless of the law, you are very foolish to go after him. He is said to have as many as one hundred men."

"He doesn't have that many," Smoke said.

"How do you know?"

"Like you said, Captain. I've already killed seven of them."

"Ramos is dead?" Keno asked Pena, who had returned to the place where Keno and his men were camped out.

"*Sí.* And so are the others who were with him."

"How can this be? Did he not go into the house in the middle of the night?"

"*Sí*, I gave him a key so he could sneak in quietly. I don't know how Jensen knew they were there."

Pena believed that Jensen may have been warned of their presence by the sound of the stick he had broken, but he wasn't about to tell Keno that. And, because the others were dead, there would be no way Keno could ever find out that he might have been the cause of the failure of their mission.

"I am beginning to think that perhaps Jensen really is a devil, who cannot be killed."

"He can be killed, *Coronel*," Pena said.

"Oh? Are you telling me, Pena, that you can kill him?"

"If you are willing to pay enough money to have him killed, I will see that he is killed."

Keno laughed. "Pena, there is not one man in my army who could not kill you. But you tell me that you can kill Jensen."

"No, *Coronel*, I can't kill him, but I can arrange for him to be killed."

"How?"

"He is an American gunfighter?"

"*Sí.*"

Pena smiled. "Then I will get a *pistolero americano* to kill a *pistolero americano*."

Chapter Thirty-three

There was an American man named Lou Tucker who lived in Cruillas. Tucker worked for the blacksmith. He didn't have the skills of a blacksmith, his work consisted of getting the fire started, cleaning up the shop, moving iron around, and other such jobs as the blacksmith might require.

Tucker had come to Mexico to run away from the law in America, and he was the one Pena went to in order to set up the deal he had proposed to Keno. He explained what he wanted, and Tucker shook his head.

"There is no gunfighter in America who can beat Smoke Jensen. Maybe you haven't heard of what happened, just a few weeks ago, between Jensen and a man named Rick Isback."

"No, I have not heard."

"Isback was fast. He was very fast, some said he was faster than Jensen. I reckon Isback began believing that his ownself, 'cause he come to San Vicente for no reason in the world, other than to face down Jensen."

"What happened?"

"Like I said, Isback was fast. Only he warn't fast enough. Jensen kilt 'im."

Pena shook his head. "Then you know of no American who can kill Jensen?"

"I didn't say that. I said there was nobody who could beat him. That ain't the same thing as sayin' there ain't nobody that can kill 'im. For that, all you need is someone who is willin' to do it. And I know who that is, if you're willin' to pay him enough."

"Who would that be, *señor*?"

"That would be a feller by the name of Rex Kennedy."

"How much money do you think he will want to do the job?" Pena asked.

"He will want at least five hundred dollars. And maybe another two hundred and fifty to kill the people who are with Jensen."

"Do you think Señor Kennedy is good enough to do this?"

Tucker laughed. "Good don't have nothin' to do with it. What you want is someone who's mean enough to do the job. You need someone who won't give a second thought to waitin' behind the corner of a buildin', then steppin' up behind a fella with a shotgun, and blowin' his head off. And if that's what you want, then Rex Kennedy is your man."

"What I want is Jensen dead."

"Oh, he'll be dead all right."

"Do you know this *hombre*? Do you know Rex Kennedy?"

"Yeah, I know 'im. I rode with 'im some down in San Saba County back a couple of years ago."

"Will you take me to him?"

"Yeah, I'll take you to him. But it's goin' to cost you five hundred pesos."

"Five hundred pesos? I don't have five hundred pesos."

"You don't have five hundred dollars either, but I told you it was goin' to cost you that much to hire Kennedy, 'n' you didn't blink none. So I figure you're settin' this up for someone else. And if you can get five hundred, or maybe even seven hundred and fifty dollars to get the job done, why, I reckon that person would be willin' to give you five hundred pesos to pay me to take you to him. 'Cause I'm tellin' you right now, without me to introduce you, he ain't goin' to talk to no Mex. And, by the way, just so that you know, Rex Kennedy ain't the kind of man you want to be messin' around with," Tucker warned. "So when he tells you how much money he wants to do the job, either tell 'im you'll pay 'im that much, or else thank him, then turn around and walk away. Don't try 'n' bargain with 'im."

"It is going to cost you one thousand dollars American to have Jensen killed," Pena said. "And I am told that the man we must hire will not negotiate."

"Who is this man?" Keno asked.

"Like Jensen, he is a *gringo*. His name is Rex Kennedy."

"And this man, Rex Kennedy, is a better *pistolero* than *Diablo* Jensen?"

"No."

"No?" Keno replied, surprised by the answer.

"He will not fight him, *Coronel*, he will kill him."

Keno thought for a moment, then he smiled and

nodded. "*Sí*, that is what I want. I do not want a fight, I want Jensen killed."

"Then Rex Kennedy is the man you must hire."

"This *hombre* Kennedy . . . he doesn't expect to be paid before he does the job, does he?" Keno asked.

"I think he will take half now, and half when the job is completed."

"All right, I will pay half now."

"What about the others? You're going to have to have them killed as well."

"How much will that cost?"

"It will be another five hundred dollars."

"All right, but that must include the woman as well."

"*Sí.*"

"And," Keno said, holding up his finger, "whatever money you get will have to come out of that fifteen hundred dollars."

"*Sí, entiendo, Coronel.*"

As Pena left the meeting with Keno, he could scarcely contain his excitement. He had just doubled the amount of money it would take, which would give him more money than he had ever had at any one time in his entire life. And if Kennedy was successful, that would end the challenge to Keno, which meant he was very likely to mount a successful revolution against the government in Mexico City.

Surely *El Presidente* Keno would reward him by appointing him governor of the state of Tamaulipas.

Rosita had overheard the entire conversation, and she was frightened by the prospect of someone killing

Señor Jensen. She had to warn him, and in order to do that, she must escape.

Rosita had given Keno no trouble for the several days she had been here, having made no attempt to escape. Because her behavior had been so benign, Keno had greatly reduced the security around her. She was able to go to the creek to get water, and even to fish. She moved freely through the encampment and had become so much a part of the operation that it was as if she had just disappeared from sight.

When Rosita initially began making plans, she considered taking one of the horses, but she realized that if she were mounted on a horse she would not be able to leave without being seen. On the other hand she was small enough that she was certain she could slip, unobserved, through the guards at the pass.

Her heart was in her throat as she left the cabin in the middle of the night.

Segundo, Texas

When Rex Kennedy was fifteen years old, his stepfather was killed by a shotgun blast, while sleeping in his bed. It was well known that Kennedy did not get along with his stepfather, and though there were suspicions that he was the one who killed him, there was never enough evidence to bring him to trial.

Kennedy left home when he was nineteen, hooking up with an outlaw gang in San Saba County, Texas, robbing trains and stagecoaches, and often killing their victims in the process. He was quick to use a gun when it suited him, and he had killed several men in saloons when arguments would erupt over whores or poker games.

Killing came easy to him, so easy that he embarked on a career as an assassin, casually proclaiming that he would murder anyone for money. He quickly earned a reputation for getting the job done quickly and efficiently, often by means of a shotgun ambush.

Pena and Tucker found him sitting at a table playing solitaire, in the Vaquero Feliz Saloon. He had just put a black jack on a red queen when he looked to see two men approaching him. Immediately suspicious, he moved his hand to the butt of his pistol as they came closer to the table. Then, recognizing one of the two, he relaxed, and smiled.

"Lou Tucker," Kennedy said. "It has been a long time."

"I reckon it has at that," Tuck said.

Pena noticed that Kennedy had not offered to shake hands, nor had he brought his up where it could be seen.

"What are you doin' with the Mex? I heard you'd gone to Mexico. You takin' up ridin' with 'em now?"

"This feller's name is Pena. He don't speak no American, so I'm goin' to have to speak for him."

"Speak about what?"

"He wants you to kill someone, 'n' he's willin' to pay for it."

"This feller he wants kilt. Is he down in Mexico?"

"Yes."

Kennedy nodded. "Good, that'll make it a mite easier. I can kill 'im, then come back across the border 'n' there won't be nobody up here lookin' for me. Who is it he wants kilt?"

"You ever heard of a man by the name of Colonel

Taurino Bustamante Keno? He is the *comandante* of the *Ejército Mexicano de la Liberación*," Tucker said.

"Keno, yes, I've heard of 'im. Big *bandido*, I hear. Is that the fella the Mex here wants kilt?"

"No, he's the one that wants you to kill somebody. Pena is just here to arrange it."

"I make it a point never to talk about business on an empty stomach," Kennedy said. "It is nearly lunchtime. Come buy me lunch, and you can tell me what you want of me."

Kennedy waited until the meal had been delivered before he brought up the subject.

"All right, who is it you want me to kill?" Kennedy speared a piece of meat and lifted the fork to his mouth.

"Smoke Jensen," Tucker said. "He wants you to kill Smoke Jensen."

The fork didn't make it to his mouth. Kennedy put the fork back down and looked at Keno.

"The same Smoke Jensen that Rick Isback tried to kill?"

"I heard about that. I also heard that Isback tried to brace him," Tucker said.

"*Qué?*" Pena asked, wondering where the conversation was going.

Tucker translated for Pena.

"Was Isback a friend of Kennedy's?" Pena asked.

"No. Men like him have no friends."

"But he knew him?"

"Yes, I knew him."

"Ask Señor Kennedy if this man Isback was good with a gun."

"He was one of the best," Kennedy replied when the question was put to him. "A lot better 'n me."

Again, Tucker translated.

"Oh. Then he does not think he can kill Jensen." It wasn't a question, it was a statement, and the tone of Pena's voice reflected his disappointment.

Tucker translated Pena's statement.

"Do you want me to fight him? Or kill him?" Kennedy asked easily.

"I want you to kill him, *señor.*"

"I want five hundred dollars."

Pena smiled. This was working out exactly as he wanted.

At first it was just a thin wisp, looking like nothing more than a column of dust in the distance. But as they drew closer to the little farm, the wisp of dust took on more substance until it became a column of smoke, growing into a thick, heavy, black cloud, filled with glowing embers and roiling into the sky.

The fire was still snapping and popping when Smoke and the others arrived, but there was little left to burn. What had been the house was blackened adobe and charred timbers with just enough fuel left to support the dying flames. In addition to the fires there had been a wanton slaughter of two burros, who lay dead in the corral.

Smoke saw a man facedown in a pool of his own blood. When he went over to get a closer look he saw that the man, who looked to be at least seventy, had been shot several times in the head and chest. He knew, even before he reached him, that he was dead. A woman was lying nearby, also dead.

"What kind of evil son of a bitch can do something like this?" Cal asked.

"*Fueron asesinados por Keno*," a voice said.

"Who said that?" Pearlie asked.

"It sounded like a young girl's voice," Sally said.

"You are *americano*?" the voice asked, and looking toward the sound, they did see a young girl, who had been hiding in a narrow gulch that cut through the place.

"Yes, we are Americans," Smoke said. "Are these your parents?" Then realizing they were probably too old to be parents, he glanced at Sally. "Grand-parents?"

"*Abuelos*," Sally suggested.

The girl understood and shook her head, then she spoke again in English. "They helped me when I escaped. They would not tell where I was, so Keno and the others with him, shot them."

"When you escaped? Are you Rosita Salinas?"

"*Sí*. You have heard of me?"

"Yes, your papa told us about you, and we have been looking for you."

For the first time, the little girl smiled. "I was right! I knew Papa would send a knight in shining armor to rescue me!"

"I'd hardly call myself a knight in shining armor."

"You are the one called Smoke Jensen?"

Smoke was shocked to hear the girl say his name.

"Yes. How did you know that?"

"I know," she said without further explanation.

Chapter Thirty-four

"Señor Jensen, Keno is going to pay a bad man to kill you," Rosita said. "I got away so I could warn you."

"Well, thank you, child, I appreciate that," Smoke said.

"The bad man's name is Rex Kennedy."

"Kennedy?" Old Mo said.

"Do you know Kennedy, Mo?" Pearlie asked.

"Yeah, I know him."

"How well do you know him?" Smoke asked.

"I rode with him for a while."

"You know him and you know Smoke," Cal said. "Come on, do you really think Smoke has to worry about someone named Rex Kennedy? I mean if he was that good with a gun, don't you think someone would have heard of him?"

"How good do you have to be with a gun if you step up behind someone with a shotgun and blow their brains out?" Old Mo asked.

"But if he isn't nearly as good as Smoke . . ."

"Cal, when are you going to learn that being good with a gun is only a small part of it. The biggest part is being willing to kill a man and think no more about it than you would about stepping on a cockroach."

"Kennedy is that kind of a man, is he?"

"Yeah, he's that kind of a man. Little girl, are you sure the name you heard was Kennedy? Rex Kennedy?" Old Mo asked.

"*Sí.* I heard Señor Keno speaking with Señor Pena. Señor Pena said he would get Señor Kennedy to kill Señor Jensen."

"Pena," Cal said. "That's the man from town."

"Yes, and Señorita Delgado warned us about him," Smoke said.

"I wonder what Kennedy plans to do about the rest of us?" Pearlie said. "Surely he doesn't think we are just going to sit by and let this happen, without doing anything about it."

"He plans to shoot you as well," Rosita said. "And you too, *señora.* He plans to shoot all of you."

"Well, he's not going to do it, because you came and told us about him," Smoke said. "That was very brave of you. And since you told us about him, it means we have the advantage. Fore . . . fore-something. Sally, what is that saying about being warned means you are armed?"

"Forewarned is forearmed," Sally said.

Smoke chuckled. "Sometimes it's good to be married to a schoolteacher."

"Smoke, what are we going to do about Rosita?" Sally asked. "You saw what Keno's men did to those poor people who helped her. If she goes home, I fear they will go there, and harm not only her, but her entire family."

"We'll keep her with us for a while," Smoke said.

"With us? Out here, in the wild, so to speak?"

"No. We're going back to Cruillas. You can stay with her in the house."

"I want to come with you," Sally complained.

"Sally, please," Smoke said. "You would be a lot more helpful to me if you would just watch out for the girl."

Sally nodded. "I'm sorry, of course I would. Please forgive me."

"Forgive you for what? For wanting to be with me? Don't be ridiculous. But, in this case . . ." Smoke let the words string out, then fade away.

"I know, sweetheart. I'll take really good care of her."

Rosita had watched and listened to the exchange between Smoke and Sally, and though she didn't follow it as closely as she wished she could, she was able to assume from the conversation that they were talking about her.

Then Smoke turned to her.

"You did say that Keno spoke with Pena, didn't you?"

"*Sí, señor.*"

Smoke smiled. "That's good to know. It has given me an idea as to how best to handle this thing."

"What have you got in mind, Smoke?" Cal asked.

"I plan to set up a little trap for our friend Kennedy."

"*Sí,*" Leticia said after Smoke approached her. "I will speak to Pena for you. He was gone from town for a few days. I don't know where he went, but I know that he is back."

"Ask him to meet me here, at your place, so you can talk for us."

When Pena came into the store a while later, Smoke could see by the expression on his face and the look in his eyes that he was a little suspicious.

"Señor Pena," Smoke said with a broad smile and an extended hand. "Thank you for coming to see me."

Leticia translated for them.

"He wants to know why you wish to see him."

"The last time we spoke he gave me some very good information. I was wondering if he had any other good information for me. Perhaps a suggestion as to where I might go, so I could wait, and maybe see some more of Keno's men."

As Leticia translated the comment, Smoke knew at once that Pena had taken the bait. He saw the expression in Pena's eyes change from curiosity to conquest. He was being given the perfect opportunity to set Smoke up for Kennedy. He was so sure of himself that it never dawned on him that he may be the one who was being set up.

"*Sí, sí!*" he said. "I will find just such a place for you."

"*Gracias, señor, muy gracias,*" Smoke said, sticking his hand out to grasp Pena's. Pena could barely keep the smile off his face as he left the store.

"Señor Jensen, I am worried," Leticia said. "I do not trust Pena. Please, be very careful when you go to the place he will say."

"*Señorita*, I appreciate your help, and your concern," Smoke said. "And I promise you, I will be very much on my toes when I go there."

* * *

Pena came back the next day with a location, which he pointed out on a map, again speaking through Leticia Delgado.

"It is called *Lugar de las Serpientes*. That means Place of the Snakes," Leticia Delgado said. "Pena says that Keno will send some of his men through this place at four o'clock today."

"Four o'clock?"

"*Las cuatro en punto?*" Leticia Delgado asked.

"*Sí, las cuatro en punto,*" Pena replied.

Smoke didn't need any further translation. "That's pretty specific, isn't it? Almost as if he is arranging a meeting."

"*Sí, señor.* Please, be very careful," Leticia said.

As Pena left the notions shop, he saw Señora Jensen going into Mama Maria's café. That in itself wouldn't have gotten his attention, he knew that the Americans had been taking their meals there. What did get his attention though, was the young girl who was with her. He was sure this was Rosita, the same girl he had seen with Keno. What was she doing here? Did Keno know she was here?

Pena smiled. This would be more information he would provide Keno, and for this information he would charge nothing. He was making enough money from arranging for Kennedy to kill Jensen that he didn't need any more right away. What he needed now was for Keno to be obligated to him, so obligated that he would remember, and reward him, after the revolution.

As soon as he told Kennedy where to go, he

planned to ride out to Keno's encampment and tell him about the girl.

After meeting with Pena, Smoke went to Sheriff Rivas's office to find out what he could about the Place of the Snakes.

"It is an evil place, *señor*. Why would you wish to go there?"

"I am just curious about it. Is it a way to pass through the Sierra Veinte Casas mountains?"

"No, *señor*, it goes into the mountains, but it does not come out. It is a dead end."

Smoke smiled. "Thank you, Sheriff."

Lugar de las Serpientes

Leaving the sheriff's office, Smoke went directly to the Place of the Snakes. A narrow, twisting gorge, it was obvious as soon as Smoke saw it that this was an ideal place to set up an ambush. Dismounting, Smoke ground-hobbled Seven, then he started into the ravine which was flanked on both sides with jagged walls. The rift twisted and changed directions so frequently that there was no part of it that continued in a straight line for more than a hundred feet or so.

It had been Smoke's plan to be here before Kennedy, but he had underestimated Kennedy's acumen as an assassin. Kennedy was here first and to Smoke's surprise, Kennedy suddenly appeared in front of him, stepping out into the middle of the gulley with a double-barreled shotgun in his hands.

Luckily, Smoke had just stepped around a bulging

rock formation in the side of the wall, and reacting quickly, faster even than Kennedy could pull the trigger on the shotgun, he jumped behind it.

The shotgun roared, and the heavy load of buckshot ripped out chunks of rock where, but an instant earlier, Smoke had been walking.

Smoke didn't know whether or not Kennedy had pulled both triggers at the same time, but he knew that he couldn't take a chance. So rather than stepping back out to show himself, Smoke got down on his knees, then did a somersault back out into the middle of the ravine. As he somersaulted, he fired at Kennedy, who, with a barrel left, shot back. Most of the shot went over Smoke, though he felt the sting of a couple of pellets in his leg.

Because he had fired from a very awkward position, Smoke had missed, though he had managed to hurry Kennedy's shot. Now, as Smoke was regaining his feet, Kennedy was pulling his own pistol, and he managed to get a shot off at the same time Smoke fired a second time.

Kennedy missed, Smoke did not.

Keno's cabin

"Jensen is dead," Pena said. "I have come to collect the rest of the money that we must pay Señor Kennedy."

"How do you know he is dead? Have you seen his body?"

"Yes," Pena lied.

"Where is it?"

"His body is at *Lugar de las Serpientes.*" Even though Pena had not seen the body as he claimed, he made the statement with absolute confidence that Smoke Jensen was, by now, lying dead at the Place of the Snakes canyon. "You can send someone to check if you wish."

"Santos, you go check on the body. If it is there, come back and tell me." Then to Pena, he added, "When he returns with the word that Jensen is dead, I will give you the rest of the money."

"I have some other information for you, *Coronel.* It is information that I will give you without charge. I know where the girl is."

"The girl? What girl?"

"The girl that was here. She has escaped, has she not?"

"*Sí.* How did you know that she has escaped?"

"Because I saw her in Cruillas. She is with Señora Jensen."

"*Coronel,* that is bad," Mendez said. "She can tell others where we are. I think maybe we should do something about her."

"Don't worry, I'll take care of her personally," Keno said.

When Smoke returned, Sally breathed a bit easier. She had immense confidence in Smoke's ability to take care of himself, and because he was forewarned about this man, Kennedy, she wasn't that worried. Still, it was always satisfying to see him return from a situation that she knew was dangerous.

"Smoke! You're wounded!"

"It's just a couple of pellets, and I don't even think

they're very deep," Smoke said. "There wasn't much bleeding."

"Let me look at them."

Smoke cut up the side of his pants leg so Sally could see them. "No," she said, relief in her voice. "It's not bad. I can get them out quite easily."

It took Sally but a few minutes to dig out the pellets, then bathe the wounds with alcohol. There was no bleeding, and the wounds didn't even require a bandage.

"Smoke, I've been talking with Rosita," Sally said. "She is a delightful and very bright young lady."

Smoke smiled. "Of course she is. She called me her knight in shining armor, didn't she?"

Sally chuckled. "Yes, she did. She also knows where to find Keno."

Chapter Thirty-five

"Pena has told the truth. Jensen is dead. I saw his body," Santos said.

"Are you sure it is his body?"

"I have never seen Jensen, so I don't know what he looks like. But there is a body lying where Señor Pena said."

"What did you do with it?" Keno asked.

Santos smiled. "I did nothing with it, *Coronel*. The animals and the birds will dispose of it."

"I told you," Pena said. He extended his hand. "May I have the rest of the money now, *Coronel*?"

"There is no need for me to give you the money."

"No need? But, *Coronel*, what about Señor Kennedy? He is not a man one would cheat."

"I won't cheat him. When I see him I will pay him the money."

"*Coronel*, do you want me to bring him here? Do you think that is wise?"

"Is he waiting in Cruillas for his money?"

"*Sí, Coronel*."

"Then, I will see him after we kill the girl and Señora Jensen."

Pena was beginning to worry. If Keno and Kennedy were to meet, it would quickly become obvious that Pena had cheated them both.

"I think it is not good for you to go to Cruillas. The people and the sheriff of Cruillas are not friendly to you as they are in many of the other towns."

"Then it is time we made them friends," Keno said. "And as *el alcalde*, you can help make them into my friends."

"As the mayor? But, Coronel Keno, how can this be? Cruillas already has a mayor. It is Stefan Valencia."

"I will tell Señor Valencia that it is time he step down from the mayor's office so that you will be the new mayor."

"Sheriff Rivas is a very good friend to Mayor Valencia. I think he will not like to see his friend step down."

"Do not worry about such things, *Alcalde* Pena. Rivas will be no more. You will appoint a new *alguacil.*"

As they started toward Cruillas, Pena was still a little worried about how he was going to handle the meeting between Keno and Kennedy. But he was so pleased with his appointment to the position of mayor, that he would find some way to deal with that problem.

Rosita had pointed out on a map exactly how to get to Keno's camp, and now Smoke, Pearlie, Cal, and Old Mo were on one of the twenty separate peaks of the mountain range, looking down on Keno's camp.

There were people milling around in the valley below them, but few, it seemed, were actually carrying a weapon. Half a dozen campfires were going, and several of the men were gathered in groups to drink. Loud talk and laughter indicated that some of them were already drunk, and none of them had any idea that they were being observed.

"I'll say this for Keno," Smoke said. "If he really is a colonel, he sure runs a loose army. Look at them. Nobody is on guard, half of them drunk, and the other half look as if they're on the way to getting drunk."

"Yes, but when you have nothin' but a bunch of outlaws, there really ain't no such thing as discipline," Old Mo said. "Don't forget, I've rode with men like these."

"I guess you're right," Smoke said.

"Smoke, look over there between the trees and the river," Cal said. Do you see those two guns on tripods? What kind of guns are those? They're too little to be cannons."

Smoke sighted through his scope in the direction Cal had pointed out, then he laughed.

"Boys, those are the machine guns they've been using."

"Damn. Wouldn't it be good now, if we could get our hands on them?" Pearlie said.

"I *can* get them," Cal replied. "Do you see how the river swings around behind those rocks? I can get down to the river there, then use the river as cover to come up to the guns, get one of them, spike the other one, then sneak back out."

"I don't know, Cal, you'd sure be exposing yourself," Smoke said. "And if you're discovered, you would be a sitting duck."

"Smoke, these are the sons of bitches that killed Katrina. I want to do this, and the only thing I ask is that, when I get the gun back up here, I'm the one that gets to use it."

Smoke chuckled. "I tell you what, Cal. If you really can pull it off, the gun is yours to do with as you please. But, I suggest that you wait until dark. I think then you would have a better chance."

"All right, I'll wait," Cal said.

The four men remained on top of the peak until the sun set, then Cal looked around at the others. "I'm goin'," he said. "All I ask is that none of you shoot me when I come back."

"Cal, you know you're on your own. We can't see you from up here, so we won't have any idea whether you're in trouble or not."

"I'll be back before you know it," Cal promised.

Cruillas

"Señora Jensen!" Rosita said. "It is him! It is Coronel Keno!"

Rosita was coming back into the house, having just stepped out back to the privy in preparation for going to bed.

"What? Where is he?"

"I saw him and another man behind the house that is there." She pointed to the building next door, the one that had been used by Pearlie, Cal, and Old Mo.

"He has come to take me back!" Rosita said, the tone of her voice betraying her fright.

"He isn't going to take you back," Sally said.

"Lock the door! Please, lock the door!"

Sally locked the door because Rosita was begging her to do so, though she knew that a locked door meant nothing. The men who had come in earlier had used a pass key, and she was sure that if there was one pass key, there would be another one.

Remembering that she and Smoke had moved into the shadows of the corner before, she decided to use the same tactic. But then both she and Smoke had been armed. Tonight she was the only one with a gun, and she had to protect Rosita.

The men who had come before had seen, at once, that the bed was empty. That gave Sally an idea, an idea that might give her an advantage.

Working quickly, she put pillows and other bulky things under the blankets to make it appear as if she and Rosita were in bed. Then she took Rosita over to a corner . . . opposite from the corner where she planned to be.

"Sit here and don't make a sound," Sally warned.

Rosita, with her eyes open wide and gleaming in the moonlight, nodded.

Sally stepped quickly to the other corner, getting there just as the door was opened. As she had suspected, there had been another key. Two men came in, though in the dark she couldn't make out their features.

The two men stepped up to the bed and began blazing away. Sally let them shoot several times before she called out to them.

"I am here!"

"*Qué?*" one of the two men shouted. Both men swung toward her but, as Smoke had done in the earlier invasion, Sally had moved immediately after calling out. The two men started shooting into the corner toward the sound of her voice. Sally fired back. Sally was an excellent shot, cool with a gun, and motivated by protecting the child that had been left in her care. She had the muzzle flashes to aim at, and it took no more than four shots before both of the men went down.

"Smoke, Pearlie, it's me!" Cal called from the darkness.

Cal had been gone for an hour and the only way Smoke and the others had to measure his success was the fact that there had been no gunshots. Smoke had taken that as a good sign, and Cal's appearance now bore that out.

"Did you get the gun?" Pearlie asked.

"I got the gun, five loaded magazines, and a whole sack full of shells for it," Cal said, the excitement noticeable in his voice.

"What about the other gun?" Smoke asked.

"I've got so much mud poked down into the barrel that it's goin' to be quite a surprise to anyone who tries to use it."

"All right, gentlemen, let's get some rest," Smoke said. "We start first thing in the morning."

By sunrise the next morning all four men were in position, looking down on the encampment. Several of Keno's men were awake, and the smell of coffee filled the valley.

"Mo, do you think you could put an arrow on the roof of the cabin?" Smoke asked.

"I can do that easy," Old Mo replied.

"Then let's wake 'em up."

Old Mo drew back on the bow, Smoke lit the fuse, then the arrow was loosed. It trailed a little line of smoke through the air as it flew down toward the cabin below. It stuck down into the roof, then, a second later, exploded with a roar.

"Cal, get that thing going!" Smoke said, and Cal started turning the crank on the gun. Smoke and Pearlie began shooting as well, and on the ground below, men ran to and fro, shouting out in fear and confusion.

"There's one goin' for that other gun," Pearlie called.

"Let 'im go!" Smoke said and they watched as the man swung the gun toward them, then turned the crank. The barrel burst with the first round fired, and the man went down.

Cal continued to crank away on the machine gun and Old Mo launched several more dynamite arrows toward them, as Smoke and Pearlie continued to shoot.

"Wait a minute! Stop firing!" Smoke said a moment later. "Look at them! They're leaving, all of them! They're running away!"

Cautiously, Smoke and the others rode down into the valley. They found weapons lying everywhere, and they counted twenty-three bodies on the ground. They didn't see one living person.

"I wonder if one of these is Keno, or did he get away?" Old Mo asked.

"I don't know, but I see our horses back there," Smoke said. "I say we gather up the guns, toss them into the house and burn them, then get the horses and go back home."

Epilogue

Smoke, Sally, Pearlie, and Old Mo were in the dining car on the train, heading back to Sugarloaf Ranch.

"Say, Miz Sally, why don't you show us that medal the Mexican government gave you for killin' Keno again?" Pearlie asked.

"It wasn't the whole government, it was just Captain Cortina and the *Federales*," Sally replied.

"Yeah, but the thing is, you're the one that got it," Pearlie said. "Ever'one would have thought it would be Smoke who killed Keno, but it was you."

"It wasn't just Keno," Old Mo said. "Him and Pena both come after her, and she got 'em both. I reckon they just didn't have no idea of what they was runnin' into."

"We didn't have to go down there, we could have just sent Sally," Smoke said. "Now they'll be writing books about her instead of me."

"Smoke, jealousy doesn't become you," Sally teased.

Smoke laughed, then leaned over to kiss her. "I'm

proud of you, darlin'. I knew Rosita would be safe with you."

"If y'all are goin' to start this lovin', maybe me 'n' Mo should leave," Pearlie suggested.

"You wouldn't want to leave before dessert, would you?" Sally asked.

"No, ma'am, I sure wouldn't want to do that. The wonder is that Cal left. I figured sure he'd be wantin' dessert."

"I think I'll go check on him," Smoke said. "Order dessert for both of us."

Smoke walked back into the Wagner Palace car and saw Cal sitting at the far end, staring through the window. Smoke moved down to take the seat across from him.

"Cal, are you all right?"

"Yeah."

Smoke didn't reply because he had the idea that Cal wanted to say something and he was going to give him time to come up with the words.

"Smoke, how long did it take you to get over losing Nicole?"

The question referred to Smoke's first wife, who had been killed by outlaws several years ago.

"What makes you think I *am* over her, Cal?"

"But you must be. I mean, you're married to Miz Sally, and I know you love her 'cause I see it every day."

"Of course I love Sally. But that doesn't mean I don't still love and miss Nicole. She is in a special part of my heart, and she will be until the day I die. Just as

I suspect Katrina will be for you. Life will go on for you, Cal. And I'm sure that someday you'll find another woman. But that doesn't mean you have to push Katrina aside."

"I'm glad to hear you say that, 'cause I don't ever intend to forget Katrina."

"You're a good man, Cal. I'm glad she found you before she died. Take heart in the fact that she died happy and in love."

"Yeah," Cal said with a wide grin. "Yeah, she did, didn't she?"

"I told Sally to order dessert for us. What do you say we go see what it is?"

Cal nodded, then stood and followed Smoke toward the dining car. The train blew its whistle then, a long, mournful wail, and Cal smiled. It was as if Katrina had just spoken to him.

TURN THE PAGE FOR AN EXCITING PREVIEW!

WILLIAM W. JOHNSTONE,
WITH J. A. JOHNSTONE,
The Greatest Western Writers of the 21st Century

They called him Preacher.

On the rolling Missouri River a riverboat of fur
traders, a U.S. senator, and Prussian royalty
are all heading to the Yellowstone from St. Louis.
Preacher's on board because the nation's fate
depends on the passengers landing safe and sound.
But it won't be easy. Two beautiful women make a
play for Preacher. So does a killer. So does a band
of river pirates. No sooner does Preacher beat back
these threats than the riverboat lands in the middle
of a blood-soaked Indian ambush—with a Prussian
nobleman and his family taken hostage.
Preacher has no choice but to go off in pursuit,
even with a traitor trying to slaughter him.
Someone wants to start a war and change the
course of American history. Only a lone mountain
man and the ambush of bullets he wields with deadly,
unerring force stand in the way . . .

PREACHER'S SLAUGHTER

by William W. Johnstone,
with J. A. Johnstone

**Coming in January 2015
Wherever Pinnacle Books are sold.**

Chapter One

One of these days he was going to just stop coming to St. Louis, Preacher told himself as he looked down the barrel of the flintlock pistol the angry black-bearded man was pointing at him. It seemed like trouble was always waiting for him every time he set foot in civilization.

Preacher dived forward as smoke and flame spouted from the pistol. The heavy lead ball hummed through the space where his chest had been a split second earlier.

Preacher landed on a shoulder and rolled over with the lithe, athletic grace of a younger man. Preacher was approaching middle age but didn't look or act like it. The life he had lived since leaving his family's farm and heading for the frontier more than two decades earlier had kept him young.

As he let the momentum of the somersault carry him back up onto his feet, he considered snatching his heavy hunting knife from the fringed and beaded sheath at his waist and plunging it into the gunman's chest.

Hell, the varmint deserved it, Preacher thought. He'd pulled a gun, after all.

But while killing this idiot wouldn't make Preacher lose a minute's sleep, dealing with the law afterward would be an annoyance. The authorities had started to frown on wanton slaughter, even in raucous riverfront taverns like Red Mike's.

So Preacher left the knife where it was, balled his right fist, put the considerable power of his body behind it, and broke the stupid son of a bitch's jaw with one punch instead.

Like a fool, the man had been trying to reload his pistol when he didn't have nearly enough time to accomplish that task before Preacher hit him. When the mountain man's punch exploded against his jaw, the impact drove him into the bar with bone-crunching force. The man's arms flew wide. The empty pistol slipped from his fingers, flew across the room, and smashed into the face of a burly keelboatman.

The redheaded whore who had started the whole ruckus by screaming in pain when the black-bearded man grabbed her by the hair and jerked her up against him now threw her arms around Preacher's neck.

"You saved me from that brute!" she gushed. She came up on her toes and planted her painted mouth on Preacher's mouth.

Preacher didn't have any objections to kissing a whore, but he knew better than to close his eyes while he was doing it too. Because of that, he saw the keelboatman leap up from the table, blood running like twin rivers from his busted nose, and charge across the room like a maddened bull.

Clearly, the fella didn't care whose fault it was that he'd gotten walloped in the snoot. The black-bearded man had collapsed in a moaning heap at the foot of the bar, so to take out his rage the riverman headed for the combatant who was still on his feet.

Preacher thought about shoving the whore at the man to trip him—after all, she'd had a hand in this mess—but that wouldn't be the chivalrous thing to do and Preacher still tried on occasion to be a gentleman.

So he took hold of the redhead under the arms, picked her up, and swung her out of the way.

"Better scoot, darlin'," he advised her with a pat on her attractive rump.

Then he turned back to the keelboatman, whose lumbering charge was practically shaking the puncheon floor under Preacher's boots by now.

Preacher lifted a foot and the fella's groin ran right into it at top speed. The shriek he let out was pretty high-pitched for somebody who was all muscle and almost as wide as he was tall. He doubled over, curling around the agony he felt, and barreled into Preacher like somebody had bowled him in a game of ninepins.

As he fell, Preacher thought again that he really ought to stay away from St. Louis in the future. There were other places to sell his furs now.

Then he was down on the sawdust-littered tavern floor and several of the keelboatman's friends came at him like a herd of stampeding buffalo.

"Get him!" one of the men cried.

"Stomp him!" another yelled.

Somebody crashed into the group from the side and with widespread arms swept the two leaders off their feet. That gave Preacher time to get his hands and knees under him and surge up to his feet once more.

He snatched a bucket of beer from a nearby table and waded into the remaining three men, swinging the bucket like a medieval flail. Two of them went down almost immediately, but the third man landed a punch to the side of Preacher's head that made the mountain man's ears ring. Working on keelboats gave a fella plenty of muscles.

One of the men Preacher had knocked down grabbed his leg and twisted. Preacher yelled more in annoyance than in pain and tried to kick the man free. The one who was still on his feet took advantage of the distraction and hammered a punch to Preacher's solar plexus that knocked the air out of his lungs.

Then he tackled Preacher around the waist and dragged him to the floor.

Preacher wound up wrestling with all three of them as he rolled around in the sawdust. A pungent blend of spilled beer, vomit, unwashed flesh, and horse dung assaulted his nostrils. He clamped a hand around the throat of one opponent and banged his head against the puncheons hard enough to make the man's eyes roll back in their sockets. He was out of the fight after that.

Another man looped an arm around Preacher's neck from behind and squeezed. The man's forearm was like an iron bar. Preacher was still mostly out of breath, and as long as the man was choking him like that, he couldn't get any air in.

Everything started to go hazy around him, and Preacher knew it wasn't just from all the pipe smoke that hung in the air inside Red Mike's.

He felt the hot breath of the man who was choking him against the back of his neck. That meant his face was right handy. Preacher drove his head back as hard as he could. His skull was thick enough that the fella's nose had no chance against it. Cartilage crunched and blood spurted under the impact.

That loosened the man's grip enough for Preacher to gulp down a breath, but the man was stubborn and didn't let go. Instead he stood up and hauled Preacher with him.

Upright again, Preacher spotted the fella who had pitched in to help him. He was part of a tangled mass of flailing fists and kicking feet a few yards away. The rest of the tavern's patrons had grabbed their drinks and their serving wenches and gotten out of the way, clearing a space in front of the bar for the battles.

"Hang on to him, Rory! We'll teach him he can't treat us that way!"

The shout came from the other keelboatman still on his feet. As his friend kept up the pressure on Preacher's throat, he closed in with his knobby, mallet-like fists poised to hand the mountain man a beating.

As the man rushed in, Preacher grabbed the arm across his throat with both hands, pulled his feet off the floor, lifted his knees, and then lashed out with both legs. His boot heels caught the man in the chest with such force that he was knocked back a dozen feet before he landed on top of one of Red Mike's rough-hewn tables and lay there with his arms and legs splayed out.

Preacher got his feet on the floor again and drove hard with them, forcing the man who held him backward. Preacher always knew where he was and what was around him. His long, dangerous life had ingrained that habit in him. Just as he expected, after a couple of steps the small of the man's back struck the edge of the bar. This time it was enough to make him let go completely.

Preacher lifted an elbow up and back. It caught the man on the jaw and snapped his head around. Preacher pivoted, took hold of the front of the man's linsey-woolsey shirt, and forced him up and over the bar. A shove sent him sprawling behind it.

The man who'd helped Preacher had his hands full with his two opponents. One man had him down on the floor choking him while the other man tried to kick him and stomp him in the head. Preacher laced his fingers, stepped up, and swung his clubbed hands against the back of the second man's neck. It was a devastating blow that dropped the man like a poleaxed steer.

With the odds even now, Preacher's ally was able to cup his hands and slap them over the ears of the man choking him, causing that varmint to turn loose and howl in pain. Freed, the man bucked up from the floor and swung a right and a left that had his opponent rolling across the puncheons. The man landed with both knees in his belly and sledged two more punches down into his face.

That ended the fight.

The brawny Irishman behind the bar, the tavern's namesake, said in a tone of utter disgust, "Preacher, does this have to happen every time you come in here?"

Preacher had picked up the broad-brimmed, round-crowned, gray felt hat that had been knocked off his head early in the fracas. As he punched it back into its usual shape, he grinned at the proprietor and said, "Appears that it does, Mike."

Red Mike grunted, reached down to take hold of the man Preacher had shoved behind the bar, and heaved his senseless form back over the hardwood. The man thudded onto the floor in front of the bar.

As Mike dusted his hands off, he said, "Well, I happen to know those spalpeens just got paid, so I'll collect from 'em for the damages, and maybe a little extra for the annoyance. Why don't the two of you move on so they won't try to start another brouhaha when they wake up?"

"You're chasin' off customers?" Preacher asked, astonished. He clapped his hat on his head.

Red Mike grimaced and said, "I prefer to think of it as limitin' the potential damage to me place."

Preacher chuckled and turned to the man who had pitched in on his side. He intended to offer to buy the fella a drink in some other tavern—there were plenty of them along the river—when he realized that he knew this man.

"Simon Russell!" Preacher said. "What are you doin' here?"

"Actually, I'm looking for you, Preacher," the man said. "I want to offer you a job."

Chapter Two

"It never turns out well when I work for wages," Preacher said a bit later as he lifted a pewter mug of beer. "I'm a trapper. I work for myself."

"I know that," Simon Russell said. "I also know there's no finer fighting man anywhere west of the Mississippi."

They were in a somewhat fancier drinking establishment now. The mighty river was several blocks away. The whores who worked here dressed a bit more discreetly and weren't as brazen in their behavior. The floor still had sawdust on it, but it was swept out and replaced more often.

Simon Russell wore a brown tweed suit instead of the greasy buckskins he'd sported when Preacher first met him in the mountains ten years earlier. They had seen each other at a number of rendezvous since then and had always gotten along well. Preacher considered the man a friend, although he wasn't nearly as close to Russell as he was to, say, Audie and Nighthawk.

A thatch of lank blond hair topped Russell's squarish head. His clean-shaven face bore the permanent tan of a man who had spent most of his life outdoors, like Preacher. They weren't really that different, Preacher mused, although obviously Russell had taken to civilization better than Preacher ever would.

"I heard you were in town and figured I might catch up to you at Red Mike's," Russell went on. "I wasn't surprised to find you in the middle of a brawl, either. Seems like you get mixed up in one every time you set foot in there. What started it?"

Preacher set his mug back on the table after taking a long swallow of beer.

"Oh, a fella was mistreatin' a woman."

"A whore, you mean. I doubt if a respectable woman has ever set foot in Red Mike's."

"She was still a woman," Preacher snapped. His first real love had been a whore, and he had never forgotten Jenny.

"I didn't mean any offense," Russell said. "I know how quick you are to jump into a fracas anytime you think somebody is being wronged."

Preacher just shrugged and didn't say anything.

"Or when the odds just aren't fair."

"I already thanked you for pitchin' in," Preacher said, "and I paid for that beer you're drinkin', even though anybody could tell by lookin' at the two of us that you got a heap more money in your pockets than I do."

"Sorry. I didn't mean for it to come out that way."

Preacher wasn't convinced of that, but he let it go. He sighed and asked, "What is it you want me to do, anyway?"

Russell didn't answer the question directly. Instead

he said, "You know I work for the American Fur Company now, don't you?"

"I might've heard somethin' about it," Preacher replied with a slow nod.

The American Fur Company was the oldest and largest fur-trading company in the United States. Founded by John Jacob Astor, the market it provided for beaver pelts had probably done more to promote the exploration of the continent's western half than anything else, no matter what the historians might say about Thomas Jefferson, Lewis and Clark, and the Louisiana Purchase. Knowledge for its own sake was all well and good, but throw in the promise of some profit and a lot more people were likely to sit up and take notice.

"The company has started sending riverboats up the Missouri to the mouth of the Yellowstone so our men can buy furs directly from the trappers up there," Russell continued. "The Yellowstone is as far as they can navigate."

"I heard about that too. Can't say as I really cotton to the idea."

"Why not?" Russell asked with a frown.

"Riverboats are smelly, smoky contraptions, and they make a hell of a racket," Preacher said. "You've been all over that country out there, Simon, just like I have. You've seen how quiet and peaceful it is. You send riverboats up the Missouri, you're just gonna scare all the wildlife, and you're liable to spook the Indians, too."

Russell leaned forward and said, "Actually, that's exactly why I wanted to talk to you, Preacher. The last few times a boat has gone upriver, it's run into problems. Some have been attacked by Indians, and some have been waylaid by river pirates."

"Pirates," Preacher repeated. "Like the Harpe brothers over on the Ohio?" He had heard plenty of stories about those bloodthirsty criminal siblings known as Big Harpe and Little Harpe.

"That's right."

Preacher shook his head.

"I don't recollect hearin' anything about pirates on the Missouri," he told his old friend.

"That's because there was never enough traffic up-river to make it worth their while . . . until now. The company has had boats attacked on the way up, while they were carrying the money to buy furs, and they've been attacked on the way back down and had a whole boatload of plews stolen. Of course the Indians aren't interested in stealing money or furs. They just want to kill the crews and set the boats on fire so they won't come up the river again."

"I'm sorry to hear that," Preacher said. "I can make a guess what this is leadin' up to. You're in charge of one of these riverboats, and you want me to come along."

Russell clenched his right hand into a fist and lightly thumped it on the table.

"That's exactly what I want," he said. "You're friends with a lot of the tribes out there, and the ones that aren't your friends are afraid of you."

"I don't reckon I'd go so far as to say that."

"I would," Russell declared. "They don't call you Ghost Killer for no reason."

Preacher inclined his head in acknowledgment of that point. In the past he had made war against the

Blackfeet, the Absaroka, the Arikara, and several of the other tribes.

The Blackfeet especially hated him. Russell was right about them fearing him too. More than once he had crept into an enemy camp under cover of darkness with no one seeing or hearing him, slit the throats of several warriors, and departed just as stealthily, so the deaths weren't discovered until morning. It was a very effective way to demoralize an enemy.

It also made legends grow up around him, which wasn't something that Preacher necessarily wanted, although he had been known to take advantage of the fact.

"And if we run into any of those pirates," Russell went on, "there's nobody I'd rather have around to help me run them off than you. Anyway, if word was to get around that Preacher was on that boat, they might decide to leave it alone."

Preacher grunted.

"You're countin' an awful lot on my reputation," he said.

"Well, of course I am. You're the most famous mountain man since Colter and Bridger."

"The day of the mountain man is comin' to an end, you know," Preacher said gloomily. "Another five or ten years, there won't be any of us left."

"I don't believe that. There'll always be a mountain man or two around, as long as there are mountains."

Preacher drained the last of the beer in his mug and wiped the back of his hand across his lips to get rid of the drops that clung to his drooping moustache.

"I hope you're right," he said.

"What about the job?" Russell prodded. "Will you take it?"

"I was plannin' to re-outfit and head back to the mountains for another round of trappin' before winter sets in."

"The *Sentinel* can get you there faster."

"That's the boat?" Preacher asked.

"Yep. Finest vessel on the Missouri River." Russell laughed. "Of course, the company only has three or four of them, so that doesn't necessarily mean a whole lot. But I'd rather be traveling on the best boat than the worst one."

Preacher couldn't argue with that logic. He said, "What about Horse?"

"That big ugly stallion of yours? Bring him along. There'll be room for him on the boat." Russell frowned and went on, "Wait a minute. Is that the same mount you had when I met you ten years ago, or a different one?"

"Does it matter?" Preacher said.

"No, I suppose not. I assume Dog's still with you, too."

Preacher just shrugged.

"You can bring Horse, Dog, and as many supplies as you want. The company will pay for them and provide cargo space on the boat for them. In addition we'll pay a fee for your help and a bonus if the boat makes it to the mouth of the Yellowstone without any trouble. Plus I can promise you top dollar for your pelts next time you sell a load of them."

"You said some of the boats had been attacked on their way back downriver," Preacher reminded his old friend. "Even if you talk me into ridin' upriver with you, I ain't sure there's enough money in the world to pay me to turn right around and come back here to this hellhole."

"Hey, St. Louis isn't that bad," Russell protested. "I've kind of gotten used to it here. But while I'd certainly like for you to make the round trip with us, I'll take what I can get. Chances are that if we have trouble, it'll be on the first half of the trip."

Preacher was torn. He liked Simon Russell, and the man *had* pitched in to help him during that fight at Red Mike's.

That wasn't the first time the two of them had fought side by side against a common enemy, either. They had been in more than one battle together against the Indians, out there on the frontier.

It was true, as well, that traveling as far as the mouth of the Yellowstone on the riverboat would get him back to the mountains considerably quicker than if he loaded a couple of pack animals and started out there on horseback.

On the other hand, he wasn't in any big hurry to get anywhere. That was one of the good things about being a trapper and working for himself. He didn't have to worry about sticking to somebody else's schedule.

And the thought of spending several weeks smelling the smoke spewing from the boat's stacks and listening to the roar of its engine and the clatter of its paddle wheel didn't appeal to him, either.

"Preacher?" Russell said.

"I'm thinkin', I'm thinkin'."

"Normally I wouldn't press you for an answer, but

the *Sentinel* is leaving tomorrow morning. I didn't even hear you were in St. Louis until late this afternoon. So time is short. Honestly, I won't hold it against you if you say no. I understand you're not that fond of riverboats, and Lord knows you've saved my hide more times over the years than I've saved yours. We're more than square when it comes to that."

Russell really seemed to mean that, Preacher thought. It wasn't just a subtle ploy.

When Preacher still didn't say anything, Russell added, "If it's a matter of more money—"

Preacher held up a hand to stop him.

"I might haggle with you over the price of a load of pelts," the mountain man said, "but not about somethin' like this. I'll just say yea or nay." He drew in a breath. "And I'll say yea. I'll go up the river with you on that damned rattletrap steamboat."